TIME CHANGE

A Time Travel Romance Novel

Elyse Douglas

COPYRIGHT

"Oh, Jerry, don't let's ask for the moon. We have the stars."

—*Now, Voyager* (1942)

For Bradley, who reads books, and
who's been in a movie or two.

TIME CHANGE

PART 1

CHAPTER 1

1948

"I'm tired of it all, Tony. The late-night parties, the Sunset Strip, the publicity department and the studio. Everybody's pulling at me, wanting something from me."

Tony made a face. "Hey, baby, nobody gets tired of being a star. Nobody. And you're almost there. Tell me, what up-and-coming Hollywood actress wouldn't die to be where you are right now?"

"And where am I?" Rita asked, dispirited.

"Where are you?" Tony exclaimed. "What the hell kind of question is that?" He held up his thumb and index finger, a tiny space apart. "You're just this far from being one of the biggest stars in Hollywood. In two years, Rita Randall will be on every schoolgirl's and every pimple-faced boy's lips. In two years, you'll be bigger than Greer Garson and Claudette Colbert put together."

They were in Tony's candy-apple-red, two-seater, 1947 Triumph 1800 Roadster, having just left the RKO Radio Pictures movie lot. Tony turned left off Gower Street onto Melrose Avenue and drove past a row of tall palms, gleaming in golden, late afternoon sunshine. Rita Randall cranked her window all the way down and presented her pretty face to the balmy breeze, her luscious blonde hair snapping and playing in the wind. She listened to the comfortable purr of the engine as Tony shifted through the gears, and she felt the usual swelling emptiness; the usual blues melody that played in her head, a sad, haunting tune, with the brooding lyrics, "*I've just wrapped a picture, and I'm as lonely as a low, mean dog.*"

Rita had just completed filming her latest movie, *Danger Town*.

Rita leaned back, eyes closed, enjoying the breeze. "I'm tired, Tony," she said wearily. "I've been making picture after picture for years now, and this last one really took it out of me. I just feel drained."

"All right, so you rest. Hey, it's Friday and you don't start your next movie for three weeks."

Tony stole another quick glance, one eye on the road and one on Rita. Tired or not, she was as gorgeous as ever, dressed in a short sleeve, light blue floral swing dress with padded shoulders. She was full-figured yet elegant, with the chiseled neck of a ballet dancer and the blue luminous eyes of a goddess.

"After a good night's sleep, you'll be good to go," Tony said.

Rita kept her eyes closed. Few people knew the real Rita—the quiet, shy loner, who was uncomfortable around crowds and smart, educated people. But the movie magazine writers never wrote about that. It didn't sell fan magazines. Instead, they wrote things like

Rita Randall projects an unspoken availability that draws the wide eyes of men and women alike. Her honey blonde hair falls in waves over thin, ivory shoulders, in a longing, in a natural invitation to touch and caress. No wonder she attracts all the bad boys and the lusty eyes of married men.

Rita sat in a gentle sorrow. "Let's face it, Tony, I'm getting nowhere. I've been doing the same B movie over and over. I'm tired of playing the bad blonde who does her man wrong and then shoots him. Or the good blonde who gets shot because her man did her wrong. Or the dumb blonde who does everybody wrong and gets shot at the end. Just once, I'd like to play a good girl. I mean a girl who is nice and meets a nice guy. A good part like Greer Garson played in Random Harvest. Ronald Coleman was the perfect man, and he loved her so much."

"Rita, you know that RKO makes more money on B pictures than on A movies. It's their bread and butter. And they love you, baby."

"I've gotta move on, Tony. I've gotta move into better parts. I don't know, maybe I just need to move on."

"Stop it with that, okay? You've been saying too much of that lately. So fine, we'll get different scripts. Better scripts. Hey, you've been making good money, haven't you? I mean for a contract player; you're doing all right."

Rita rolled her head toward him, eyes slitted open. "We've both been doing all right from those pictures, Tony."

"Hey, okay," he said with a shrug. "So, we help each other. What's wrong with helping each other? And speaking of good scripts, didn't I get you in that picture with Robert Mitchum? That was a good part. And your reviews were hundred-proof, baby. I memorized Dolly Gold's review of you in that picture. And you know how nasty she can get with actresses. Anyway, I quote that review at every meeting I get with producers, directors and studio bosses. 'Rita Randall in *Dark Detour* comes swaying onto the screen with heat and sultry magnetism.'" Tony barked a laugh. "Hey, don't you just love how the writers out here find words like that? I mean, you never hear words like that back in Brooklyn. And then, get this, Dolly Gold goes on to say 'Rita Randall, cavorting in her most iconic and vampish role yet, is the despised, drop-dead-desirable vixen of every man, both on screen and off screen.'"

Tony looked at her with a sharp gleam of satisfaction. "I mean, come on, Rita, it don't get no better than that. You and Mitchum were a killer team."

"That's been a year already. And, anyway, Bob strangles me at the end of that picture."

"So, what do you want, some knight in shining armor?"

Rita smiled, wistfully. "Yes, maybe I do. So, what if I do? Why not? Maybe I do want a guy like that. I almost had it once, but then…" Her voice trailed away.

"That's over and done with, Rita. Don't let yourself go back there. It's a deep, dark cave that leads nowhere."

Rita's stomach knotted up at the old memory that often came boomeranging back on her, whenever she thought about the war. They sat in silence for a time.

Tony finally spoke up. "Hey, do you want me to take Mayberry Road and drive down to the beach?"

"No, I just want to go home, take a bath and sleep for a few months."

"Rita, baby, you say you want to meet a nice guy. You

want to meet a knight in shining armor. Okay, then how about me?"

"You're not the knight type, Tony."

Tony looked insulted. "And so what am I then? So, I'm not a knight? How many times have I asked you to marry me? Three. Four. Five even? Hey, you keep working, don't you? Haven't I always been there, Rita baby? I've done good for you, haven't I?"

Rita softened. "Yes, you have."

"So why not marry me? We're a winning team, you and me. Look at us. We make a beautiful couple. You got the looks of Lana Turner and Ava Gardner. Look at your honey blonde hair and that goddess of a face. I'm telling you the camera loves you, Rita, and so does your knight in shining armor, Tony Lapano. So why not marry me?"

"You don't love me, Tony. You've got more girl-friends than Errol Flynn. I know you spend a lot of time at Flynn's Mulholland Drive mansion."

"It don't mean nothing, Rita. You know it don't mean nothing."

Thirty-one-year-old Tony Lapano wore a blue striped, double-breasted suit, white shirt and gold and blue striped tie. His raven hair was smoothed back with pomade, parted on one side, and combed over and slightly back to create a wave. He had good shoulders, a flat stomach, and he presented an easy, suave confidence and flashy smile, that were calculated to win favor with the rich, the powerful and the dames.

His good looks had been stroked, flattered and daily confirmed by his feisty Brooklyn mother, his back-home girlfriends, and the lusty, half-hooded gazes of itchy, older, rich California women.

He was a Hollywood agent, not a big-time agent, but a

player nonetheless. Tony's big media smile, revealing pearls of glowing white teeth in a proud, tanned face, oozed with gushing delight. His fast New York accent and gesturing hands got attention, if not always movie roles, for "his sweetheart girls," as he called them.

He managed mostly innocent girls from all over small-town America, who had come to Hollywood looking for their big break in the movies. Most wound up in bit parts in low budget movies, or in Las Vegas reviews, or working as waitresses, hoping to be discovered like Lana Turner. She was discovered on the Sunset Strip at Schwab's Drugstore counter in 1937, when she was 16 years old, by Mervyn Le Roy, the famous movie director, who happened to be seated at the counter that day.

Tony flashed Rita one of his dazzling grins. "I'll give up all the broads for you, baby, if you just say 'yes.' Just a simple 'yes' would be all it takes. Those dames don't mean nothin' to me."

Rita stared ahead. The late afternoon sun made a track of shadows across the road.

She shrugged. "No, I don't think so, Tony."

Rita sighed, looking away. "Maybe I need a vacation. A good, long vacation. I talked to Everett Claxton, and he offered me his beach house on Long Island for a couple of weeks in July. I'm thinking of taking it."

"Everett Claxton is a washed-up director. When I saw your rushes, I could see that your lighting was all wrong in *Danger Town*, and he shot you too much on your right side. Your best side is your left, but then a guy like me likes both your sides, Rita baby."

"Everett has always been nice to me, and I trust him. Anyway, I think I'm going to go back East, see my mother and spend some time at his beach house."

"You don't need a vacation, baby. All you need is that

break-out script, and old Tony's gonna make sure you get it. Now I've been keeping this as a surprise until after the meeting, but I gotta cheer you up. Look, I've got a meeting scheduled at Chasen's next week with none other than Howard Hughes, the new RKO owner himself."

Rita shot him a glance. "Howard Hughes?"

"And he's got a thing for you, Rita. That's what I heard. That's why I got the meeting."

Rita felt a sudden chill. She knew what it meant for Howard Hughes to be attracted to a girl. Rita knew he had relationships with Virginia Mayo and Linda Darnell, and she didn't want to have to date Howard Hughes to get better roles. She'd heard that not only was he possessive and obsessive, but he was also a little crazy.

"So don't worry, baby. I'll tell him we've got to get better scripts for you."

Rita stared longingly out the window. "Listen to me, whining. I've never been a whiner, Tony. I've always been grateful for the breaks I got. That's how my mother raised me."

"You're just having a bad day, Rita baby. That's all."

"You know what?" Rita said. "I don't think it's the movies so much. I think it's me. I've been trying to be a movie star ever since I was 16 years old."

"And you're almost there, baby. Almost."

She turned to him, her beautiful face empty and sad. "But I've never really lived. I've never had the time to be truly in love… to really care about somebody other than myself. Go figure, a girl who has dated most of the big stars in this town, and I haven't fallen in love."

"Don't go there with the love thing, Rita. It's way over-rated. Take it from me. I've had two wives already." "I never finished high school, Tony. I don't know anything but the movies. I want time to read a book or, I don't know, go to a museum or something."

"Forget the books and the museums. There are too many of them as it is. And as far as high school goes, I never finished high school neither, and I bet I make more money than any of those sons of bitches I went to high school with back in Brooklyn. That's why you and me get along, Rita, we're the same kind of people. We're both Brooklyn, no matter where we go. You, Flatbush. Me, Brooklyn's East New York. We're real, you know? Genuine like. You know what's wrong with this town? Too many phonies and smart guys. You and me, Rita, are the real thing. The real gold coins."

Tony glanced over. "You say you're tired, we could go to the Biltmore or to Santa Barbara for a long weekend. That will be good for both of us, baby."

Rita's voice thickened. "No, I just want to go home and take a bath, just slip down into the hot water, close my eyes and sleep."

"Okay, kid. I'll come and wash your back."

"No, Tony. None of that."

"None of what? What did I say?"

"Home, Tony. I just want to go home."

Tony frowned a little. "You know what, Rita? One day you're gonna say 'yes' to me. One day you're gonna realize you love Tony. Hey, and by the way, when you meet with Howard Hughes, don't mention anything about Laura. I don't think he approves of that kind of thing."

Rita snapped him a look. Her eyes flared. "What kind of thing? Laura is my daughter, and the best thing that ever happened to me. If Howard Hughes doesn't want me in his movies because of Laura, then he can go straight to hell."

Tony lifted an eyebrow, surprised by her outburst.

"Hey, hey, baby… take it easy. Don't worry, Tony will fix everything. Just remember me once in a while that's all. Remember that you and me are gonna get together someday. It's in the cards, baby."

Rita shut her eyes, suddenly lost in a thicket of emotion. She never had and never would let Tony touch her. He was a snake in the grass, and she knew it.

Maybe it was time for a new agent? Would Tony get violent, like he did when Mary Clifford wanted to leave? Rita sank down into the seat. Would he shove her around, slap her and give her a black eye like he'd done with Mary and a couple other of "his girls?" Maybe, but maybe it was time to move on anyway.

CHAPTER 2

2019

Thirty-two-year-old Clint West stood in his 18th floor condo, staring out through the floor-to ceiling wraparound tempered windows. He had good south and east views of Los Angeles, and from his perspective, the bustling, rambling city appeared still and quiet in the evening haze. The light of the dying day was pink and orange, with a scattering of gilded clouds and distant soaring birds.

Clint was only vaguely aware that Amy Parks was seated behind him on the L-shaped white couch.

"So, do you like it?" Amy asked.

Clint, barefoot, wearing jeans and a sky-blue t-shirt, turned only slightly. "Yeah, I'm getting used to it. You know, little by little. It's a bit bigger than I need. The master bedroom with the round en suite bathroom and open windows is extravagant… but whatever."

"I thought you'd especially like the 2000 square foot

corner loft with the skylights."

"Yeah, it's nice," Clint said, with little enthusiasm.

Amy tried to inject some, raising her voice and indicating, with a sweep of her arm.

"Hey, you're living in LA's premier South Park neighborhood, with a 24-hour concierge, a pool, a spa, a deck and not one, but two, parking spaces."

"Yeah, you did good, Amy. It helps to personally know one's real estate agent."

"I thought maybe you'd work in the loft. I thought that would be your main room. It's spacious, so you can jog around it and maybe shoot some hoops."

She'd hoped a little humor would awaken him from his mood. It didn't. He seemed even more distracted.

"Might. Yes."

"Have you been working?"

"No... Not yet. I guess I should shop for furniture or something. The place looks pretty empty, with all this space."

"I can help, you know. Just say the word."

"Thanks, Amy..."

Amy was a 30-year-old brunette with a Cleopatra hairstyle, wide wondering dark eyes and a fit, willowy body. "How about this weekend?"

"Yeah, maybe." Clint pocketed his hands, hunched his shoulders and watched the lazy glide of a helicopter in the distance.

"Are you happy with the price?" Amy pressed, knowing she was pressing, trying to get some positive response from him.

"Yeah, good price. Yeah, you did real good, Amy. I appreciate all your help."

Feeling shut out and a little frustrated, Amy got up. "Do you want me to go, Clint?"

Clint lowered his head and slowly turned to face her.

Amy took in the man she'd had a crush on from the first time she'd met him. Many people believed that Clint resembled a younger Jeff Bridges, with his thick, long, reddish-brown hair; the trimmed beard; his deep, gorgeous, almond eyes, watchful and intelligent. Now those eyes were sad, as they had been ever since Jenny had died, more than six months before.

"Sorry, Amy. Aren't we supposed to have dinner?"

"Only if you want to. You don't seem in the mood."

He pulled his hands from his pockets, took a step down to her level and approached her with a weak smile.

"Sorry, it's just not one of my good days. Maybe it's leaving the old place and moving in here. It just seems so, I don't know, empty."

"So, we'll fill it up. I have lots of ideas. I majored in interior design, you know, my first passion. Selling real estate with my mother pays the bills, and she needs the help."

"Do you know how many times you've told me this?" Clint said lightly.

Amy ducked her head. "I'm sorry. There's nothing worse than a woman who repeats herself."

"Don't apologize because you make money, Amy. Don't apologize because you love your mother and you're a good daughter."

Clint glanced around. "Well, anyway, I have to finish my novel or I'm going to be asking you for a job."

Amy brightened. "You'd be a good real estate salesman, Clint. With your name and looks, you'd make a fortune."

Clint shook his head. "No, too bookish. Not a good networker. Not that good with people."

"I'd do all the networking. I'm good with people. We

could work together."

Clint saw a familiar flicker of desire in Amy's eyes. He knew she found him attractive and always had, although she'd never acted on it when he was married to Jenny.

And then Amy said something she often repeated, and he never knew how to respond.

"Jenny told me to take care of you, Clint. I know I've said this before too, but she was so worried about you. She was afraid you'd become a kind of recluse. Is that what you're trying to do?"

"I don't know."

"Because it's not good for you to spend so much time alone. Jenny always got you out. She used to say that if she didn't force you to go to parties and dinners and book readings, you'd never go out."

Clint inspected Amy's face, a face he hadn't really studied all that much in the last few months. She was attractive and ambitious, and if her first marriage had failed, according to Jenny, it hadn't been Amy's fault. She'd tried to make it work, but her ex liked the bars and the girls, and spending Amy's money in Las Vegas.

Amy's a good soul, Clint thought. He wished he felt something for her. His eyes rested on her softly. "You were a good friend to Jenny, and you've been a good friend to me."

He turned his face from her. "It's just that I can't get her out of my mind."

"You will, Clint. In time, you will, and when you do, I want you to know that I'll be here for you. I'll always be here for you. I'm going to be bold, Clint. I fell in love with you before Jenny did. She said you were too brooding and too much of a loner, just like most writers. She said your relationship would never work, because she was such an extrovert."

Clint lifted his broad shoulders and resettled them. He lowered his eyes. "Yes… Well, somehow it did work. Jenny brought out the best in me, didn't she?"

"I could too, Clint. I know I could, and in time, I know you'd fall in love with me. You can do whatever you want. Be who you are and write, and be a loner, I don't care. I'll support you no matter what."

Clint saw the intensity and the pleading in her eyes, and it made him sad and irritated at himself. Amy would make a good wife, a good friend. But his heart was stone cold. He felt nothing.

He shifted his eyes down and away. His voice was nearly at a whisper. "Amy… I'm thinking about leaving LA."

Amy was so startled that she didn't answer.

"I see Jenny everywhere here. She was born in LA and she loved it here. No matter where I go, I remember her, I see her. I can't get away from her and a part of her will always be here."

Amy's voice took on an urgency. "But… Clint, you just have to give it more time. I mean, you just moved in here a couple weeks ago."

Clint stared into her misty eyes. He dreaded the tears that were sure to come.

"Amy, I want to go home. I want to go back to New York. This was Jenny's home. Our home. New York is my home, and I think it's time I go back."

Amy stared down at the floor, tears running down her cheeks.

Clint continued. "I thought maybe I'd rent a beach house on Long Island and spend the rest of June and most of the summer out there. Maybe out there, away from all this, I'll finally be able to finish my book and make my agent happy. Hey, I'm a lucky guy. Netflix is waiting for the book too. It's the final book in the series, and they want to start working on the script for release sometime next year. I just haven't been able to write a word. I've got to try another place, another town. I've got to get away from here."

Amy struggled to find words, her voice breaking with emotion. "I could go with you. I mean, I could... well, go with you."

Clint reached and brushed her cool cheek with his fingers. "I'm no good to anyone right now, Amy. I feel like a block of cold marble. After a few months out there on the ocean, maybe I'll finally be able to let Jenny go and move on with my life. I've got to move on. I know it's what Jenny would want me to do. So, it's time for me to go home."

CHAPTER 3

1948

Rita Randall lived in a secluded, 1927 Spanish Colonial residence, the only house at the end of a quiet cul-de-sac in Brentwood. As Tony turned into the circular drive, five-year-old Laura came bursting out of the front door, arms extended, face stretched in ecstatic anticipation of hugging her mother.

Rita flung open the door and pushed out in time to gather her daughter up into her arms.

"Hello, princess," Rita said, all sunny smiles. "How's my darling princess today?"

Rita's full-time housekeeper/babysitter, 50-year-old Maude Bleckendorf, appeared in the doorway, wiping her hands on a hand towel. Her square face and sturdy build suggested a no-nonsense woman, but her expression held kindness and humor.

"She was singing Christmas carols today," Mrs. Bleckendorf said.

Rita held her excited daughter at arm's length. "Laura, this is June. It won't be Christmas until December."

Laura's round face, perky smile and blonde curls reminded many people of Shirley Temple, although Rita didn't see the resemblance.

Laura brushed a blonde curl from her eyes. "But I like Christmas songs. I like those snowmen. Can we build a snowman on Christmas?"

Tony left the car and walked over. "Hey, Laura, don't forget your Uncle Tony."

Laura looked up at him, squinting, blinking in the sunlight. She didn't say "hello."

"Do you like snowmen?" she asked.

Tony spread his hands. "Does Tony like snowmen? Of course, I like snowmen. I used to build the biggest, fattest and tallest snowman in the neighborhood."

"I want one," Laura said.

"Okay, so when Christmas comes around, Tony will take you up into the mountains and we'll build a snowman. Now give me a hug already."

After hugs, Mrs. Bleckendorf asked Tony if he was staying to dinner and, to Rita's relief, he declined, saying he had meetings. Rita knew what those meetings were. He had a date with a woman. Maybe two.

Before he slid in behind the wheel, he pointed at her. "Get some good sleep, Rita baby, don't forget I've got a meeting with HH next week, and I know he's gonna want to meet you. So rest and look your best."

During dinner, Rita fought a gloomy depression, but she forced smiles and happy chatter with Laura. Later, while Maude cleaned up, Rita and Laura sat nestled in the couch, listening to the polished oak Philco radio, the dial set to KNX-FM. They listened to *I'll Dance at Your Wedding* by Ray Noble and *It's Magic* by Doris Day, while

Laura rambled on about her favorite radio shows and her new friends in the neighborhood.

After Rita bathed Laura, tucked her under the sheets and kissed her goodnight, she met Maude at the front door.

"I'll be in at ten in the morning," Maude said.

Rita thanked her, then closed and locked the door.

Twenty minutes later, Rita was luxuriating in a hot soapy bathtub, allowing all the stress and fatigue to drain out of her. She slid deeper into the water and closed her eyes. Her thoughts and emotions were all mixed up, and she felt things shifting inside. If she didn't meet Howard Hughes, would he cancel her contract? He'd already canceled others. She'd heard from the crew and other actors that he was reviewing everyone's contract and testing everyone's loyalty. If he distrusted anyone, he fired them.

The thought of having to date him and lie to him about Laura sickened her. What would happen if she was fired? Would another studio put her under contract?

What if she severed all ties with Tony and went with another agent?

At some point, deep into the night, Rita heard a pounding on the front door. She sat up abruptly, heart thrumming. Instinctively, she swung her feet to the carpeted floor, switched on the side lamp, yanked open the side table drawer and reached for her .38 caliber Smith & Wesson Snub nose handgun.

When the hammering on the door persisted, Rita swallowed, feeling the cool walnut grip of the gun. With mounting anxiety, she crept to the bedroom door, open it and peered out into the dimly lit hallway. She left her room, barefoot, and approached the front door with caution.

"Rita, let me in!"

It was Tony.

She breathed in her annoyance and marched toward the door, hearing his fists thudding into it.

"Let me in, Rita!"

She turned the lock, grabbed the doorknob and yanked it open, handgun still at her side.

There he was, shiny faced, loose-limbed and lazy-eyed drunk.

"Hey, baby, I've come to see you," he said in a slurred voice.

"Do you know what time it is?" Rita snapped.

"Hell, no. It's early I think."

"It's two-thirty in the morning. What's the matter with you? Go home and sleep it off, Tony."

A spark of lusty mischief filled his narrowing eyes. "No, baby…It's time you and me get down to the basics. It's time you and me start having some real fun together. No more make believe, like in the movies."

Incensed, Rita went to slam the door, but Tony swiftly inserted his foot and stopped it. In one violent move he put his shoulder against the door and drove it open, the force shoving Rita back-peddling, struggling to stay on her feet.

Tony entered and kicked the door closed, breathing hard. With only a plank of light coming from Rita's bedroom, Rita saw the dark intent in Tony's black eyes. For the first time in the four years she'd known him, she was scared.

"Go home, Tony," Rita said, glancing behind her. "You'll awaken Laura."

"She sleeps like a rock, Rita. You know it, and I know it. Don't bullshit me. It's time you and me finally do what I've wanted to do for years. You know you want it as bad as I do, baby. You know you belong to me."

Rita needed to stall him. She needed time to think. The handgun felt heavy in her hand, the walnut grip damp in her clammy, trembling hand.

"Why now, Tony? After all these years, why now? Why tonight?"

"Because Howard Hughes is going to get his hands all over you, doll. Yes, that's right. He has it bad for you, baby, and he's gonna get you. Well, not before Tony gets his first. Do you hear me?"

As she backed away from him, a breath caught in her throat. "Go home, Tony. You're drunk. When you wake up in the morning, you're going to hate yourself for this. Hey, we'll both laugh about it. Go home."

He jabbed an angry finger at her. "Don't bullshit old Tony, baby. I'm not going anywhere until I get what I came for. Now, we're going to your bedroom nice and friendly like. Just you and me, because I found you. I discovered you and I made you who you are. It was me! Me, okay? Tony. And now I'm going to get what's coming to me. I'm going to do what I've been waiting to do for a long time, baby."

Rita licked her dry lips, glancing about for an escape. But there was no escape, and anyway, Laura was asleep in the back bedroom. Rita was not going to leave her to this drunken lunatic.

Tony scowled at her, speaking through clenched teeth. "You were always so high and good—maybe you think you're too good for Tony. Don't forget where you came from, doll face. You're from Brooklyn, just like me, and I say you're just a tramp just like all the other tramps in this town. So now I'm gonna take what's mine, so old Howard will know he can't push me around."

The handgun felt like a lead weight. Like a threat. Like a friend. Rita's heart drummed against her ribs as she tried to make sense of this nightmare. She felt sweat on her forehead and under her breasts.

And then, from somewhere deep inside, outrage welled up, and a call-to-arms determination willed her to fight back. She was not going to let Tony, or any other man, push her around. Not Tony and not Howard Hughes, with all his money and power.

In an instant, before Rita could react, Tony sprang at her, hands splayed for attack. In one violent motion, he seized her shoulders and flung her onto the couch. As she tumbled hard into the back cushion, the gun bounced from her hand, hit the floor and slid away. Tony was on top of her in seconds, his clawing hands ripping her pajama top. Her full right breast was laid bare, her chest heaving.

She battled him, but he pinned her arms, a crooked, ugly grin revealing white shark teeth. Rita gasped for breath, twisting, ramping and kicking, but Tony was too strong. He slapped her hard across the face. For a moment, it stunned her. She tasted metallic blood. The blow briefly paralyzed her, and she went limp. Tony tugged down her pajama bottoms, grinning when he saw there were no panties.

Rita slowly came to, as Tony crushed her lips with his. She gagged at his foul-smelling breath, and when he sank his tongue into her mouth, she bit down hard. He screamed, drew back and belted her again. The blow whipped her head sideways, and everything blurred and went fuzzy. She fought to stay conscious, thoughts of Laura returning her back to the horror of the nightmare.

For a second, Tony relaxed his grip as he felt his injured tongue. Rita seized the moment. Like a coiled snake, she struck a blow—a knee to his groin, just missing a direct hit. It disabled him just enough for her to free her hands. With adrenaline pumping and filling her with new strength, she wrenched and lurched, and in a violent attack, she shoved Tony off the couch to the floor. She heard his body thump, and she thought he might have banged his head. He cursed.

In a heartbeat, she leaped up, her eyes darting about, searching the dimly lit room for the gun. She only had seconds. The shadow of the gun loomed large, and she dropped to the floor, grabbing for it. She heard Tony scramble to his feet.

Rita snatched up the gun and, on her knees, she swung around, gun raised, finger on the trigger, second hand bracing the grip.

Tony screamed out curses. He was a large, violent animal about to pounce.

"Stop, Tony, or I'll shoot!"

"You bitch!"

He charged.

Rita squeezed off a shot. She heard the POP. Flinched at the recoil. Saw the sharp, angry flash explode from the barrel.

CHAPTER 4

1948

The Triumph's headlights tunneled the night, as Rita drove the twisting Palisades Road toward Tony's sprawling cliff-side house. She was a mass of nerves, her hands trembling on the steering wheel. She longed to stop her mind from galloping, from thinking, but she couldn't. It ran and re-ran the scene with Tony repeatedly, in slow motion, and then in time-lapse photography, where everything was speeded up. And then she re-ran every possible scenario and alibi.

Rita refused to look right, where Tony sat slumped in his seat. It had taken all her strength, and then some, to tug and drag him out of her house and into his car. She'd glanced about tensely, every shadow a person, every sound a threat—a dog barking, the drone of a single airplane engine overhead, the wind whooshing across her ears. Had anyone heard the single gunshot? No one had appeared. She heard no sirens. Thankfully, her house was private and isolated.

As she turned and motored up Tony's winding driveway, she prayed the house wouldn't be ablaze in lights, with a wild party underway, and a woman waiting for him.

She was in luck. The house was eerily dark. She'd never seen it so dark. Normally, it was lit up like a birthday cake, with some party throbbing on into the wee hours.

She drew up to the garage and parked. After one quick, distasteful glance at Tony, she killed the engine and got out, chucking the door shut. Her watch revealed it was after four. Not much time. She'd have to work fast.

Rita had been in enough bad B crime movies to know that the best way to confuse detectives was to create complications and diversions.

After she'd fired the bullet into Tony's chest, she'd frozen in horror. Then, after she'd stuck her fingers into Tony's neck and confirmed there was no pulse, she'd sat back against the couch, shaken and stunned. She struggled to find any reality. Was it a movie? Was this the final scene? Would the director holler "Cut"? Would Tony get up? Would they say, "What a great scene"? Did she hear the director say, "Print it"?

Minutes later, she gathered herself, corralled her chaotic thoughts and set to work. First, she hurried to Laura's bedroom door and peeked in. Thankfully, she was sound asleep, as usual. Next, Rita hurried back to her bedroom, beating back panic. She dressed down in a frumpy dress, a pair of old pumps, and an old black scarf that she tied around her head. A pair of black-rimmed glasses finished the outfit. Once she had Tony inside the car, she drove away, not speeding and not too slow.

Now, at Tony's two-car garage, she walked to the side entrance door, found the hidden key under the round mesa planter and opened the door. Inside was Tony's second car, and one she'd driven home several times after one of his late parties, when no one else wanted to leave.

She saw the spare car, a midnight black 1945 Cadillac Fleetwood, and found the key under the passenger floor mat. *Tony had never been clever*, Rita thought. When the garage door was open, she climbed in, cranked the engine and backed out. As she turned the car to drive away, the car's headlights swept over Tony's parked Triumph. She saw his slumped silhouette, and it brought tears. How in the world had this happened? She'd never been overly fond of Tony, but he had been good to her in many ways. She thought they were, at the least, friends. She would have never believed he'd attack her and try to rape her. It had never entered her mind.

Rita felt like the lowest person on the Earth as she drove out of his driveway and turned onto Palisades Road.

Fifteen minutes later, she stopped near the beach. Glancing back over her shoulder to make sure she wasn't being watched, she left the car, hurried across the sand to the edge of the tide, hearing the waves rumble in. The moon was white and nearly full, casting eerie light onto the beach and charging surf. Reaching into her purse, she drew out the handgun that had killed Tony. She swept her eyes up and down the abandoned beach once more, and then heaved the gun into the ocean.

It was time to implement the next part of her plan. Also, in her purse, was Tony's necktie. As she tramped back across the sand, she paused and then tossed the tie away. It fluttered and settled like a dead snake, the wind snapping at it, the tail flicking about like a tongue.

Back in the car, she drove along Beach Road, parallel to the ocean. Minutes later, through the open window, she flung Tony's fat wallet away. It held nearly two hundred dollars in cash.

When she was within three miles of her home, she shut off the headlights and turned onto South Bay Road, a quiet, dark street. The second house she saw, she pulled the car into the driveway, stopped and shut off the engine. She waited. All was quiet. With a hanky, she wiped the steering wheel and door handle, ensuring there were no fingerprints.

She left the car, shutting the door softly, and walked purposefully away under faint, watery moonlight. Dawn would be breaking at any minute, and she had to be back at the house before Laura woke up, and before anyone saw her and recognized her.

Rita moved steadily ahead, wondering what she would have done if she hadn't had Laura. Would she have turned herself in and pleaded self-defense? Yes. But she'd made her decision. If she did turn herself in, it was likely she'd get jail time. Tony wasn't liked by everybody, but he was connected to the LA mob, to the cops, and to the studio bosses. Yes, she would surely get jail time.

Then what would happen to Laura? And even if Rita was found innocent, the media circus surrounding Tony's death would be dreadful, and Laura would be pulled into it. It would take months before the whole ugly thing finally blew over, and surely, by then, Rita's career would be over, and any hope of her finding a good husband and father for Laura would be finished.

About a mile from home, she grew faint, her legs wobbly, as stress, shock and exhaustion finally struck, nearly overwhelming her. She stopped, bent at the waist and inhaled deep breaths.

One thing was for sure. She couldn't leave town until she was cleared by the police. When they arrived, she'd have to appear shocked and innocent. It would be the ultimate test of her acting ability. She had to play the scene perfectly. She had to do it for Laura. It was her only hope.

After that, Rita and Laura would have to leave town for perhaps weeks, perhaps forever. She could only hope and pray that the LAPD wouldn't be able to find some piece of evidence that would tie her to Tony's death.

CHAPTER 5

2019

Clint West rambled the beach, pausing often to stare at the sea and watch sails topping and tilting in the late June wind. The breeze was salty and warm, the day bright with sun, and the squealing seagulls were loud, gliding the restless currents of wind. Kids scrambled across the beach with ecstatic expressions. They tugged at long strings holding kites that danced and trembled in the infinite blue sky.

Clint smiled at the lovely scene—and it felt good to smile and be back on the East Coast, away from LA; away from his past. Dressed in shorts, a golden t-shirt and old comfy sandals, he indulged his love of sand, sun and sea, finally tugging on a Yankees' baseball cap when the baking sun began to sting his neck and face. He pulled his cell phone from his short's pocket and took a video of the scene: kids playing badminton; lovers hand-in-hand, charging the curling waves; the sandpipers skittering along the tideline.

He'd arrived only four days before, on June 24th, and after spending a few days with his parents in White Plains, he drove to Amagansett, Long Island. While still living in LA, he'd rented the beach house sight unseen from an online ad. Amy had helped arrange the deal and, as ever, she'd found just what he was looking for.

The three-bedroom house had character and a history. Built in 1946 as a refuge for the celebrated Broadway producer and movie director, Everett Claxton, over the years it had gone through several owners and renovations, but it had never expanded into a modern, arrogant beach house like many that hugged the upper dunes. It was currently owned by a Wall Street banker who loved old movies and wanted to preserve some of the "old school" style.

Clint loved the simplicity of the place, the bright, airy bedrooms and the sunken living room, with the stone fireplace and swallow-you-up couches and chairs. The exposed beams added a rustic, beachy atmosphere, and the timber and glass kitchen had French doors with easy access to a broad, screened-in deck with an awe-inspiring view of the dunes and sea.

Clint's writing room was private, a textured stone-and-wood den, with a sturdy oak desk that faced the sea, and a delightful mix of old and new furniture. The autographed black and white photos on the wall revealed old-time Broadway and Hollywood stars: Greer Garson, Humphrey Bogart, Ginger Rogers, Veronica Lake, Henry Fonda, Rita Randall and Helen Hayes. Centered below the others hung the glossy photo of a heavy-faced middle-aged man with a pencil mustache, salt and pepper hair and an expression of fastidious pride. The gold nameplate on the frame read Everett Claxton.

Clint couldn't have been happier with the place. It was his dream house come true. If he couldn't work here, then he was in big trouble.

Clint's older brother Jack, a recently divorced attorney, had invited himself for the weekend. That was alright with Clint. He and Jack had never been close, but they always got along and, now that they were both single, they'd have time to catch up and bond a little.

Clint finally left the beach, returning to the beach house about 11 a.m., feeling refreshed but lazy. He wandered into the den and sat behind his laptop for a time but only daydreamed, staring out the angled blue venetian blinds into the golden glory of the day. He couldn't write one simple sentence. The natural intoxication of the place offered little desire to work, and the morning had left him relaxed and drowsy. Within minutes, he was on his screened-in deck, asleep in a chaise.

Jack arrived late that afternoon, Friday, June 28, and Clint gave him a tour of the house.

As they entered the den, Jack put hands on hips and appraised the room. "It's old and new all mixed up together," he said, "But somehow it works. You said it was originally built in 1946?"

"Yes, by some Hollywood movie director."

Clint pointed to the autographed black and white photos of actors and actresses and Jack strolled over, hands behind his back, studying them.

Jack was 36 years old and, though slight of build like their mother's side of the family, he was trim and in good shape. He had blue, intelligent, perceptive eyes, an angular face with good cheekbones, and a friendly manner.

"I love this Veronica Lake photo. She was fantastic in *The Glass Key* with Alan Ladd."

Clint stepped over. "You and Dad always loved to

watch old movies together."

Jack nodded. "Yeah, Dad loved the noir films, especially *Out of the Past* with Kirk Douglas and Robert Mitchum, *The Postman Always Rings Twice* with Lana Turner and..." Jack stopped when he saw Rita Randall's photo.

"Wow, look at this photo of Rita Randall."

Clint nosed forward. "Yeah, she was a beauty."

"Both Dad and I loved her in *Danger Town*. She was brilliant in that one."

Jack looked at his brother.

"Did you ever see it?"

"A long time ago on *Turner Classics*."

Jack shook his head. "Rita Randall should have been one of the greatest stars of her time, but something happened... some scandal. I can't remember. I'll *Google* it later. Anyway, she did a lot of film noir, playing the pretty bad girl or the femme fatale. Of course, they didn't call them that back then. They were just classified as melodramas. Dad used to say that the term *film noir* didn't stick as a genre until sometime in the 1970s."

Clint took Rita Randall in for the first time, newly entranced by the black-and-white photo. All that lovely hair was scattered across her shoulders. She had arched her head back, and her face expressed surprised recognition and longing. She wore a black satin, low cut dress, revealing a slim, chiseled neck and plenty of cleavage. Her eyes suggested bright intelligence and stormy depths, and Clint was sure he saw a spark of mischief in those eyes. His eyes lingered on her full, inviting lips, moist with gloss, and he felt an unexpected rise of desire.

Jack smiled at his brother's obvious attraction. "Rita Randall was a sexy beauty and a mystery."

"Why do you say mystery?" Clint asked.

"If you watched more old movies and read fewer

books, you might know that after the scandal, Rita Randall just seemed to vanish."

That night for dinner, Clint pan-fried fresh fish, baked two potatoes, steamed broccoli and tossed a salad. They ate on the deck, taking in the pink and orange sunset sky, washing their dinner down with a cold bottle of Chablis. They retold stories from their childhood, laughed at new jokes and grew solemn when they gently touched on their marriages.

"So how are you holding up?" Jack asked, wine glass poised at his lips.

"Better, now that I'm out of LA. I don't see her everywhere and remember all the good times. I've got to move on. That was one of the last things Jenny said to me during those last days."

Jack raised his glass in a toast. "Here's to both of us moving on."

Their glasses chimed.

In the middle of the night, Clint awakened with a start and sat up. He blinked into the darkness, feeling as though someone was there, watching him. He heard the distant hiss of the sea and saw soft moonlight leaking in from an upper window.

As he settled back down in bed, his mind flashed upon the old photo of Rita Randall. There was something about her that captivated him. He rolled over on his side, recalling the words she'd inscribed on the photo, written to Everett Claxton.

To my best friend, Everett. Thanks for keeping the secrets.

CHAPTER 6

1948

"I'm Detective Sergeant John Briggs, Miss Randall, and this is Detective Hadley."

In late Saturday morning sunlight, Detectives Briggs and Hadley produced their shields for Rita's inspection.

Rita wore tan cotton slacks, a yellow blouse and leather slip-on loafers. Her makeup was light, no lipstick or eye shadow, and her hair was tied back with a bright orange silk scarf. They stared at her, and she at them; theirs with glint-eye appraisal, hers with suspicion and curiosity.

"How can I help you?"

Detective John Briggs was a tall, thin, middle-aged man, dressed in a dark double-breasted suit, a gray tie and gray fedora with a black band. He had a ruddy face and steady eyes. He had the tight mouth and narrow eyes of a worrier and the expression of someone who had little time for humor.

Briggs removed his gray fedora, revealing oiled and

wavy salt and pepper hair. Hadley removed his hat, revealing a mostly bald dome.

"May we come in? I'm afraid we have some rather bad news," Briggs said.

Rita blinked nervously. "Why, yes. Come in."

She stepped aside, and the detectives entered.

Hadley was a stout man in his early 40s, who seemed uncomfortable and distracted. His eyes wandered, as if he couldn't trust them to focus on Rita for any length of time, afraid they would begin undressing her. His pinstriped suit fit him loosely, as if he'd recently lost weight.

Rita indicated toward the couch. "Please sit down," she offered.

Hadley remained standing, behind the couch, and Rita wasn't sure why.

Before sitting, Briggs took out a worn black leather notepad and an expensive looking pen.

"Are you alone, Miss Randall?"

"Yes, my housekeeper took my daughter, Laura, out to the beach."

"We won't take up much of your time. I just have a few questions. Some may seem obvious; some may seem a bit intrusive. Please bear with me and just answer them the best you can."

Rita lowered herself in the armchair opposite Briggs, her hands resting in her lap, pulse increasing, her expression expectant. She'd had little sleep, and she hoped it didn't show. After arriving home early that morning, she'd had to clean the blood off the red-patterned carpet where Tony had fallen.

She'd rubbed vigorously, until her hands were red and sore. Knowing the wet spot wouldn't dry before a visit from the police, which she knew was imminent, she'd rearranged the spot under the couch, so it wasn't visible.

She was certain they wouldn't search the house. At least not on a first visit.

Thankfully, the bullet had not passed through Tony's body and slammed some place into the wall. From the movies, she knew that detectives noticed details like that. Tony's suit must have slowed the bullet, and it lodged in his body. Not a happy thought, but one she'd had to consider when cleaning up, as the first light of rosy dawn appeared.

Rita saw Detective Hadley cast his eyes about the room, as if searching for anything suspicious: the floor plants; the hanging South American tapestry; the carpet; the fireplace she never used. Did they approve of her color scheme? The evergreen walls with red accessories scattered about the room, because Laura loved Christmas colors?

Briggs fixed his eyes on her. "Miss Randall, have you received any calls from the studio with regard to Tony Lapano?"

"Tony? No. What's happened?"

Briggs stared somberly. "I'm afraid that Tony Lapano is dead."

Rita did not scream out. She did not gasp. She did not faint. She swallowed and reacted as if she hadn't heard the statement properly.

"I'm sorry. Did you say Tony is dead?"

"Yes, Miss Randall."

Again, she just blinked, as her eyes widened. "I don't believe it. Tony? What happened?"

"He was shot."

"Shot? How? By who?"

"We don't know. We've just begun our investigation."

"When was he shot?"

"According to the coroner, sometime early this morning, between 2 a.m. and 4 a.m."

Rita looked down and away. Then she stood up, putting a knuckle to her lips. She stood frozen for a moment, as if she didn't know whether to stand, sit or walk. She had played this very scene in the 1946 movie *Deadly Restitution*.

"When did you last see Mr. Lapano, Miss Randall?"

Rita looked at the detective with a faraway look in her eye. "He was my agent…"

"Yes… when did you last see him?"

"Yesterday. He came by the studio and picked me up. He brought me home."

"What time was that?"

Rita stared at nothing. "What time…?" she asked, her voice trailing off.

"Yes, what time did he bring you here?"

"Oh… about 5:30 or so."

"Did he stay?"

"No. He said he had a meeting."

"Did he say who the meeting was with?"

"No. No, he didn't say."

"Did he return at any time last night? Did he come back here to see you?"

"No…"

Rita eased back down in the chair. She shut her eyes. "Who would shoot Tony?"

"Miss Randall, did you and Mr. Lapano have an argument yesterday?"

"An argument? No. Tony and I never argued."

"Were you upset with him in any way?"

"No… Not upset."

"Why didn't you drive your own car to the studio yesterday morning?"

"I don't like driving. I only drive when I have to. The

studio sent a car."

"What kind of car do you own, Miss Randall?"

"A 1946 Alfa Romeo."

Briggs' left eyebrow lifted. "That's quite a car."

Rita stared coolly, without responding.

"What did you and Tony Lapano talk about when he drove you home from the studio?"

She shrugged. "We talked about what we always talk about. I wanted him to try to get me better scripts. He said he was going to meet with Howard Hughes."

Briggs blinked slowly. "Howard Hughes? When was this meeting supposed to take place?"

"Next week sometime. I don't know exactly."

"Do you know if Mr. Lapano had any enemies?"

Rita looked Briggs straight in the eye. "Most people liked Tony. Okay, so maybe some people didn't like him, but I don't know who they are."

Briggs scribbled notes, occasionally looking up at his partner, Hadley, to gauge his reaction.

"Miss Randall, do you own a gun… a handgun?"

"Yes."

"May I see it?"

Rita swung her gaze first to Hadley, and then to Briggs. "Yes, of course."

She left for the bedroom, returning minutes later with a .22 caliber handgun. Detective Hadley pulled on his hat and rounded the couch. She handed it to him. He examined it expertly, checked the empty cylinder, sniffed the barrel, then hefted it. Briggs waited for his partner's assessment.

Hadley said, "Harrington & Richardson 22 special, 6-inch barrel, wood grip, single action. Not been fired recently. Maybe a 1933-34 model."

"Where did you purchase this, Miss Randall?" Briggs

asked.

"Tony got it for me. He said I should keep a gun for protection."

Briggs noted her answer in his pad.

Hadley said, "Miss Randall, you should load it if you're going to use it for protection. A gun is no good without bullets."

Briggs threw him a disapproving glance, and Hadley lowered his eyes as he handed the gun back to Rita.

Briggs continued. "Miss Randall, did you and Mr. Lapano ever have a romantic relationship?"

"No."

"Not ever?"

"No. He wanted to marry me, but I turned him down."

"When was this?"

Rita lowered the gun on the coffee table and returned to her chair, sitting, pausing, staring thoughtfully. Again, from the movies, she'd learned to speak the truth as much as possible. The detectives would check and cross-check her answers. Rita was sure that Tony had blabbered to several people about his asking Rita to marry him, and he had no doubt added, with his usual arrogant confidence, that someday she would come around and say "yes." How could she refuse him?

"Well… he asked me again yesterday. I told him no."

Briggs considered that, keeping his steady eyes on her. "Have you ever been married, Miss Randall?"

"Yes. Once. In 1943."

"And where is your husband currently?"

Her eyes dropped, then came back up. She was positive that Briggs already knew the answer. Her sad story had been printed many times in newspapers and magazines all over the world, especially after the war.

"He was killed in 1944. He was a bomber pilot and was shot down over Germany."

Briggs didn't react as he wrote. "My condolences, Miss Randall. What was his name?"

"Ted Carlton. Theodore Thomas Carlton."

A chilly silence hung in the air.

At the front door, Detective Briggs turned back to Rita. "I'll need to come back and speak with your housekeeper."

Rita seemed preoccupied. "Of course, Detective Briggs. By the way, I just completed a picture, and I was planning a vacation back East to see my mother and sister. Now, after this… Well, I think I'd still like to take that vacation, after Tony's funeral. Will that be all right?"

Detective Briggs threw a glance to Hadley. "When do you plan to return?"

"Three weeks. I'm starting a new picture. Of course, I've got to be here for the funeral, don't I? I've got to be here for Tony. Afterwards, I think getting away will do me good."

Briggs gave her a warning stare. "Don't leave the country, Miss Randall. I'll need your phone number and address where I can always contact you. This is an ongoing murder investigation. Normally, I wouldn't allow you to leave the state."

Rita gave him her mother's address and phone number and stood motionless in the door as she watched them drive away, their black sedan glinting in the sunlight.

When the detectives were gone, Rita returned to the house, dropped down onto the couch and broke into tears, not holding back the tremors of regret and fear.

CHAPTER 7

1948

On the Douglas DC-6 airliner, Rita sat with Laura in First Class luxury en route to LaGuardia Airport, flying over Pennsylvania at 13,000 feet. Laura was asleep, her head resting against her mother. Rita sat stiffly, her face registering confusion and dismay, but not self-pity.

She was relieved to finally be away from Hollywood and the media frenzy that had descended on her and the studio. The LAPD had stationed two cops at her house, day and night, to keep away reporters, the curious and the autograph seekers.

Rita was constantly on the phone with the studio, the publicity department, and friends and family, who were calling at all hours. Even Howard Hughes' secretary had phoned, wanting to set up a meeting. Rita said she was leaving town and wouldn't return for three weeks. It was reported that Howard Hughes was upset and irritable over the whole incident, stating, "What does it have to do with me and RKO?"

Rita had also heard, through the grapevine, that he was interested in dating her, now more than ever, now that Tony was dead and she didn't have any other man in her life.

On the plane, Rita stared out the window, absorbed by the mountains of creamy clouds, the quilted farmland below, and the winding rivers flashing in sunlight.

Tony's funeral had been a media frenzy, and it had been mentally and emotionally exhausting. She'd had to endure hours of sad, weepy faces from his family and friends and colleagues: actors, directors and producers. The guilt in her swelled and throbbed. As she lay awake most nights, she wondered if she should have just let Tony rape her. It had happened to other actresses—most actresses—at some point during their careers. The studio couch was a common and constant reality throughout the movie industry.

If only she hadn't grabbed the gun from her bedroom. Tony would have raped her, and then none of this raging, endless nightmare would have happened.

The funeral was held at the Forest Lawn Memorial Park Cemetery. The police, including Detectives Briggs and Hadley, were everywhere. Every move Rita made was written about, watched and photographed. She felt like a specimen under a microscope. She was almost ready to confess when Bette Davis came up to her, cigarette poised at her mouth.

Bette's prominent eyes looked Rita up and down. Though they had met a couple of times, they weren't friends. "You look exhausted, Rita. Why are you losing sleep over this? Should I say I'm surprised?" Bette asked, bluntly. "Rita, honey, Tony was a son of a bitch, and I think everybody in this town knew it but you. If you ask me, one of his girlfriends shot him, and she probably laughed while she pulled the trigger. My question is: why did she fire only one shot? She should have emptied the gun in his chest."

Bette took a drag on her cigarette and blew a plume of smoke into the air.

"Well, one should never say bad things about the dead. You should only say good. I say, Tony is dead. Good."

Rita spent four days with her mother at the Flatbush, Brooklyn, two-bedroom home that Rita had purchased for her. Gladys Haskall—Haskall being Rita's birth name—begged Rita to leave Laura with her a few more days. Reluctantly, Rita agreed, only if Rita's sister, Martha, brought Laura to the beach house that following Friday for the weekend.

Rita arrived by private car at the Amagansett beach house on Monday afternoon. The stout, taciturn driver with a wandering eye carried her suitcases, and the groceries she'd purchased in Flatbush, into the house.

After he drove away, Rita entered the living room and turned in a circle, inspecting her new, three-week home. She instantly fell in love with the place: the screened porch, the stone fireplace, the white sofas and pillow soft chairs resting on polished wood floors. The bedrooms were filled with simple wooden furniture, light yellow curtains and throw rugs. Ceiling fans whirled lazily. The views of the private beach and ocean were breathtaking.

Feeling a wave of excitement, Rita quickly unpacked a yellow, one-piece swimming suit, a pair of flat sandals and her 35mm Kodak camera. After pulling on the suit and pinning her hair up under a white, wide brim hat, she reached for a thick blue towel and hurried off. She left the house, walking briskly across the deck and down the stairs, looping the leather strap of the camera around her neck. Crossing the warm sand, she quickly removed her sandals, left them in the sand and ran toward the ocean.

Under the full flood of sunlight, Rita roamed the tide-line, presenting her face to the sun and hazy, blue sky. It was the best she'd felt for months, perhaps years.

Later, she fluttered her towel onto the sand and sat, pulling her knees up and wrapping them with her arms. When she saw a sailboat with a red and white sail tracking across the sea, she snapped several photos of it. A black Labrador galloped by, tongue waggling, not lingering. She snapped photos of him as he splashed through the surf and finally loped away to meet his owner, a small spec in the distance.

Time seemed to stand still as Rita allowed all the tension, guilt and regret to drain out of her. Later, she strolled through the golden sunshine of evening into a rising mist that arose from the sea. She continued snapping photos of the peaceful, glorious scene until she ran out of film.

That night for dinner, she warmed the chicken dinner her mother had sent with her, opened a bottle of white wine, and took her dinner and a glass of wine to the screened porch. She lit a candle in the enclosed tabletop holder and ate leisurely, contentment filling every cell of her body.

The next morning, Rita bicycled to the quaint little town and drew up to the local drugstore. She handed off her used film to be developed and asked how long it would take. Fortunately, the owner, a man in his 60s, was a fan, and he told her he'd put a rush development on the order. Instead of the usual two-week window, he said it would be ready for pickup in a few days.

On the way out of the drugstore, Rita bought a newspaper and stepped outside.

Standing near her bicycle, she snapped open the paper and read a headline on the third page that startled her:

**LAPD Find New Evidence in Notorious
Hollywood Agent Murder!**

.

CHAPTER 8

2019

"Who's the girl?" Jack asked. "I thought you had some privacy on this beach."

"What do you mean?" Clint answered as he entered the living room from the kitchen, two bottles of beer in hand. He handed one to Jack.

Jack was sitting on the couch, a modest fire gleaming in the fireplace to help burn off the morning chill. The temperature had dropped into the 60s and it had threatened rain since early morning. It was early Saturday afternoon, and Jack had returned to spend another weekend with his brother.

Jack held Clint's cell phone, swiping through recent photos Clint had taken of the beach house, dunes and sea.

As Clint sat down next to his brother, a bowling ball of thunder rolled across the sky, and rain was soon lashing the windows.

Jack presented the phone so Clint could glimpse the photo. "See? In the background, walking along near the water. It's not a clear shot of her face, but she has one hot body. You can see her face clearer in some of the other photos."

"What other photos?"

"There's more than one."

Clint took a swig of beer then leaned forward, studying the photo. "I don't know who she is. I've never seen her."

Clint watched Jack's throat working as he tipped the beer back, drinking long. After he placed the bottle on the floor, and still gripping the cell phone, he swiped backwards, looking for other photos of the girl. "Like I said, she's in more photos. See… here, and here," Jack said pointing. "She's one hot-looking blonde, and I love that canary yellow swimsuit. You must have seen her. I mean, how could you miss her? She's in at least six photos."

Clint stuck the bottle between his knees and took the phone from Jack. The wind groaned and, in the distance, the sea rumbled and pounded the beach.

Clint stared, mystified. He shook his head. "I've never seen her. How many pictures is she in?" he asked, swiping back and forth.

"I told you, at least six, maybe more. I thought maybe you were keeping her a secret," Jack said, with a wink.

"No… I'm telling you; I've never seen her."

"Well, whoever she is, she's a beauty."

Clint had a sudden idea. He snatched the phone from his brother and searched his gallery for his more recent videos and tapped one. It was of a panoramic view of the surrounding area he'd taken that morning after a quick run on the beach.

His breath caught. Jack leaned in for a better look. The lovely creature entered the frame from the left, wandering the beach, this time in a royal blue swimsuit that defined a shapely body, full breasts and long, lovely legs.

Clint was captivated. He re-ran the 45-second video and his eyes sharpened on her as she rambled the edge of the water under a buttery sun. She paused to pluck a shell from the sand and study it, as seagulls hovered. After dropping the shell into her canvas bag, she faced the glistening sea, shading her eyes with a hand. As she started back up the beach, she replaced her sunglasses and removed her wide-brimmed hat, shaking out her thick, shoulder-length blonde hair, lifting her face to the sun.

Jack stared at his brother, waiting for an answer. "So, bro, who is she?"

Clint shook his head in a wonder. "I have no idea. I've never seen her."

"Are you blind? How could you miss her? I mean some people you can miss, like our Aunt Edna, but not this girl. She's Hollywood gorgeous."

Jack snatched the phone back from his brother, searched the photos until he found the one he wanted, then tapped to enlarge it. He pushed the phone into his brother's face.

"Do you know who this woman reminds me of? The girl in your den."

"What girl?"

"Rita Randall. When you enlarge that photo and see her face, I'm telling you she could be her sister—her twin sister. Clint, man, you have got to get out of your head and find out who this blonde goddess is. I mean, come on. Do you even know who your neighbors are?"

Clint grew a bit defensive. "No, I don't, and I don't care to."

"I bet she knows who *you* are. She's probably hanging around hoping you'll go over and introduce yourself. I mean, she's like photo bombing you in every other picture, trying to get your attention, and you don't even know she's there. Come on, Clint, you're a bestselling author. She's probably dying to meet you, and you should be dying to meet her."

By late afternoon, the storm went rattling off to the east, leaving behind a squealing wind and cooler temperatures. Clint decided to put on a rain slicker and his baseball cap and return to the beach. Maybe he'd see her. He'd snap more photos and take a video or two.

He stepped onto the screened porch in a frown of concentration, feeling a mounting expectation. He wanted to see her. Maybe he even wanted to meet her. He squinted out to the horizon and started off.

CHAPTER 9

1948

"Who's the handsome man in the background, standing near the edge of the water?" Martha asked. She was sitting on the white couch, shuffling through Rita's recent photographs.

Rita sat on the floor with Laura, both involved in a *Gulliver's Travels* coloring book. From the humpback radio resting on a white radio stand, Kay Kyser sang *On a Slow Boat to China*.

"I don't know who he is," Rita said.

Laura said, "Mommy, let's use red to color his face."

"Red? Maybe brown would be better."

"No, I think he's been in the sun a lot. I think he's hot and sweaty, like we were this morning."

An early July heat wave had moved in, smothering Eastern Long Island in currents of wet humidity. A big hot sun baked the world, blistering the backs and shoulders of swimmers and sunbathers.

Rita's older sister, Martha, was a perky brunette, shorter than Rita. Though not as attractive as her younger sister, she had a round, friendly face and pleasant manner. Instead of being jealous of Rita's looks and success, Martha was proud of Rita, protective and loving. Always quick to smile, she smiled when she found two additional photos with the attractive man in the background.

"He's in these other photos, too, Rita."

"Yeah, I know," Rita said, not looking up, helping Laura color Gulliver's face red.

Martha rested the photos in her lap, staring at her sister with curiosity. "And you don't know who he is?"

"No… I've never seen him."

Martha laughed again. "Rita, how can you miss this guy? The camera didn't miss him. This is not the kind of man you can easily miss. He is very nice to look at. All right, so maybe he should shave and get a haircut, but…"

Rita cut her off. "I like the beard and long hair. He's very masculine."

Martha's eyes lighted up. "So you *have* seen him?"

Rita sat up cross-legged. "No, I haven't. Only in the photographs."

Martha snatched a photo, held it up and studied it. "Where do you think he lives?"

"I have no idea."

"Maybe your friend, Everett Claxton, knows him."

"I would assume so."

"Have you met any of your neighbors?"

"No…"

"None?"

"No. This is Sunday, Martha. I've only been here since Monday. And, anyway, Everett told me that everybody out here likes their privacy. I also like my privacy, especially now with all that's going on back in Hollywood."

Martha slapped the photo with two fingers. "Then why is this guy walking across your beach? Hey, maybe he's a reporter or something."

Rita met her sister's questioning gaze. "I thought about that. Anyway, I don't know who he is, and if I see him, I'll ask him to leave."

"I'm not sure I'd ask him to leave," Martha said, jokingly, patting her curls and waves flirtatiously. "Maybe you should invite him over for a glass of iced tea?"

Rita gave her sister a doubtful glance before returning to color Gulliver's tunic green, while Laura colored his legs purple.

"Well, if I wasn't married, I would certainly take a little stroll on the beach and see if I could spot him. He looks quite tall, doesn't he?" Martha said, still engrossed in the photo. She tipped her head right and then left, in careful examination. "A nice face, from what I can see of it, and he looks as though he's put together rather well, kind of like a younger Joseph Cotton. But then, who can really see with that beard... and he's too far away."

"Go ahead," Rita said. "Go back out in that heat and see if you can find him. But put on a hat and cover your shoulders. They're already sunburned. If you find him, bring him back and we'll all have some iced tea and a nice little chat."

Amused, Martha stood up, laughing, enjoying her sister as she always did. "And what would you do if I did?"

Rita flashed a mischievous grin. "I'd make some iced tea, sister dear, and maybe I'd spike it with a bit of that whiskey Everett keeps in his liquor cabinet."

Martha gathered up the photos and reached for the morning newspaper. She picked it up, suddenly turning serious.

"Are you finished with the paper?" Martha asked.

Rita nodded.

"Did you read the latest about Tony's murder?"

Rita nodded again, not looking up.

"The police aren't getting very far. I thought they'd have caught the girl by now. Poor Tony."

"Why do you say caught the girl? And why poor Tony?" Rita snapped, hotly.

Martha was surprised by Rita's reaction. "Well, I only meant that..."

"Tony wasn't so nice, Martha. You only saw the smiles and heard the jokes—the funny Tony. He wasn't always so nice or so funny. That's all I'm saying."

Martha lowered her head. "I only meant that..." Her voice dropped.

Rita puffed out her cheeks and blew the air out, raising her softening eyes on her sister. "I'm sorry, Martha. It's just that the whole thing has been... I just can't get it off my mind."

Martha nodded sympathetically. "I shouldn't have brought it up. You came out here to rest and forget, not to listen to my big mouth."

Rita rose to her feet, went to her sister and gave her a little hug. "Forget it. I'm just so happy you're going to spend a week with us." She held Martha at arm's length. "Are you sure Ben doesn't mind?"

Martha smiled. "No, I told you, as long as Mom takes the kids this week, and I agree to a week's vacation in Maine so he can fish, he's fine with it. Of course, I get to clean the fish, you know."

"He's been a good husband, hasn't he?" Rita said. "And he's good with the kids."

Martha shrugged, smiling in a private way, as if remembering some naughty thing. "Yes… and I love him to death."

Laura was coloring Gulliver's boots black, humming along with the radio. Without looking up, she said. "Why did Tony die?"

Rita looked stricken. She turned to Laura. "It was an accident, honey. Like I told you when the police came. It was just a bad accident."

Of course, Rita hadn't told Martha the truth. She hadn't told anyone the truth and, God willing, she never would.

"I miss him, Mommy. Tony was funny."

Rita folded her arms, staring off into the distance.

Two days later, on Sunday evening, July 11th, Rita was straightening up the living room when the phone rang. In a gruff voice, Detective Briggs said she needed to return to LA as soon as possible.

"There have been some significant developments in our investigation, Miss Randall."

"Can you tell me what they are, Detective Briggs?"

"Not over the phone. When can you return? What date?"

Rita felt herself grow cold. She tensed up. "Well… I'm not sure."

"The sooner the better. I can send someone to accompany you."

"That won't be necessary. If it's that important, I'll

catch the first plane out tomorrow. Is that soon enough?"

"Yes. Call me when you arrive. I'll send a squad car for you."

"No, thank you. I'll come with my attorney."

"I think that's a good idea," Briggs said coldly.

After Rita hung up the phone, she dropped down onto the couch, shutting her eyes and massaging them. It was apparent that the police had new evidence, and it concerned her. It was something definite. What could it be?

She heard Martha and Laura laughing in Laura's bedroom.

She called out to them. "I'm going for a quick walk. I'll be back before Laura goes to bed."

"Better make it short," Martha answered. "I think there's a storm coming."

Rita left for the beach, though angry storm clouds were piled up on the horizon, sliding ominously across the sea. It didn't matter. Rita liked storms, and she needed the walk to help still her nerves after the phone call with Briggs.

While lightning clicked in the distance, Rita decided she'd tell her attorney the truth when she returned to LA. Perhaps she'd get off with a plea of involuntary manslaughter or self-defense. If the worse happened and she was given jail time, she knew Martha would take Laura, and since her mother lived nearby, Laura would get the care and love she'd need.

Rita wandered the beach aimlessly, her lovely face lit up by the descending gloom of purple light. Waves curled and crashed, climbing the beach in smooth, spreading blankets of watery foam. The last of the fleeing sandpipers flitted away over the dunes.

In the wheezing, blowing wind, Rita's blue summer gown trembled, her rich blonde hair stirred about her face.

When she first saw a blue shimmering tube of light dancing along the upper dunes, she stopped to draw a breath, dazzled by it. What was it? She'd never seen anything like it. Its mesmerizing light sparkled and flashed like the flashbulbs from a camera. She glanced about, searching for its source. Was it a low cloud from the storm? Was it low-lying misty fog?

As she watched it expand and gather force and density, she grew uneasy. It seemed like a live thing, searching, aware of her, seeking her. It started toward her. Rita stumbled backward, glancing toward the house, measuring distance. In an instant, the tumbling wave leaped over the dunes, all iridescent light and force, wriggling toward her like a great twisting snake.

In hot panic, Rita pivoted and sprinted off in the opposite direction, glancing back over her shoulder, her breath loud and fast. She heard a crack of lightning overhead and flinched. The world trembled as thunder boomed. Still, the relentless wave charged her.

She screamed for help, running, weaving from side to side, seeking escape. But there was no escape. The wind blew sharp gusts that burst into her and all about her, like wind bombs. Her last thoughts were of Laura, and then the swelling blue wave opened its wide shimmering mouth and swallowed her.

CHAPTER 10

2019

Sunday night, after Jack was gone, Clint lay propped up in bed, staring into his phone, perplexed. He'd watched the same video over and over again, the one he'd shot that afternoon. He tapped the video and watched it again.

There she was, the same blonde wandering the tideline, her hands locked behind her back, seemingly deep in thought. The sun was bright, the waves calm, the beach deserted except for a single little girl who was busy building a crude sandcastle, much too close to the approaching surf. The castle walls would be breached within a half hour.

The woman's floppy hat was low on her forehead, shadowing her face, and her sky-blue bathing suit was still damp from a swim.

Two things bothered him: first, when he'd taken the video, it was cloudy. It was misty. Low, clay-heavy clouds lay over the horizon. In this video, the day was sunny and bright, not a cloud in the sky.

Second, there was no way that woman and her little girl were on the beach when he took the video. Absolutely no way they were there. Impossible. He'd searched the beach. He had climbed the dunes, snapping photos. He'd tramped both ways, until dune fences became barriers, and dogs burst from around houses with low rusty barks, warning him away.

So how could it be that this woman and this child appeared on his phone in this video? Impossible.

Clint was completely baffled and disturbed. He hadn't shown the video to Jack. He was afraid his brother would do something silly, like clamber into his Mercedes and drive around, stopping to get out and knock on doors, asking if there was a good-looking blonde parading about. Jack did have a crazy, fearless, and often adolescent streak. Many of Jack's colleagues said it was what made him a good trial attorney.

Clint had tried to sleep, but he couldn't. The whole thing was weird and unnerving. Not only had the woman appeared in the video, but she had also appeared in additional photos he'd taken that morning. Again, the day was bright, no clouds, and in one photo, she had turned and seemed to be looking directly at him. She had briefly removed her hat, revealing a beautiful, striking face framed by gleaming blonde hair, a refined aristocratic nose, and a long, chiseled neck. She blazed with magnetism and mystery, with a soft exotic glow, like the starlets of the 1940s and 50s; that mysterious mixture of fire and ice. Clint had looked at the photo repeatedly, and she seemed to be looking back at him, as if to say, "Can you help me?"

Was all this his imagination?

And even more astounding, in one of the last photos he'd taken, the woman was standing in the screened porch—his screened porch. In that photo, the furniture was completely different. There was no designer table with stainless steel top and wooden base; no metallic gray, futuristic deck chairs. In that photo were striped canvas deck chairs, exotic floor plants and a vintage patio table with a blue and yellow striped umbrella. Where did those come from?

What the hell was going on? If Jack hadn't seen the woman in the photos as well, Clint would have thought he was losing his mind. But Jack had seen her, right in his phone.

Clint threw back the sheet and swung his feet to the floor, the phone gripped tightly in his hand. He searched the walls for answers, scratched his beard and paced the room. Whenever he thought about the woman, he felt a pleasing anticipation and a private satisfaction that he'd somehow found her. But where was she? Was she a ghost? As silly as that sounded, it seemed to be at least one possible explanation. Perhaps she had died out here at some time in the past and her ghostly body still lingered. But what about the little girl? Was she a ghost too?

Standing there, grappling with his swirling thoughts, Clint again flipped through the photos. Whenever he stared into her eyes, he felt a grab in his chest. A longing. An aching.

When Clint clicked off his phone, the room turned eerily silent. Was she standing in his room at that very instant?

The next morning, Clint was seated on a stool at the kitchen counter, his face in his laptop, searching blogs, chat rooms, articles and *YouTube*, hoping to find anything remotely similar to what he was experiencing. He read about time slips, time travel, ghost stories, string theories, parallel universes, out-of-body experiences and near-death experiences. Except for occasional hazy images of the dead—mostly children in Victorian photographs—he came up empty.

As Clint sipped coffee and munched a bagel, he continued the search, clicking on a link that caught his eyes. *The Philadelphia Experiment and Montauk Project.* Montauk was only about twenty miles away, at the eastern end of Long Island. Clint was a voracious reader as a boy, and he recalled now reading an article that documented strange experiments that had occurred in Montauk.

Clint clicked on the link and began to read. The more he read, the more improbable the article sounded.

According to the writer, there had been secret government time travel projects undertaken at an air force base in Montauk during the 1940s and after. The Philadelphia Experiment was one of them. A man named Oscar Bates had been intricately involved with several projects and, later in life, he claimed there were secret files at Los Alamos, New Mexico which stated that time travel had been accidentally discovered in 1936 by a U.S. Navy ship, near the Bermuda Triangle. Apparently, the ship disappeared and reappeared two months later.

In Montauk, time travel experiments expanded on what was previously learned, and during World War II and after, there were several time travel adventures to the past and the future. The Montauk Air Force base finally closed in 1981. Reading on, Clint also learned that Oscar Bates had lived in Amagansett during the late 1940s and early 1950s.

Clint sat back, lacing his hands behind his head. Could there be any possible connection? There was only one way to find out.

On impulse, Clint typed in Oscar Bates' name. To his surprise and excitement, he saw that Oscar Bates was still alive at ninety-six years old, living in a nursing home in Massapequa Park, Long Island. Clint pushed away and stood up, moving toward the open French doors. He gazed out at the shimmering sea, his mind filled with speculation.

Clint shut down his laptop and paced the kitchen, working on a thought. Would Oscar Bates be mentally present enough to answer some of Clint's questions? Would the man be able to shed any light on what was going on?

Clint released a heavy sigh. Maybe he was going crazy. Maybe he was getting way ahead of himself. Maybe there was a logical answer for the photos, even though he had no clue as to what that might be.

But maybe, in some weird and inexplicable way, Clint had plugged into some strange phenomena. It was worth a visit to Oscar Bates. Massapequa Park wasn't that far away. Clint found the number of the nursing home and called.

CHAPTER 11

2019

Oscar Bates' great granddaughter, Wendy Korman, at first refused Clint's request to see the elder Mr. Bates. The nursing home had agreed to give Clint Wendy's phone number only after he shamefully used "the author" card. "I'm a best-selling author. I promise not to intrude and to be respectful."

Wendy called the next morning, her voice filled with agitation. "I don't let writers or reporters interview my great-grandfather," she said, crisply. "They have written awful things about him. What do you want?"

"I promise you, I'm not interested in writing about him."

"I've heard that before. Are you writing a book about Montauk and the Philadelphia Experiment?"

"No... Mrs. Korman, I'm not."

"Then why do you want to see him? He's not well. He's very ill. We don't expect him to live much longer and I don't want him disturbed."

Clint considered his words carefully. "It's difficult to explain, but something has happened… I can't explain it. I'm living in Amagansett, and something has happened that is, well, kind of strange. It was an accident that I found your great-grandfather's name. I was hoping he might be able to help me."

There was silence on the other end.

Clint continued. "I just want to ask him a couple of questions, that's it. I promise to be respectful, and I won't take up much of his time.

"I looked you up, Mr. West. Believe it or not, I've read two of your books."

Now Clint was silent.

"Be honest with me, Mr. West, are you using my great-grandfather for research?"

"No, I'm not. It's beyond that. I can't explain it over the phone. I can't explain what is happening, but I hope your great-grandfather might know. At the very least, he might be able to explain what's going on."

Clint was in the kitchen, stalking back and forth, cell phone in hand, his entire body tense.

"I liked your books," Wendy said softly.

Clint felt hope rise. "Thank you."

"Will there be a third in the series, the *Finding Summer* series?"

"Yes… I'm working on it… It's been going slow."

"I read that your wife died. I'm sorry. I didn't know."

"Thanks. That's why I'm out here. I'm trying to finish the book."

"Like I said, Mr. West…"

"Call me Clint. Please."

"My great-grandfather is not well."

"How is his mind?"

"When he's awake, it's good. His body is weak, but his mind is still amazingly good. Okay, can you come tomorrow… early afternoon, say around 2 p.m.?"

"Yes," Clint said, enthusiastically. "I'll be there. And thank you. Thank you very much."

Pleasant Valley Nursing Home was a low, sprawling place, with salmon brick buildings surrounded by tall trees, rows of manicured shrubs, and a little pond.

Inside, the place was clean, with the smell of lemon disinfectant mixed with floor wax. The polished, gray tile floors shined, and wide windows, which looked out on a gentle sloping green lawn, let in plenty of light.

Wendy met Clint at the reception desk, looking him up and down to ensure he was the same writer she'd *Googled*, and not some imposter. Wendy was heavy-set, in her early 40s, with short red and blonde hair, dancing alert eyes and a broad mouth. She wore jeans, an off-the-shoulder print top, and red sneakers.

Clint saw a woman who radiated confidence, practical authority and a no-nonsense manner. They shook hands, discussed the weather, "It's been cool for this time of year," Clint said, and then Wendy led the way to Oscar Bates' room.

Oscar Bates was seated in a soft, black leather chair, in a cool, air-conditioned room, with his back to the windows. Sunlight colored the closed white draperies yellow, giving Oscar a waxen complexion. He was thin, bent and yet watchful. His eyes were still young and curious, though inside a body that had long since withered. His frosty hair was sparse, his face plowed with lines, and his lips thin and tight.

While Wendy introduced him, Oscar didn't stir. Clint outstretched his hand to shake, but Oscar didn't take it or look at it. His watery eyes studied Clint, sizing him up.

Wendy offered a chair and Clint sat opposite the old man. She remained standing, as if to referee, just in case Clint had lied to her about his reason for coming. Clint had no doubt that, if provoked, she had both the sturdy strength and the will to grab him by his polo shirt collar and toss him out into the hallway, like a bouncer dealing with a rowdy drunk.

Clint gathered his thoughts, keeping his voice low and measured. He glanced up at Wendy. She nodded for him to begin.

Clint looked directly into the old man's eyes, then swallowed and leaned forward.

"Mr. Bates…I've rented a house in Amagansett. I know you lived there for a time back in the 1940s and 1950s."

Oscar Bates didn't move. He kept his frosty stare fixed on Clint.

"Mr. Bates, something strange has been happening."

Wendy took a half step forward, all ears.

"I know this is going to sound weird, but I think there is someone occupying the same space as me. I don't know if it's a ghost or what. I… well I…" Clint's voice trailed off, as he searched for the right words. "I don't even believe in this kind of thing."

Oscar hooded his eyes, as if recalling something.

Clint struggled on. "I take photos of the beach and my beach house, and in some of them, a young woman appears somewhere in the background. But she wasn't there when I took the photo… I'm certain of it. I've taken countless photos and videos and she appears in at least a third of them, but she wasn't anywhere in the area when I took the photos. I'm positive about it. I just don't know what to think."

Oscar's still sharp eyes flared with sudden interest.

For the first time, Oscar moved—just a shaky hand to scratch the end of his nose. He slowly turned his head toward Wendy. When he spoke, his voice was a hoarse whisper.

"Leave us alone, Wendy."

Wendy's eyes enlarged. "Leave?"

"Yes… Please… And close the door behind you."

Wendy's mouth tightened and her face fell in disappointment. She threw Clint an inquisitive glance as she left the room, shutting the door softly.

Now alone, Oscar sat up a little straighter, narrowing his eyes and examining Clint more closely. He folded his liver-spotted hands in his lap, and Clint noticed that the old man's thread-thin body seemed to awaken.

"Are you cold?" Clint asked. "Can I get you a blanket or something?"

Oscar stared, and Clint saw the hard metal of his eyes.

"Talk… Tell me," Oscar said, speaking with some difficulty.

Clint tugged out his cell phone and tapped on his gallery. He carefully and concisely explained everything that had happened, pointing often to the phone.

Oscar sat in a placid dignity; his cool expression unchanged.

Clint stood up. "Would you like to see the videos? Through an App, I was able to create a time-lapse movie that shows the woman in various times and places on the beach. Even occupying my house, but all the furniture is different."

Oscar slowly, mechanically nodded, and Clint stepped over.

Oscar watched the video with a keen, excited interest.

After Clint returned to his chair, silence ensued for a time, as Oscar's eyes grew distant with thought.

Finally, to Clint's surprise, Oscar smiled sadly. He looked at Clint and then beyond him, into unknown worlds.

"I miss it," Oscar said, weakly. "Those days… those impossible days."

Clint sat as still as a statue.

When Oscar's eyes again settled on Clint, they were changed. They were brighter, but somber.

"Be careful," he said.

Clint adjusted himself in the chair, feeling the weight of the moment. He was sure the old man knew what was going on.

"What is it? What's happening?"

Oscar placed his left hand over his right, to still the weak right hand's trembling. "What's happening? A time portal."

Clint's uncertain eyes blinked. "Time portal?"

"I assume you've read about me and the experiments I was involved with?"

Clint nodded.

"In the early 1940s, we accidently discovered two portals… running from Montauk to Amagansett. Well, running is not truly correct. They appear randomly, which is why we remained in Montauk and did our experiments there. These portals were known by the Montauk Indians, who had lived there for hundreds of years, or so we learned when we delved into the history of that area."

"What are time portals?" Clint asked. "I mean, I vaguely know what they are… but… not exactly."

"Time portals connect the present with the past, or with the future. They're natural doorways that allow time travel, if you know how to navigate them. Well, that's not entirely true. They allow time travel, even if you don't know how to navigate them. They can be random, and if one is present at the right time and place, one can find themselves swept up in them and propelled into another time, past or future. In our experiments, we found that there is a kind of eccentric intelligence about them, as if they are aware of the time traveler and what he or she is intending."

Oscar paused to cough. Talking was hard for the elderly man, and he reached for a glass of water and took several sips before continuing.

"They're not easy to find or see. They are volatile and unpredictable, as we learned. We lost people during several experiments. We had no idea where they went or what happened to them. I was lost once myself, in the future, and I was lucky to get back. When I did get back, I was all banged up and I had lost my memory. I didn't know who I was or where I'd been."

"How long did it take before your memory returned?"

"A month or so. I was in the hospital for a week."

Clint gripped his phone tightly, stress building in his gut. "But how does it work? How could it work? I mean, how is it that this woman appears in photographs and videos on my cell phone? It doesn't make any sense."

Oscar looked away, uncertain. "I suspect you have somehow linked to the identical digital phase. In other words, your phone has dialed her number, so to speak."

Clint strained to understand. "How is that even possible?"

Oscar's gaze was inward, as he smiled. "You have engaged the portal. My best guess is that you have linked to this woman. I'm too tired to explain."

Clint had many questions, but Oscar was losing energy. His shoulders sagged, and his eyes fluttered closed for a time.

"Can she see me?" Clint asked softly.

Oscar's eyes opened, and his forehead knotted into a frown. "Perhaps, if she has the right device."

"What kind of device?"

"A radio. A phone. A camera. Does she appear as someone in the past or in the future?"

"I'm not sure. The past I think."

Oscar's eyes twinkled with a new pleasure. "At least she's pretty."

"So what do I do about this?" Clint asked, knowing it was a stupid question.

"Easy. Turn off your phone, but it may be too late for that."

"Too late?"

"I suspect you've engaged the portal."

Clint didn't like the sound of that. "Then why don't I see the portal?"

Oscar tugged on his ear and again stared into space. "Full moons and thunderstorms often make them visible. People mistake them for mist, fog or low clouds. They hover near the sea and over the dunes toward early morning and at twilight."

"What do they look like?" Clint asked.

"A blue, translucent, scintillating light. They twist and leap, like large rolling snakes. The mouth of the thing can expand to as much as 20 feet."

Clint swallowed away a lump. "Well... I guess I won't be taking any more photos or videos."

Oscar smiled weakly. "Wherever she is, I'm sure she's already received your call."

Clint's body turned cold. He suddenly wished he hadn't come. "What does that mean?"

Oscar looked away, shrugging a shoulder. When he spoke, it was nearly at a whisper.

"To keep it simple and in modern language: you've most certainly got each other's number."

"But through a cell phone? By taking photographs with a cell phone?"

"Back in the 1940s, we used radio waves and monitors to connect to past power stations and future telepathy. The past and future are very different things, but they operate in similar ways, although, again, portals are highly volatile and dangerous."

"How did you know where to go?"

"Focused thought. We developed telepathy. We cleared our heads from the constant static of thought. It wasn't easy. In your case, you have somehow connected to this woman. Not such a bad thing, I'd wager from the looks of her."

Clint tried to shake off the weirdness of the thing, the improbability.

Oscar managed a wan smile. "If you think you know the world, and understand the world, then you don't know anything or understand anything."

Clint looked at him carefully.

Oscar held his smile. "I do miss those days… those impossible days."

CHAPTER 12

2019

Later the next evening, Clint stood near the ocean, shirtless, in blue trunks, with a towel wrapped around his neck. He'd gone for a swim, hoping to clear his mind from the prior day's conversation with Oscar. It hadn't worked. Clint's head was a storm of thoughts and emotions.

As he hovered on the edge of a decision, he gazed out at the setting golden sun and the turquoise sea. Should he leave—go back to LA? He certainly wasn't getting any work done. No, he couldn't return. He couldn't face the memories of Jenny yet. Should he move to Manhattan? No, too hot and sticky this time of year.

Clint had hoped a conversation with Oscar would confirm that there was nothing paranormal going on, but it hadn't. Oscar had spoken with clarity and directness. But could he believe him? No. The whole thing was just too fantastic and out of Clint's practical and comfortable reach. It was a bridge too far.

Time portals? It was the stuff of fiction, not reality, and he knew the difference. Clint dealt in imagination nearly every day of his life. He was a novelist who made up stuff. This sounded made up to him, as if he were a character in a novel.

So why was he still filled with anxiety? Because he'd had little sleep, and he still had no "real" explanation for the beautiful woman who appeared in his photos.

He was seriously considering a visit to a shrink. Maybe his mind was playing tricks on him. Maybe Jenny's death and his grieving had taken a strange turn. Maybe he was simply hallucinating.

But the same old undeniable fact kept circling back: Jack saw the photos too. He'd seen the same beautiful woman, and he'd seen her first.

Jack had called earlier in the day, and Clint was growing annoyed with him, as he often had when they were kids. On the phone, Jack's voice had been sugary sarcastic.

"Any more of those photos of the hot blonde, bro?" he'd asked, taunting humor in his voice. "And don't say you haven't taken more photos. I know you have. I know you're lying to me, little brother, but that's okay. You've got her tucked away somewhere in that house, and you're keeping her all to yourself. Hell, I'd keep her hidden too if I was in your shoes."

Clint was irritated. "I'm not hiding anyone... certainly not her."

"Okay, whatever you say. Do you mind if I come this weekend and bring a girl? She's one of the paralegals. Her name's Linda. She's smart and has a good body and a wicked sense of humor."

Clint was not in the mood to see Jack or meet his new

girlfriend. "Not this weekend, Jack. I've got to work on the book."

Jack made a tsk-tsk sound. "Yeah, Yeah, I know what you're really going to be working on. It's not nice to hide things from your big brother, you know."

"Look, Jack, I have to go."

"I know you do, bro. I'll be in touch. You know I'm going to have to meet her someday."

That evening, Clint stared into a sunset sky that looked tragic, all red, orange and purple. After the sun finally sank, a soft, bluish light covered the sea, sand and dunes.

Clint wandered for a while, feeling a lovely ocean breeze wash over him and cool some of his agitation. He'd purposely left his phone at the house, and now he was tempted to hurry back to flip through the photos again. He had to face it: the woman had a hypnotic, dreamlike quality that left an impression he couldn't shake off. She'd awakened something inside—something he hadn't felt since Jenny's death.

He'd dreamed about her during an afternoon nap. She appeared on a hillside, bathed in brilliant sunlight, wearing a flowing, white diaphanous gown. He watched, transfixed, as she meandered through a field of yellow daisies; he was caught by her graceful figure and the gentle sway of her hips. He watched breathlessly as she waved, beckoning him to join her. He started up the hill, only to watch in agony as she dissolved into a shimmering blue mist, drifting away in a puff of wind.

Clint returned to the house through the screened porch. He entered the kitchen, opened the fridge, and reached for a bottle of water. As he took a first swallow, he felt a warm stirring across his skin. He had the sudden feeling that he wasn't alone, and he glanced about uneasily. Something on the porch grabbed his attention. He saw a scintillating light, as if someone had tossed a handful of glitter into the wind. It scattered, sparkled and flared.

To his utter shock, something began to take shape within the light. Against the backdrop of blue twilight, a swirling flame of sapphire light danced and expanded, filling the place with millions of bright sparks.

Clint dropped the plastic bottle. It bounced on the tile floor and rolled away, water gurgling from it. He shrank back from the spectacle, shading his eyes from the sharp glare, as the room exploded into light.

A spiral of sparks began to spin, like a small galaxy, and from its center, a form emerged. From a smoky fog, the indistinct shape of a woman gradually appeared, gleaming with life.

Clint fixed his astonished eyes on her—on her lovely face and shining blonde, shoulder-length hair. She stared back, luminous, as if lit from within by a glorious blue light, her pool blue eyes round with baffled surprise.

Timeless minutes passed while Clint stared, his heart kicking in his chest. As the light flared and fizzled about her, he saw her clearly. She was an elegant beauty, and to his utter shock, she was the same woman who had appeared in his photos. He advanced slowly toward her, feeling strange and spellbound.

She gazed sightlessly, as if stunned and lost, her body radiating an otherworldly enchantment. All at once, the dazzling light vanished, and she stood before him, real, present and trembling.

CHAPTER 13
2019

Rita struggled to breathe as she swallowed the heat of terror. It seemed only seconds before that she was on the beach, watching in horror as a wave of blue, rolling light charged her. Filled with panic, she'd darted off, glancing back over her shoulder to see the blue surging wave thunder toward her. It seemed to have intelligence and an infinite range. There was no escape. If she ran right, toward the sea, it adjusted and followed. If she climbed the dunes, it was there. And then it engulfed her. She tried to run in and out of rays of brilliant light, but it was no use.

The force of impact swept her off her feet, flinging her about like a rag doll. She crashed through prisms of light, tossed about like a twig in the ocean, waves tumbling over her, through her and around her.

She was hurled, helpless, fighting for breath, chest heaving, as desperate thoughts of her daughter, Laura, flashed through her mind. If Rita was drowning, dying, what would happen to her? Rita cried out in desperation, calling Laura's name.

Rita had nearly recovered her balance when a massive blue moon appeared ahead, racing directly toward her. She braced for a collision but, to her cold surprise, she passed through it. Again, she struggled to find balance and stand.

And then she was running again—racing down an old asphalt road, between columns of massive tree trunks that seemed to stretch up into infinity. She ran on, heart pounding, as the sun slanted down in threads of spinning gold. Without warning, the road buckled and she dropped, limbs flailing, falling into an endless blue light. Far below, she saw an emerald pool, no larger than a swimming pool. Holding her breath, she dropped like a stone, splashing into its rippling water, plunging down, and down.

Rita stood on rubbery legs, feeling drugged and disoriented. How did she get here? Where was here? Who was he? As objects began to take shape, her mind was a muddled mess of fear, memory and confusion. The man before her was only vaguely familiar, and her eyes strained to focus on him.

"Where am I?" Rita said, her voice hollow, as if she had no air in her lungs.

Clint resettled his shoulders, hardly aware that the cold, damp towel he'd used for his earlier swim was still around his neck.

He stared at Rita with a splendid wonder. He tried to speak, failed, cleared his throat and tried again. "What was that light? Who are you?"

Neither seemed to have answers, and so they fell back into a thick silence, their wide eyes trying to make sense of the extraordinary moment.

Rita presented a façade of bravery as she willed herself not to faint. For several minutes, Rita's and Clint's eyes connected, each startled and exploring.

Rita studied the tall, handsome, bearded man with the guarded, captivating eyes, with the considerable breadth of shoulder, and the smooth, naturally muscled arms.

As the silence between them expanded, Rita slowly took in her surroundings, her body quivering, feeling the shock of displacement.

"Where is this?" Rita asked, as she worked to steady her breath.

Clint didn't move. "Where? Long island."

Rita stared with a certain suspicion and reluctance. "Amagansett?"

Clint lifted an eyebrow. "Yes…"

"I don't understand," Rita said.

"What happened to you?" Clint asked.

"I don't know…"

Clint struggled to shake his thoughts lose. "What was that light?"

Feeling weak, Rita touched her temple and shut her eyes. "Can I sit?"

Clint moved toward her as she lowered herself in one of the gray, futuristic deck chairs. He stopped a few feet away.

"Can I get you something? Water? Coffee?"

Rita's eyes fluttered open. She looked up at him, staring, her eyes glassy and unfocused. She began to shiver uncontrollably.

Clint left for the bedroom, soon returning with a blanket. He wrapped her shoulders with it and she sighed in relief, tried to thank him, but failed, her voice lost somewhere in her throat.

Minutes later, he brought her a mug of coffee. She'd recovered enough to accept it with trembling hands. Clint stood by, waiting.

"Feeling better?" Clint asked.

After a few sips, her eyes cleared, and she looked him over. Where had she seen this man? "… Yes, a little."

Darkness had nearly descended, and the lantern light hanging above the patio deck flickered on. Surprised, Rita gazed up at it, curiously.

Clint drifted away to his room to shimmy out of his trunks and slip into a black t-shirt and a pair of cargo shorts. He'd left her on purpose, wondering if she'd still be there when he returned. Wondering if he had somehow created the whole incident in his wild imagination.

Minutes later, when he rejoined her on the deck, he hesitated. She was still sitting there, eyes shut, hardly moving, completely wrapped in the blanket, her hands clutching the coffee mug, as if to warm them.

With a little sigh of unease, Clint decided to let her rest. He made a detour into the kitchen, soon returning to the patio with his own mug of coffee.

She sensed his presence and opened her sticky, heavy eyes. "I think I'm having a crazy dream," she said.

Clint blew on his coffee, taking careful sips. "Certainly crazy," Clint added.

Rita brought the coffee mug to her lips, drank, and swallowed with some effort. Her body felt punished, her voice strained and hoarse.

Clint angled a chair to her right and eased down. Neither spoke for a time as they struggled to relax, trying to understand what had happened.

Rita nodded toward the LED lantern. "How does it light?"

The amber light caught the side of her face and cast a

soft golden glow that accented her lovely hair.

"It's an LED, solar powered."

His gaze lingered on her. He couldn't pull it away.

Rita felt the stir of the night breeze across her face, heard the voice of the sea rise and fall, heard the echoing bark of a dog down on the beach. She longed to ask questions, but her mind was in a kind of shock, as if her wires were crossed and the words were stuck somewhere in her mushy brain.

She lowered the coffee mug to the table, her hands still trembling.

"Getting warm?" Clint asked.

She looked at him somberly. "Yes... I don't know what has happened to me. I don't know where I am."

Clint thought of Oscar Bates and he reran their conversation about the time portal. What had he said?

"*Your phone has dialed her number, so to speak. You have engaged the time portal. My best guess is that you have linked to this woman.*"

"What's your name?"

"Rita."

"I'm Clint."

"Clint? Not a common name."

"Not so much."

"Rita... how did you get here?"

She reached for her coffee and drank before speaking, in a voice low and reflective. "The last I remember, I was on the beach. There was a storm. A kind of rolling blue light came at me. I ran."

Clint's jaw tightened. He pushed his hand through his hair. "Does this place look familiar?"

She looked about uneasily. "Somewhat."

Clint set his coffee mug aside, stood up and walked toward the patio door. He looked up at a night now heavy with stars. He felt unsettled and yet aroused by Rita. If Oscar was right, if Rita had time traveled—and that thought seemed absurd and impossible to him—then where had she come from? He didn't face her when he spoke.

"What year is it?" he asked.

"What year?" she repeated.

He turned to her. "Yes, what year is it?"

"… It's 1948."

Clint steadied himself with effort. It was an incredible moment.

Rita sensed his anxiety. Something was wrong. Very wrong, and she was slowly rising to the surface of her normal functioning mind, not the one that had been blunted and submerged by the trauma of the blue rolling wave.

"What's going on?" she asked. Her stomach churned with dread as she anticipated his answer. "What's going on and who are you?"

Clint inhaled a breath, speaking over the surf roar of high tide. "Rita… this is 2019. Somehow, you have traveled into the future."

Rita felt the blood drain from her head. She swayed unsteadily for a few seconds, as if she might faint. Clint rushed over to help.

"Laura…" she said in a desperate whisper, and then her head dropped to her chest.

CHAPTER 14
2019

Rita sat up with a start. Where was she? She glanced left to see a glowing green digital clock. *Odd*, she thought. It was a little after seven o'clock. Sun leaked in from under the unmoving, cream-colored curtains. No breeze coming through the windows? She heard a low humming sound. What was that? The room was cool and pleasant.

The bed was large. Queen-sized. Her mind jumped from one thing to the other until she recalled, with a sudden intake of breath, the night before, and her eyes popped fully open.

She threw back the blanket and, to her relief, she saw she was fully dressed in the same blue summer gown she'd worn the night before. The night before when? Was it the night before? Where?

All of yesterday's memories crashed in on her in an avalanche of emotion and fear. She made a little sound of panic as she swung her legs to the floor, noticing a wide, flat screen facing her. It sat on a mahogany bureau next to some large headphones. She stared at it, eyes wide. What had the man said—Clint—that was his name, wasn't it? What had he said? Something about the year being 2019? Impossible. Time travel to the future? Completely ridiculous. She had to find out what was going on. Was Clint a reporter, or worse, a policeman? Was she being held a prisoner? Were the LA detectives coming for her?

Her heart was loud in her ears as she fought to control her chaotic thoughts. She pushed up, crossed to the window and parted the curtains. She lifted the window, inhaled fresh air and peered out into a sun-drenched morning: a broad expanse of ocean blinking in the sun, double-decker dunes, wandering dune fences. She ventured a look right, where in the middle distance a beach house lay, a wide and sprawling magnificent thing with winding deck stairs, patios, glistening windows and plenty of trees and hedges. Even in Malibu, she hadn't seen anything quite like it.

A timid knock on the door jarred her. She pivoted to see Clint in the doorway. Yes, that was Clint, the man from the night before. The man she now recalled was the same man who had appeared in the photographs she'd taken. Martha had commented about him, hadn't she?

"Good morning, Rita," he said, softly. "Hope you're feeling better."

She couldn't find her voice. She gaped at him, as truth struck like a hammer blow. She finger-combed her hair, sure she looked a mess.

"How did you sleep?" Clint asked.

Still she couldn't speak.

"I made coffee. I can scramble up some eggs if you like. I have bagels too. They're fresh. I went out early this morning. I left you a note in the kitchen, in case you woke up and wondered where I was… or where you are."

That was considerate, she thought. His warm, probing eyes seemed to bore into her and hold her. Despite her still dizzy fatigue and confusion, she couldn't ignore his striking face, the long thick hair and the deep, masculine voice. She'd never seen any man quite like him. Maybe it was the attractive hair and beard or the style of shorts he wore, revealing his long legs. He had a fine body and a diffident manner that relaxed her, and the weary sadness in his eyes was intriguing.

She was good at appraising men. Maybe it had come from working in the movies with such a wide variety of actors, directors and producers.

In Clint, she sensed a sad tenderness and darkness, as if he were fighting inner demons, struggling to stay afloat. But she also sensed a strong, passionate man, wrapped in a cool demeanor, who hid inside himself until some spark of desire or inspiration ignited his passion. She suspected Clint was, at his core, a very passionate man.

From out of nowhere, she recalled a line from *Danger Town*, spoken near the end of the movie. Her male star had a gun pointed at her, as he spat out the angry dialogue. *"You hide inside yourself, baby, all calm and bad, until the right man charms you with a wicked wink. Then your match of desire flares, and you break out and burn down the town."*

Clint said, "I helped you to bed and left the door slightly open in case you needed anything. You collapsed and instantly fell asleep."

Rita folded her arms across her chest. "Thank you. I hope I wasn't too much trouble."

"Not at all. Sorry I don't have any clothes or toiletries. If you like, we can go shopping or look online. I recommend shopping online. You might draw more than a few curious looks, dressed like that."

Rita had no idea what "online" was, and she didn't ask.

She cleared her throat. "Last night, you said this was 2019... Is it, truly?"

Clint nodded. "Yes. It is 2019. I can explain some things to you over breakfast, if you like. Many more things, I can't explain."

Rita lowered her eyes, her mind filled with thoughts of Laura.

"I know it sounds crazy. For me too," Clint said. "It must be difficult for you."

Rita felt the irrational animal impulse to escape, to stampede away and run until she dropped. She snapped him a look, her voice suddenly filled with a desperate force.

"I don't believe it. I don't believe any of this. I need to get out of here. I need to get home. Just tell me how I can get home."

Clint pocketed his hands. "I don't know. I don't know much more about all this than you do. Let's talk about it over breakfast. Together, maybe we can come up with something."

Rita lowered her arms, clasped her hands and turned back to gaze out the window. She spoke in an emotional whisper, so that Clint barely heard her.

"What is going on? How the hell did I get here?"

They ate on the deck in silence. Rita stabbed at the eggs as if angry, and Clint said little. As they were draining the last of the coffee, Rita gave him a frank look.

"Are you married?"

"I was. She died, about seven months ago."

Rita's mood shifted, and her eyes softened. "I'm sorry. She must have been young."

"Yes, thirty-two. One of those weird things. She had

a urinary tract infection that somehow turned into septicemia."

"I don't know what that is."

"Simply put: it's a bloodstream infection or blood poisoning. It all happened fast. One day she was there, the next, she wasn't."

Rita lowered her head. "I am truly sorry."

Clint nodded, distracted. "Well, they say you have to move on, don't they?"

Rita sat back and sighed over the whispering wind. "Yes, they do say that."

Clint looked at her. "You're Rita Randall, aren't you? The actress?"

Rita twisted her hands, watchful and skeptical. "Yes, I am. Don't tell me that in 2019, if this is 2019, the actress Rita Randall is so well known."

"You'd be surprised."

"I don't believe it."

"Your photograph is hanging in the den, where I work."

Rita sat up erect. "What?"

"Everett Claxton built this house in 1946. Look around, it must look familiar, despite the changes."

Rita slowly put her face in her hands, as if she needed to escape. Clint wanted to say something to comfort her, but nothing came.

Finally, Rita lowered her hands and looked up with moving, questioning eyes. "Did you arrange all this? Did you bring me here? Do you have the power in this time to do things like this?"

"No, of course not."

"Then how did this happen? How did I get here? I just... I just don't believe any of it. Things like this don't happen. They can't happen."

Clint rearranged himself in the chair. "Do you know what a time portal is?" He held her eyes to get her reaction. She blinked slowly, trying to understand.

"No."

"I'll paraphrase the *Wiki* definition. Time portals are vortices of energy which allow matter or people to travel from one point in time to another by passing through the portal. It's like a doorway that leads down a hallway to another time."

Rita's eyes filled with interest. She thought about it, remembering her ordeal. She turned to stare out at the sea, while the wind played in her hair. Under her breath she said, "The rolling blue tunnel of light..."

"Yes," Clint said. "You mumbled about it in your sleep. I couldn't sleep last night, so I went to check on you. You thrashed about as if you were trying to run away, and you kept talking about the tunnel of blue light."

Rita slowly got to her feet, her nervous eyes searching for answers. "So, it's true then," she said, not as a question but as a final resignation.

"I'm afraid so, Rita. Whether either one of us believes it, the fact is, you are here."

She whirled about. "Then how do I get back? If I got here, then there must be a way to get me back. Where is that doorway?"

Clint shook his head. "I have no idea."

Rita's shoulders sank. "I have a daughter. I have a life back there."

"There might be a way. I know a guy who may be able to help us."

CHAPTER 15

2019

"He's in a coma," Wendy said. "He's been moved to hospice and they don't expect him to live more than a few days, if that."

Clint was in the den, standing by his desk. He kept his eyes on Rita while she studied her autographed, glossy black-and-white photograph.

"I'm sorry, Wendy."

"It's okay. He's tired. He said he's ready to go. It's his time."

After a brief pause, Wendy said, "Was he able to help you with your situation?"

"Yes, he did help. He's quite a man, isn't he?"

"He never talked to me about those things. He didn't talk to anybody about it for years. He had so many crazies trying to get at him, some genuine, some just plain out of their minds. You were lucky he talked to you. It really grabbed him, so it must have been something out of the ordinary."

Clint was quiet.

"Was it out of the ordinary?" Wendy pressed.

"I don't know. Maybe... Well, yes, it is out of the ordinary."

After he hung up, Rita turned to him, worried. "Laura was five years old in 1948. She'd be 76 now... if she's still alive."

She stared, entranced and shaken. "I just can't take it all in. My friends, family... all the people I've worked with are dead and gone."

Rita sat in the leather chair, the energy drained from her. She stared at the floor, distressed. "God in heaven, Laura might still be alive..."

Clint took a few steps toward her. "Rita, we know the portal exists. You're proof of that. It's just a matter of finding it again."

"Finding it?" she said, lifting her gloomy eyes to him, her lovely face creased with anxiety.

"Last night, you said you had been walking in a storm when the rolling light engulfed you, right?"

She nodded.

Clint sat on the edge of his desk. "A friend... a knowledgeable friend I talked to recently, knew about these portals. He lived out here in the 1940s and he and others did experiments with them in Montauk. He said he'd even time traveled to the future. Anyway, he mentioned that the time portals often appear during full moons and thunderstorms. They hover near the sea and over the dunes at early morning and during twilight. So, during the next thunderstorm or full moon, we'll go out and search."

Rita stared numbly. "I feel like I'm in a nightmare and I can't wake up. I don't even know what day it is."

"It's Sunday, July 7. I just checked, and the next full moon is on July 16. We'll be ready for it."

"What do I do in the meantime?"

"We make the best of it."

Suddenly self-conscious, they both glanced away, realizing that they'd have to stay together, plan together and live together for days, weeks or perhaps even months. Without money, ID or a place to live, Rita couldn't leave. And, anyway, where would she go? She didn't know anyone, and the world had completely changed since 1948: the fashion, the technology, the culture. It was as if she'd been rocketed to another planet. And if she used her real name, and if someone recognized her, as remote as that was, what would she say? *"Yes, I'm Rita Randall. I haven't aged a day since 1948 because I time traveled"*?

Clint was wary, wrestling with this new reality that included a gorgeous Hollywood movie star from 1948. Again, he heard Oscar's words rattling around in his head: *"If you think you know the world, and understand the world, then you don't know anything or understand anything."*

At that moment, Clint didn't know or understand anything except that Rita Randall was sitting in his den, staring at him, in a pleading, expectant way, hoping he could come up with the answers and find a way to send her back home. She was also a distraction. She was more magnetic and beautiful in the flesh than she'd been on the silver screen; her hair was still fragrant, her skin glowing, her eyes filled with allure.

Clint rounded his desk and sat behind his laptop. "You'll need clothes and things."

She looked at herself. "Yes. I feel like I've been wearing this gown for weeks. Well, I guess it's been decades, hasn't it?" she said, trying for a little joke.

"You mentioned a store called online. Is it close by?"

"Yes. I'll show you how it works. I'm sure the sizes have changed since 1948, but fortunately, we can return whatever doesn't fit."

For the next hour, Rita sat next to Clint, mesmerized by the magic of the laptop. Clint patiently explained the internet to her, but she had no foundation or common vocabulary. She was overwhelmed by the depth and infinite possibilities, and nervously frightened by it all. She was startled by the prices of clothes, jewelry and cars, and often distracted by the color TV on the other side of the room. Though it was set on mute, it blazed with bright, clear images, projecting the news of the day from all over the world.

Rita went into overload. "This is impossible," she exclaimed, holding her head with both hands.

She shot up abruptly, feeling as though her head were about to explode, and swept out of the room and headed for the kitchen to fill her coffee mug, leaving behind the faint scent of perfume.

The power of her lingered in the room, alive and pulsing. She exuded a natural animal magnetism Clint had never experienced, and it was arousing and disconcerting.

As they'd surfed the internet, he'd worked to keep his anxious attention on the shopping sights and not on her, especially when he was clicking through various styles of lingerie. Even with Jenny, he'd never shopped for lingerie. It felt oddly thrilling and voyeuristic with a stranger— a sexy, gorgeous stranger from another world.

At first, Rita had been engrossed in the styles and colors, pointing and commenting. She was not as self-conscious as he. After all, she had spent hours in wardrobe, being fitted for film roles by both men and women. She'd been eyeballed and touched and nudged and pushed and pinned so many times she couldn't count.

She'd glanced at Clint several times, measuring his expression, but his eyes were glued to the monitor, not allowing them to stray, to steal a look at her. She purposely edged in close to him, enjoying the smell of his cologne. Had he splashed some on just for her? In a small way, she enjoyed watching him squirm, as she leaned in toward the monitor. She found it sexy, and a welcome escape from her fraying nerves and churning stomach. She had the quirky image of the two of them being marooned on a desert island and, in a way, that's just what it was.

But then, it had all been too much. Clint, the laptop, the internet, the TV. She had definitely followed Alice in Wonderland down the rabbit hole. She had to get out of that room to clear her mind, collect her thoughts and cool her emotions.

While she was away, Clint stood, stretched and pondered. He'd spent a near sleepless night wrestling with himself, wondering what he was going to do with Rita. When Jack returned, and he would return, what would Clint tell him? No matter what he said or how much he explained or lied, Jack wouldn't believe him, because Jack didn't believe anybody. He had been naturally suspicious since they were kids. Becoming a trial attorney had only made him worse.

Rita soon returned. She paused, leaning alluringly against the doorframe, tinkering with a thought, coffee mug near her lips. He waited for her to speak, and when she didn't, he did, wanting to fill the silence.

"I have some old t-shirts and sweatpants you can wear until the clothes arrive."

She didn't seem to hear. She sighed heavily, shining her soft, blue intelligent eyes on him, awakening his dormant desire.

"Clint... you said that this internet thing could look up

all kinds of things. It's like a big infinite library that can find out almost anything, past and present. Is that right?"

"Yes… almost everything."

"Can it find out about me? Can it tell me what happened to my daughter, Laura? And what happened to me?"

Clint weighed the loaded moment. He had *Googled* Rita Randall last night when he couldn't sleep, and after reading about her and her daughter, he decided not to tell her what had happened. She was already unsteady and weak, and who wouldn't be?

"I don't think it's something you want to know about right now. Maybe you should give it a few days."

"How is giving it a few days going to change anything?"

"It's not going to change anything but being more rested when you hear it might help."

"Is it that bad?"

He breathed in, averting his eyes.

"If this is about Laura, I've thought about it. Whatever happened, I'll find a way to get back to her and change the past. Now, please, will you read it to me? I would do it myself, but I don't know how to make that thing work."

He admired her courage and determination. He nodded.

Rita stepped fully into the room and returned to the chair, sitting erect as a soldier, as if expecting an attack.

Clint surfed until he found the *Wiki* article he'd read the night before. He cleared his throat and began to read.

"Rita Randall (born Rita Haskall) was an American film actress who is perhaps best known for disappearing, without a trace, after her agent Tony

Lapano was found shot to death in his car in June 1948. Although initially not a suspect, detectives later received information that implicated her in Lapano's murder. Rita was vacationing on Long Island, New York, with her daughter and sister, when the LAPD asked her to return to Los Angeles as soon as possible. She never did.

"Miss Randall is remembered for her film noir roles, her most celebrated being *Dark Detour*. There she played the femme fatale, Della Bain. She was also celebrated for her portrayal of Delores Wagner in the 1948 film noir, *Danger Town*.

"Randall was born in Flatbush, Brooklyn on October 22, 1922, to Evelyn and William Haskall. William was a doting father for young Rita until his death when she was only seven years old. 'Lucky Billy,' as he was known, was a gambler, making most of his money in side-alley poker games and crap games. After one such crap game, where he'd won a handsome amount of cash, he was found beaten to death in a side alley in Flatbush. His robbery and homicide were never solved. Rita said his death had a profound effect on her, and that she never quite overcame the loss. As a result, she "grew up too fast."

"A beauty-contest winner and professional model from her teens, Randall began her show business career as a big band singer, singing with the Eddie Kempton Orchestra.

"It was the Broadway producer/movie director, Everett Claxton, who spotted Rita singing at the Tangerine Club in Brooklyn and put her in her first Broadway show, as a dancer/singer. A year later, she had the second lead in the musical *It's All about Nancy* and received favorable reviews from the New York Press.

"Tony Lapano, a Hollywood agent, signed her and arranged a screen test at RKO Radio Pictures. Rita signed a fifty-dollar weekly contract in 1941 with RKO and began working in as many as three movies at a time, mostly uncredited.

"After appearing in *Don't Make Waves*, a musical, Everett Claxton cast her in her first starring role with Humphrey Bogart and Edward G. Robinson in *Deadly Restitution*. Receiving rave reviews as the bad girl trying to go straight, she was soon being cast in a series of films, including *Back Street Confidential, Payback on Front Street, Bad Girls Don't Die, Goodbye Lover Girl, Dark Detour, Wrong Turn to Waco, and Danger Town*."

Rita interrupted, in a low sarcastic voice. "You can tell from the titles that none of my movies were quite up to the quality of *Gone with the Wind*."

Clint glanced up, coming to her defense. "They've become classic Film Noir. Many modern film critics say that you were one of the best film noir actresses at that time."

"What's that? Film Noir?"

"Oh, that's right, they weren't called that in your day."

"We called them B pictures or hard-boiled melodrama. Film Noir sounds fancy. What does it mean?"

"As my brother, Jack, would say, and he loves the old Film Noir movies, they're a style or genre marked by a mood of pessimism, fatalism, and menace."

Rita grinned with satisfaction. "Yeah, they were that all right. Ironically, that's how my life turned out."

Clint waited for clarification, but Rita didn't offer any. "Shall I read on?"

Rita turned somber and still. "Tell me what happened to my daughter."

CHAPTER 16

2019

Clint gave Rita a few seconds of evaluation, concerned that what he was about to read would emotionally damage her.

"Read it, Clint," Rita insisted. "I can take it."

Clint focused on the laptop screen and began to read, slowly and reluctantly.

"This section is titled Personal Life.

"Rita Randall married First Lieutenant Theodore Thomas Carlton, a B-17 bomber pilot, in 1943. Soon after their one-week honeymoon, First Lieutenant Carlton was deployed to Europe to fly bombing missions. Tragically, a few months later, his plane was shot down over Germany, killing the entire 10-man crew.

"Rita fell into a depression that led to heavy drinking. She stopped when a doctor told her it could damage the baby she was carrying.

"Laura Carlton was born on May 23, 1944 and Rita insisted on taking time off from the movies to be with her.

"When Rita returned to work, her career fell into familiar roles of playing the tarnished beauty with an irresistible sexual allure.

"By 1948, she was quoted as saying '*Danger Town* is the last picture I'm going to make where the heel slaps me around, or shoots me, or I shoot him. There are good scripts out there, and I want to make a movie about the good people in the world and not just about the low-class rats.'"

Rita stood up and began to pace the length of the room.

"Do you want me to stop?" Clint asked.

"No… Keep reading."

"The strange disappearance of Rita Randall has never been solved. In June 1948, her long-time agent, Tony Lapano, was found shot to death in his car in the driveway of his home. An investigation by the LAPD revealed little, although a Detective Briggs said later that he'd suspected Rita had shot Lapano.

"Lacking proof, Rita was permitted to leave town to vacation on Long Island, New York to rest and escape the press. While there, detectives received a tip from none other than Ava Gardner, who stated that the night of Tony's murder she'd seen him at about one in the morning at Barney's Beanery, in West Hollywood. Miss Gardner stated that he was drunk. He told her he was going to drive to Rita's house because she owed him. When Gardner asked what he meant by 'she owed him,' he shouted at her. 'All you bitches are the same.'

"Gardner further stated, 'Then Tony stormed out, stumbling and lurching about like a drunken sailor.'

"The police called Rita in Long Island and asked her to return. Accordingly, she agreed to leave the next day for Los Angeles.

"Rita's sister, Martha Haynes, later told the police that her sister left the house around twilight to take a walk on the beach. A violent storm blew in, and Rita Randall never returned to the house. Her body was never found, and she was never heard from again. Even to this day, there is much speculation as to what happened to her. Various investigators speculated that she hired a boat to pick her up on the beach. From there she motored to a cargo or transport ship, where she escaped to South America. Others believe she hired the boat and was taken to a private airport, where she was flown to South America. There have been many sightings of Rita Randall over the years, in the United States, Europe, Canada, Asia and Argentina, but none have ever been proven or substantiated.

"Martha Haynes stated, emphatically, that her sister would have never left her daughter, Laura. It was her belief that Rita went for a swim, probably swam out too far, was caught by the sudden storm, and drowned.

"Laura Carlton's future was eventually decided by the courts. Laura's grandparents, Helen and Raymond Carlton, were awarded custody of Laura in 1949. Martha Haynes was forced to release Laura, even though she tried for many years to regain custody, but to no avail.

"Laura grew up and was educated in Boston, Massachusetts. Possessing much of her mother's beauty, when she was 18 years old, against her grandparents' wishes, she traveled to Hollywood, hoping for a movie career. Unfortunately, movie roles were scarce, and she spent much of her time doing bit parts, dating single and married men and frequenting night clubs and bars.

"She married playboy Nickie Karn, but they divorced six months later. Two years later, she married Mario Cipolletti, a known Las Vegas Gangster. The marriage lasted less than a year, when he was gunned down by two hitmen who, it was believed, worked for the infamous Moe Dalitz.

"Depressed and addicted to pills and alcohol, Laura took an overdose of narcotics and was found dead in a motel room south of San Diego in June 1970. She was 25 years old."

Clint raised his eyes to gauge Rita's reaction. She was staring ahead, her eyes misty, fixed and hard. Her face turned white, her hands trembled. There was a sharpening of focus as if she were remembering something, as if it were playing out on a movie screen before her.

She stood with effort, and her wet eyes flitted about in glassy shock.

Concerned, Clint pushed up and started across the room toward her. "Are you all right, Rita? Can I get you something?"

She didn't seem to hear him. She stood shakily, weeping into a fist, lost in agony. Mechanically, she started for the hallway as Clint watched helplessly. Rita left the room without another word.

Minutes later, Clint stopped outside her closed bedroom door and knocked lightly. In the heavy silence of the house, he heard her anguished, deep sobs.

He returned to the den, found a glass and a bottle of bourbon. He splashed in some of the brown liquid, swirled it around in thoughtful appraisal, then downed it in one quick swallow, feeling the fire slide down his throat.

He stood staring, the booze warming his chest. With unblinking eyes, he allowed himself the uncomfortable possibility that they might never find the time portal and, even if they did, would it return her to 1948?

CHAPTER 17
2019

On Tuesday July 9, Rita left her room and found Clint on the patio eating breakfast. Clint arose, and they held each other's eyes for a time, not speaking. He pointed to an empty chair.

"Have a seat."

She sat.

Since Sunday, Rita had hardly left her room. They had said little. When her clothes arrived, Clint had knocked on her door, told her they'd come, and walked away, leaving the boxes and bags.

Rita appeared rested. Her lovely hair lay natural and careless, as if dried by the wind. With light makeup, the color had returned to her cheeks, and she looked back at Clint with a milder gaze and a small, shy smile that touched him.

She wore designer capri jeans, a yellow cotton shirt and sandals.

Clint swallowed away a lump, again moved by a tender desire to kiss those moist lips, run his fingers through her shimmering hair, and inhale the natural spring scent of her.

There was the hint of a breeze, a warm summer breath, fleeting, but it stirred her honey hair, lit by the morning sun.

"Feeling better?" Clint asked.

She nodded.

"Hungry?"

She nodded again.

"What would you like? As you can see, I'm having oatmeal, a bagel with cream cheese, watermelon, orange juice and coffee."

He reached for the glass pitcher of freshly squeezed orange juice. "I set the table for you, just in case. Juice?"

She nodded again, not speaking.

"Bagel?" Clint asked.

She lowered her eyes on him, smiling faintly. She took a fresh breath. "Do you know, no man has ever cooked or waited on me? I find it very attractive. Men in my time would never wait on a woman, at least none that I ever knew, unless they were waiters, of course."

"Okay, then I'll be your waiter."

"No… be the first man who ever waited on me."

Clint nodded. "Didn't you have servants? A butler?"

"A housekeeper, no butler. I like privacy."

Clint poured her juice glass full. "You're looking much better this morning. How do the clothes fit?"

"Not bad. Some too small, some too large. I love the fabrics. We have nothing like these fabrics in 1948."

"As I said, we can return them and order different sizes."

"How much were they?" Rita asked.

"Don't worry about the money."

Her eyes held gratitude. "Why are you so nice to me?"

"Truth?"

"Of course. Always."

"You're my guest, and you're a beautiful woman. But then you know that. You're also a mystery, but we both know that."

Clint eased back, folding his arms across his chest. "I also just happen to like you. You're straightforward, courageous, and very intriguing... I mean, you are a time traveler from the past—a past I know very little about."

A little breath of laughter escaped her lips. "Perhaps I am intriguing. Courageous? Yeah, I've had to be. Straightforward? No, if the word means truthful. I guess I'm not so truthful, am I? Otherwise I wouldn't have lied to the LAPD, and I wouldn't be here right now, and my daughter would still be alive."

Clint decided to be bold. "Did you kill Tony Lapano?"

Clint watched her changing expressions. "Yes, because he was going to rape me. He was drunk, and he was ugly and violent. He was so violent I thought he might even kill me."

"Why didn't you tell the police what happened?"

"Mostly because of Laura, I think. I didn't want her pulled into the whole ugly mess. I didn't want her to think bad of me. I didn't want her friends to point fingers at her and call her names. Selfish, yes, but that was only part of it."

Rita raked away a loose strand of hair that had fallen over an eye.

"I don't know how things are in your time, but in 1948, the courts weren't always so forgiving of these kinds of things. And if I am very honest, I knew the studio would dump me, because Howard Hughes didn't like bad publicity or scandal. The press and fan magazines would print rumors and lies, and the gossip columnists would rip me to pieces. I would be box-office poison. No one would hire me. Everything I'd built up would come crashing down. Tony was well liked by the corrupt and powerful men in that town. Innocent or guilty, those power men would never let me make another picture. So, there it is, bald honesty. As you can see, nearly all for selfish reasons. If I could do it over again, would I shoot Tony?"

Rita's eyes narrowed. "Knowing what I know now about Laura, I'd let him do whatever he wanted to me."

"And if he killed you? How would that have helped her?"

Rita avoided his eyes.

Clint got up and left for the kitchen. He returned with a mug of fresh coffee for Rita in one hand and a bowl of watermelon in the other. He placed them down before her and slid the bagel and square of cream cheese next to her plate.

"Anything else? Oatmeal?"

"No oatmeal. I despise oatmeal. I had to eat it with Laura, otherwise she wouldn't touch it."

They ate in silence, absorbed in their thoughts. The morning breeze stirred across them, the sea fell softly upon the beach, and the ocean shimmered like millions of silver butterflies.

Rita held the coffee mug to her lips and sipped thoughtfully.

Clint said, "We have a week... before the next full moon. A week from today."

Rita looked at Clint, a glimmer of hope in her eyes. "Do you think I can get back?"

"I hope so. If not next Tuesday, we'll try again."

They held each other's gaze, and Clint got lost in her eyes. If he let himself, he could easily fall hopelessly in love with this woman, and the absurdity of it nearly made him laugh. Rita was all magnetic allure and heat, an apparition of unexpected desire that disturbed and thrilled him. The longer he stared into her crystal blue eyes, the more he fell into a pool of inebriated emotions that were unknown to him. If he touched her, if he kissed her, he knew he'd never be the same, and he'd never want to let her go.

Rita experienced the moment as a drowsy seductive peace; as distant night music, as a kind of new drug that blunted the pain and alarm in her chest and raised the temperature of her desire.

Clint was kind, and good, and so very attractive. So very handsome, with an understated masculinity that brought awakened passion. Despite the nightmare she was living, her body was simply taking over. She wanted his lips on hers, his body pressing against hers, his hands exploring her breasts, legs and thighs.

Her body had lain fallow, had slumbered for years, finding no man appealing, wanting no man in her bed. Staring at Clint, she had the startling realization that since Ted's death, she'd been in mourning. His sudden death in 1944 had smashed her desire and beliefs, leaving her in pieces. She'd been angry at God, at life and at herself.

Perhaps Clint was just an escape, a port in the storm, a fleeting dream, and since she was decades away from her past life, she could drop her guard and let him in. She could allow him to caress her, explore her and make love to her. The bare truth was, it had been a long time since she had been with any man, and Clint heated up her cold passion. He intoxicated her. His eyes were marvelous, and she sensed a moment rich with sexual possibility.

Did he see the invitation in her eyes? Did he feel her warm request for a kiss?

"How did you meet your husband?" Clint asked.

Rita readjusted her mood, pushing away desire. She sipped the orange juice, keeping her soft eyes on Clint. "It was one of those fast wartime romances that happened to many couples at that time. Most of us felt an urgent need to experience as much life as possible, because so many men and women were dying. Death was so close, and time so short. Do you know much about World War II?"

"Some… In our time, your generation is known as the greatest generation."

Rita nodded. "Well, anyway, Ted and I met at a USO dance in Hollywood. We girls weren't supposed to fraternize with the soldiers, but that didn't stop me. There was an attraction and Ted and I acted on it. He took me out on the town, and the fan magazines loved it. I remember one headline that said *Beauty and the Pilot*. A week later, he learned he was going to be shipped overseas. He didn't know where. I was hopelessly in love, and we were married three days before he shipped out. I got completely swept up in the romance, believing that nothing could, or would, happen to him. I just knew he'd live. I prayed to God every day that Ted would live, and I believed in my heart of hearts that he would live and come back to me."

Rita turned her head toward the sea. "It rained the day he left, and I hated that rain. I cried my eyes out. I didn't know Ted all that well, how could I? We'd only met a little over two weeks before. But he was a good and gentle man, perhaps a bit serious at times, but then, everyone was all laughs one moment and all serious the next in those days."

Rita swiped away a tear. "His family was wealthy. They were completely against the marriage and were outraged when they learned about it. I never met them."

She forced a bright smile. "But I have Laura, and she keeps me smiling and happy."

She faced him, eyes imploring, full of emotion. "I have to get back to her, don't I?" she said, her eyes shimmering with tears.

"Promise me, Clint, that you'll help me get back to Laura."

Clint felt his throat tighten. "Of course, Rita. Of course. Whatever it takes."

CHAPTER 18

2019

Rita and Clint spent the next few days sunning on the beach, taking twilight walks, and driving through the Hamptons so Rita could experience the look and feel of 2019.

Naturally, she was astonished by the changes: by the colorful, large cars that looked "like little trucks;" the crowds; the cell phones; the thumping, driving music that puzzled her. She said that the pace of life was faster, the fashion more explicit and bold. Everything was "so futuristic."

"People dress so casually in this time," she said, her attention riveted on the young women in shorts and leggings. "No one is smoking, and the streets are so clean. I feel like an alien."

Clint took her to a movie, a new *Mission Impossible*, and she found it frantic and jarring, devoid of much real acting.

On Saturday night, Clint drove them into Montauk for dinner. The restaurant was a remodeled three-story house with a generous wrap-around porch that ran the length of the place, wide enough to accommodate tables for dining. With an easy turn of the head, one had a commanding view of the sea and sky. Christmas lights were strung in the eves and through the hedges, adding cheerfulness, and hanging plants swung leisurely, scenting the breeze.

A boyish male host seated Rita and Clint at a table on the porch and presented them with menus. Through the open windows, they heard the rattle of dishes and the murmur of conversation, while a guitarist strummed and wailed sad Irish tunes in a high, lilting tenor.

Rita sipped her water, observing a black cat prowl the gravel parking lot, entranced by movement in a rosehip bush near the road.

"I like this place," Rita said. "I can smell the honey-suckle."

Clint looked at her with new pleasure, feeling expanded in her aura. It was difficult to pull his eyes from her lovely face. She was over-dressed for the casual summer crowd, but she dressed as she would have in 1948. She dressed like the star she'd been, wearing a royal blue crepe strapless hourglass dress, silver dangling earrings and 2-inch satin pumps that gave her height and elegance. Her luxurious hair was twisted up and braided artistically, her nails a polished red. Her eyes were highlighted by a de-fined brush of eyebrows that added a seductive, enigmatic beauty.

There was not a man in the place who wasn't stealing looks at her, and few women who weren't studying her unique clothing style and effective make-up.

After they'd ordered, she the sole, and Clint the lobster, he chose a bottle of Chardonnay. As Rita sipped the wine, she gazed out to sea, her eyes distant, her body still, her face moving through an array of expressions.

"What are you thinking?" Clint asked.

"This reminds me of a little restaurant in Malibu. I often drove there after I wrapped a picture. It was my own little private discovery, and I always went alone. The maître d' sat me in an inconspicuous spot away from the public, where I had a spectacular view of the sea."

She smiled into Clint's eyes. "I like this place. I like it very much. Thank you for all you've done. Somehow, I will have to reimburse you for the clothes and the jewelry and the make-up. I hope I haven't been too extravagant."

Clint took her in completely. "No, you haven't, and I haven't had this much fun in years… maybe never."

Rita leaned a bit forward, holding her wine glass up by the long stem, peering at Clint through the cloudy, straw-colored wine. "We have had fun, haven't we?"

Suddenly the moment was deliciously intimate. They'd avoided moments like this all week, often retreating to their rooms: Rita to her bedroom and Clint to the den where he wrestled to finish his book.

"Do people consider you to be a good writer, Clint?"

"You tell me. You read the first book in the *Finding Summer* series."

Rita smiled with pleasure, lowering the wine glass to the table and lowering her voice to a seductive whisper. "I loved the book, Clint. I started the second."

"You didn't say. I mean, I wasn't even sure you'd finished it."

"Why do you think I was in my room so much or out on the beach?"

"I didn't know."

"Do you know what I thought while I was reading it?

I thought, I'd like to play the part of Lisa Graham."

Clint raised his voice. "You'd be perfect. The three-book series is going to be adapted for a movie. Of course, I have to finish the third book."

"Have you written for the movies?" Rita asked.

"No, but two other novels I've written were made into movies."

Excited, Rita's eyes widened. "What were they?"

"The first was *Tear down the Moon*, a romantic drama that did well with the critics but didn't make much money. The more successful adaption of my novel, *Island of Dreams*, is about an elderly couple who are the only survivors of a plane crash. They are marooned on a strange, beautiful island and they soon discover they are not alone, and that as the days pass, they grow younger and more beautiful."

Rita lifted an eyebrow. "I like that one. Tell me what happens."

He shook his head, grinning mischievously. "No way. You'll have to read the book or see the movie."

Rita drew back in playful irritation. "Who would have thought you could be so mean?"

He winked at her and she laughed, a girlish laugh that Clint had never heard. It said much about her. There was lightness and playfulness behind those often sad eyes.

"You can bet I will read that book," Rita added.

She ran a finger around the rim of her wine glass. "Yes, I would like to play Lisa Graham in the *Finding Summer* series. It's a good part. I never got parts like that."

"You'd be perfect. Lisa is vulnerable, smart and ambitious. Of course, she's also a beautiful woman."

Rita shifted her gaze, noticing climbing yellow roses on a trellis, seeing stately ferns and potted plants on an adjoining terrace. It reminded her of her home back in Brentwood.

Rita took a generous drink of the wine, its soothing buzz making her bold, enticing her to want to touch, to kiss, to make love. Being in such close quarters with Clint, and straining not to show her feelings, had been nearly impossible. With an eager restlessness, she'd kept secret eyes on him as he moved through the house. Every night, she wished he'd open her door, enter the room and slip under the sheets beside her. She'd dreamed about playing with him, teasing him, loving him. Despite everything that had happened, and all that was surely to come, the temptation of being with Clint had become a near obsession.

After their entrees arrived, they said little. They avoided each other's eyes, aware that their swelling passion was filling the space and the silence.

After they finished the wine, they declined dessert and left, driving home mostly in silence. The red sun had disappeared into the far edge of the sea by the time they arrived in Amagansett. They drove on, meandering along two-lane roads that skirted the sea. On the beach, fireworks were rocketing up and exploding, spraying white and blue flecks into the gray-blue sky, as a broken piece of moon began to rise over the ocean.

"What are the fireworks for?" Rita asked.

"Probably some sweet sixteen's birthday party or a wedding. They do that kind of thing out here."

As the high from the wine dissipated, Rita began to think better of starting any kind of relationship with Clint. She was going to have to leave, or at least try to leave. Why break both their hearts? What good could come from a few nights of love making? She wasn't a saint, but she was also not the one-night-stand type or the two-or three-night- stand kind of woman.

When she'd married Ted, it was because she'd intended their marriage to last until death did them part, and that's just what had happened.

With Clint, she wished things were different. She could easily fall in love with him, and if he did make love to her, she would fall hopelessly and helplessly in love. There would be no going back.

"Do you mind stopping the car over there?" Rita asked, pointing to the shoulder of the road that skirted the beach.

Clint did, looking over. "Is everything all right?"

She didn't look at him. "If you don't mind, I think I'll walk along the beach back to the house."

"Want company?"

She looked at him, tenderly. "I've got some things to think about."

He nodded, disappointed.

She got out and closed the door, stooping to look through the window. "See you soon."

Clint managed a tight smile, put the car in gear and drove away.

Rita peeled off her heels, entered the dunes and advanced, feeling the warm, sinking sand give way as she worked her way down to the beach. With shoes in hand and her purse swung over her shoulder, she strolled along the edge of the tide, feeling some of the hot emotion slowly drain out of her. Fireworks were exploding further down the beach, bonfires were flickering, and lovers strolled by arm in arm. Families were out, kids were racing around playing, pointing and screaming up at the booming, spreading streams of light.

Rita stopped and tilted her head back, looking skyward. She felt so far away from her life in 1948. She felt so attracted to Clint that a deep, aching desire heated her chest.

Rita was nearly asleep when she heard her door squeak open. In the dim light, she saw Clint's silhouette framed in the doorway, just as she'd dreamed it.

"Clint... is that you?"

"Yes..."

He didn't move for a time. The room was alive with quiet and pulsing hearts. Clint stepped into the room and closed the door behind him.

Rita sat up, expectation and desire throbbing. She'd prayed for this moment, and now she felt the hot fluid of love. As he approached, she tossed back the sheet in invitation.

Without speaking, Clint removed his underwear and sat down on the edge of the bed, looking down at her. Her face was upturned toward his, her body willing him to touch her. When he did, stroking her face, neck and breasts, she sighed, all warm with dizzying pleasure. He slid in beside her, their bodies pulsing with the electric brush of hips.

Outside, they heard thunder. The first click of lightning strobed the room. He brushed his lips against her. Kissed her.

Both were vaguely aware that a thunderstorm had begun to rage. Both were aware of what Oscar Bates had said about the time portal: *"Full moons and thunderstorms often make them visible."* But they deleted his words from their minds as their bodies and their desire swept them away.

Clint kissed her again, hungrily, their tongues exploring, as wind squealed and groaned around the house. Then the storm began to gather force. When Rita pulled back from Clint, lightning flashed and her eyes were shining, catching his attentiveness.

"I want you, Clint. Make love to me."

Clint touched her lips with the tip of his fingers and she kissed them, and then she held them against a breast, feeling a new passion when Clint arched to kiss her stomach.

Thunder rolled heavily over them, and the ugly sky was cracked open by jagged flashes of lightning. Rain pelted down, lashing at the windows and drumming on the roof.

Rita reached for him, pulling him down on top of her, eager for their joining, already feeling thrilling tremors of easy pleasure.

Afterwards, they lay close, listening to the gentle tap of rain and distant thunder. Rita felt the steady beat of her heart, so full of love. She felt the pulsing of her life force that already seemed joined to Clint's. Her surprising love was rich and calm and hot, the stuff of poetry and imagination—something she'd always desired but never known.

Her eyes were still damp with the shock of loving tears. The kind of love she was feeling had always been the stuff of movies and dreams, a delicate flimsy, a wonder of a thing like a butterfly's wings. Yet here it was, alive, strong and fluttery.

This was the way lovemaking was supposed to be, wasn't it? It was the gentle, yet driving and passionate play between two lovers, so right, so warm, so secret.

Rita heard Clint's breathing beside her, and she knew his eyes were open and staring at the ceiling. She stared too, but she was sleepy, so very sleepy. Her eyelids fought the urge to close into a peaceful sleep, but she resisted, wanting to own this moment for a while longer—

this remarkable feeling—this sterling and precious moment.

Clint spoke at a whisper. "What are we going to do, Rita?"

Rita let the silence draw out. "I love you, Clint. I love you as if I've always loved you."

He turned over on his side, lifted up on an elbow and kissed her, stroking her damp face, feeling the wetness of her tears.

"We have some thinking to do, my love."

"Do you love me, Clint?"

He kissed her again. "Haven't I always loved you?"

CHAPTER 19

2019

"Clint! Hey, where the hell are you?"

Clint jerked awake.

Rita sat up abruptly, sleepy eyes wide open. "Who is that?" she said, in a scared voice.

Clint cursed, slid out of bed and bent to retrieve his undershorts.

"It's my brother, Jack. What the hell is he doing here?"

"Your brother?"

"Dammit! I don't have any clothes in here."

Rita was naked. She yanked the sheet up to cover her breasts. "Did you know he was coming?"

"No…"

Jack was right outside the door. He knocked, hard. "Clint… Are you in there?"

Clint huffed out an exasperated sigh. "Yes, Jack. Don't open the door. I'll be right out. Why didn't you call?"

"I didn't think I needed to."

"Yes, from now on, you need to."

"Okay, hey, bro, whatever. I brought Linda with me. I'll be out on the deck. She wants to go for a swim."

Clint circled the space, his mind racing and leaping. "Okay. Fine."

Clint and Rita exchanged glances. She shrugged. "I'll get dressed. Anything I should know?"

Clint shook his head. "Whatever you do, don't tell him you're Rita Randall. He knows who she was... I mean is." Then he stressed, "He knows who you are, so make up a name. Anything. Make up a story, any story. I'll tell him we met last week on the beach."

She nodded nervously as she left the bed and scrambled into the bathroom.

Clint crept to the door, cracked it open, waited, then opened it enough to hear muffled voices out on the deck. He slipped out and skittered across the polished wood floor to his own room, closing the door behind him.

Ten minutes later, an edgy Clint made his way slowly to the deck, gathering himself for his encounter with his brother. He stopped to look back at Rita's closed door and sighed.

Jack was slouched in a deck chair, bathed in the summer sun. His eyes were closed, and his hands were folded across his middle. Linda stood staring out to sea.

"Come on, Jack," Linda said, "Let's go to the beach before the sun goes behind that dark cloud."

"Take it easy... I've got to see who's shacking up with my brother."

Clint frowned.

Linda was a compact, voluptuous brunette, "Jack's type," with a short, bobbed haircut and purposeful mouth. Clint sensed a harsh practicality about her, a trait Jack had always found attractive in a woman, but one he could never live up to. Despite being a successful attorney who dealt in facts and the law, he was also a bit of a dreamer.

Linda wore a white strapless bathing suit under a lacy white cover-up, and black studded ankle-strap heels that added height and proportion to her broad hips.

Linda pivoted to see Clint, and she brightened. "Hi, there. I'm Linda," she said, producing an outstretched hand.

Jack's eyes slitted open as he watched Clint and Linda limply shake.

"Hope you don't mind that we came," Linda said. "Jack said you wouldn't care."

Clint passed his brother a disapproving glance. "You're welcome, Linda. I'm Clint. Can I get you anything?"

"If you have a Bloody Mary all dolled up and spicy, I wouldn't say no."

Clint had never heard that expression before. "Sorry, I don't. I have wine and beer."

"A beer is good. IPA?"

"Yes."

"Make that two," Jack said, still not moving.

As Clint left for the kitchen, he heard his brother call out. "Who's the girl, bro?"

Clint ignored him, feeling his chest tighten with anxiety and irritation.

Back on the deck, Clint handed off the beers.

Linda stepped about, glancing nervously skyward, her body energetically eager, as if sitting were a near impossibility for her. Clint wondered if she was high on some drug. Her sea-gray eyes seemed to have trouble focusing.

"Jack, come on. It might rain later."

"You go ahead, doll, I'll meet you down there."

The word "doll" seemed to hang in the air like a bad odor, but Linda didn't seem to mind.

"Yeah, okay. You don't mind if I meet your girlfriend later, do you, Clint?"

"No. Not a problem."

Linda kicked off her sandals, grabbed a towel Jack had brought for her, snagged the beer by the neck of the bottle, and marched off toward the sea.

Jack drank his beer with closed eyes. "That crazy girl is wearing me out, bro. I'm exhausted. Hey, am I getting old or something?"

Clint stood with fists on his hips. "Why didn't you call first, Jack?"

"Hey, I didn't think I had to. How did I know you'd be shagging some girl?"

Jack opened his eyes and sat up. He gestured with his beer. "Hey, I'm happy about it, you know. I mean, it's about time you hang out with a woman. It's just that the last time I saw you, you didn't seem in the mood."

At that moment, Rita appeared, wearing yellow shorts, a light blue cotton top and white sneakers. Vast quantities of shining hair fell on her shoulders, framing her lightly tanned face and high-impact shine lip gloss.

When he saw her, Jack sat up like he'd been touched by a live wire. He flipped his eyes up to her, in an instant flash of recognition.

He shot to his feet, spilling his beer. "Holy shit. It's... It's you. It's Rita Randall!"

Clint stiffened.

Rita played the scene perfectly, all cool and smiles. "Who?" she asked, innocently.

Jack swallowed and pointed. "You... You..." He

struggled to find words. "How can you be Rita Randall?"

Rita kept her innocent smile, batting her eyelashes. "Are you Jack, Clint's brother?"

He nodded, still gawking at her.

Rita moved toward him, hand raised. "I'm Cynthia Collins."

Jack took her hand, eyes blinking fast, unable to put the name with the face. "Cynthia?"

"Yes... Cynthia."

Jack shook his head in a stunned wonder, his face unable to release the shock. "Did anyone ever tell you that you look just like Rita Randall?"

"I'm afraid I don't know who that is."

Frustrated, he jabbed a finger toward the interior of the house. "Haven't you seen the photos in the den? Her photo is in there. She looks just like you... or you look just like her. Whatever."

"No," Rita said, batting her eyes again. "I haven't seen it."

"Well, she was only the greatest Film Noir actress of all time."

Clint glanced into Rita's eyes and saw a flicker of pride.

"Oh was she now?"

Jack shot his brother a look. "Clint, didn't you show her the photograph? Didn't you tell her she looks just like Rita Randall?"

Clint stood casually, offering a complacent smile. He scratched his head. "No, I didn't. I guess I didn't notice."

"What the hell do you mean, you didn't notice?"

Before Clint could stop him, Jack seized Rita's arm and tugged her away, down the hallway to the den, with Clint fast behind.

"Jack, what the hell are you doing? Stop it."

Jack burst into the den, with Rita in tow. He led her across the room to the photo, pointing an emphatic finger at it. With a firm jerk of his chin, he said, "Now tell me if you are not the living image of the woman in this photograph?" he concluded, throwing his hands to his hips.

Clint drew up, standing next to Rita in a protective stance. "What is the matter with you, Jack?"

Rita inspected the photo of herself, squinting, her mouth twisted up for dramatic effect. "I guess there's some resemblance."

"Some resemblance?" John blustered. "Bullshit! You're identical. You and the woman in that photograph are identical!"

"My nose is crooked, and her eyes are wider apart than mine. My mother always said my eyes were much too close together."

Jack heaved out an exasperated sigh. Before he could protest, Clint gently took Rita by the elbow and led her away, with Jack now trailing behind.

Back on the deck, Jack wiped sweat from his forehead with a paper napkin. He kept shaking his head. "And you were the woman Clint was taking photos of all over the place, and then he was lying to me, pretending he didn't know who you were." Jack pointed a guilty finger at his brother. "I knew you were lying to me, bro. I knew it. It didn't take a trial attorney to figure that one out."

Jack flopped back down in his chair, blowing out another deep sigh. "I tell you, it's uncanny. I mean, I know you're not Rita Randall, because she died back in 1948, and even if she'd lived, she would be, I don't know, about 100 years old by now, but you must be her reincarnation or something. You must be related to her in some way. Have you ever looked up your family tree?"

"No," Rita said, with a new innocence, looking at Jack with pity. "I never did anything like that."

Clint cut the conversation short. "Jack, Cynthia and I haven't had breakfast and we're starving, so we're going out. We were just about to leave when you came. So, you and Linda enjoy yourselves. Rita…"

Rita shot him a stern glance.

Clint swiftly recovered his mistake, ignoring Jack's awakened eyes "…I mean Cynthia and I will be back later."

"How much later?"

"Don't know."

"Hey, bro, don't be rude to your brother and leave me like this."

"You'll be fine here with Linda. Cynthia and I have things to talk about."

Jack lit up. "Are you talking about marriage?"

"Not yet, Jack. Other things," Rita interjected. "Please tell Linda I said hello, and that I'm looking forward to meeting her."

"Yeah, sure."

Clint touched Rita's arm. "I'll just grab my cell phone. I'll meet you at the car."

Jack hitched one leg leisurely across the other, his eyes boring into Rita. She didn't flinch.

"It was nice to meet you, Jack."

His hot gaze traveled from her mouth to her breasts. "You'll be seeing more of me, you know. I come out often. Oh, and by the way," he said with a wicked grin, "Clint and I share everything. Always did, ever since we were kids."

Rita grinned back, darkly. She'd heard this line before

in one of her movies. A co-star, Tom Neal, had spit it out at her in the movie *Payback on Front Street*. She recalled her line in response, and now she was going to use it on Jack.

She faced Jack squarely, and in an instant, she'd transformed into Roxy Tucker, the icy, sultry blonde in the shadowy, cynical, hard-boiled film, *Payback on Front Street*. Her pretty face was now hard, her jaw set, her eyes blazing.

"I heard that Clint is the man and you're the boy. Now I see it's true. Well, I stopped playing around with dirty-faced boys a long time ago, pal. Clint gives me dream kisses. Kisses that count. Kisses that don't give up. Kisses that say you're mine, baby. So go peddle your song and dance to some other tramp, Jack. This one has her man, and tonight, we're catching the last train out of town to nowheres-ville."

Rita left Jack with his mouth open, and a dumb look on his face. He blinked and blinked, and he was still blinking in disbelief when he heard Clint's engine roar to life and drive away.

CHAPTER 20
2019

On Monday, Rita and Clint wandered the quiet beach, arm in arm, under lazy clouds and a white sun that began to sting their backs. They returned to the beach blanket and sat side by side under a flapping beach umbrella. Rita screwed off the cap and poured a French rosé into paper cups, and they toasted.

"Here's to the full moon tomorrow," Rita said.

"Hear, hear," Clint said, softly, with little enthusiasm. They sat for a time, excited by the intimacy and the soft breeze. They drank and took in the sky, the seagulls and the moving clouds.

Clint took a sip of the wine and looked down at his cup. "The wine's not so bad for a screwcap."

"You've been quiet today," Rita said.

"Yeah… You've been distracted too."

Rita met his gaze. "Have you made your decision?"

He nodded. "I can't stay, and I know you have to go,

so I'm going with you."

Rita leaned, resting her head on his shoulder. "I'm selfish, Clint. You're leaving your entire life behind."

"And I'm gaining a new life with you. A better life with you. There's nothing for me here if you leave."

Rita wrapped an arm around his shoulder. "How could it have happened so fast? How can it be that I love you so much in such a short time?"

Clint said, "Like the poets say, love is about feeling, not about thinking. It's not rational. The heart leads and the head struggles to make sense of it."

Rita took his hand and squeezed it. "Do you think it was fated? I mean, the way we met, two people living in completely different times. It's so crazy and weird and wonderful." She laughed. "What are the odds of that happening?"

Clint turned serious. "I wish Oscar Bates was still alive. I wish I could talk to him one more time. I could sense that he knew a lot more than he was telling me or would tell me."

"Let's not be scared, Clint. As long as we stay together, there's nothing to be scared of."

Clint kissed the tip of her nose. "Aren't you the romantic?"

"I didn't used to be. I used to be cynical and skeptical of anything that had to do with love, especially after Ted was killed. You made a romantic out of me. You made a lover out of me."

Clint gave her a soft kiss. "I still wish we'd gotten married."

She lifted her head from his shoulder, facing him. "I know, darling, I do too, but we're out of time. Like the fellow said over the phone, there's a 72-hour waiting period."

Clint looked at her earnestly. "So let's pretend we're married."

"That's easy," she said. "I feel married when you make love to me."

A fat seagull waddled by with one beady eye turned up, as if curious about Clint's response.

"So we'll get married in 1948."

Rita's eyes shifted away. She pulled her knees up and wrapped them with her arms. She rocked, gently swallowing back fear of the approaching full moon.

"Why didn't you and Jenny have children?" she asked.

"We were going to in a year or so. Jenny wasn't quite ready. She was involved in so many things, friends, clubs, work. She was always on the go, and she wasn't ready to be tied down."

"Do you like children, Clint?"

"Yes, I do. I wouldn't mind having a couple."

Rita adjusted her sunglasses and smiled at him. "I'd love to give you a son. I think I'd like to name him Nathan. I've always liked that name."

"Okay, Nathan it is. What's Laura like?"

"She's a beautiful child, bright like her father; active and curious about everything. She's also a very sensitive and loving child."

"Does she ever ask about her father?"

"Once in a while. I tell her he's gone to heaven. I tell her he's happy up there."

Rita laughed. "She once asked me if we could go and visit him."

"What did you say?"

"I didn't know what to say. I said heaven was too far away."

The wind circled and blew sand, and the fat seagull sprinted and lifted off, swinging back over them, beating slow wings toward the dunes.

Rita removed her sunglasses and tightened her lips, her eyes dreamy and a little sad. "I shouldn't say this, but part of me wishes we could forget about that damned time portal, get married and build a life here. We could have a couple of children and forget about the past."

Clint removed his sunglasses and gave her a quick and narrow look of calculation.

"You know it would never work. You'd always be thinking of Laura."

Rita slipped her sunglasses back on and stretched her legs out. "Yes, of course I would."

A minute later, she reached for him. "Hold me, Clint. I'm so scared."

He drew her up into his arms, kissing her perfumed hair, wondering what the next day would bring.

Clint stared out into the vast sea—vast like time itself, he thought. "It's going to be all right. Whatever happens, we'll work it out. Right now, we should get out of the sun before we both get sunburned."

Late in the night, Clint was awakened by the sound of the shower. His hand patted the empty space next to him. It was still warm. The clock said it was 5:20 a.m. The full moon would not be exact until 11:12 a.m.

Clint hitched himself up and ran a hand through his mussed hair. *Why was she up so early? Must have the jitters*, he thought. He settled back down, feeling plenty of his own jitters as he laced his hands behind his head. The impossible reality struck him again as it often had in the last few days. Had he seen to all the details? He'd written Jack a letter, explaining, as best he could, the whole story. Clint had included a letter to his parents and one to Amy. He'd leave a separate letter for his agent, with a condensed fiction about how he'd left for the Far East and didn't plan to return for many years.

Clint had left a will, leaving everything to his parents. It would make a nice retirement. He had been a successful writer and the royalties from his books and movies would pay dividends for years to come.

Rita left the bathroom, wearing a silky robe belted at the waist. A plank of yellow light fell on the floor.

"Can't sleep?" Clint asked.

"No… Too many nightmares. Too many memories. Too many everything," she said, a small quiver in her voice.

"It will be over soon."

"Not soon enough. This whole thing, time portals, falling in love… I mean, the whole thing is just crazy. It's all too much and all too crazy."

Clint had never seen her so stressed. He patted the bed. "Want to join me?"

She didn't look at him. "Don't come with me, Clint."

He lifted, concerned. "What?"

"Don't come. I don't feel good about it. If we do make it back, the police will arrest me, and I could wind up in jail for years. Your whole life will be ruined. And for what?"

"For what? I love you. Anyway, let's not get ahead of ourselves. We don't know where we'll wind up, or if we'll wind up anywhere."

Rita walked across the room to the door. She paused before opening it, not looking back.

"I don't want you to come," she said tartly, disappearing into the darkness of the house.

CHAPTER 21

2019

At ten-thirty in the morning, gray quilted clouds hung over a gun metal sea, and a fine mist was falling, making the world a living, impressionistic painting. Rita stood on the deck by the front windows, gazing out to the sea, lost in her own stare.

Clint stood behind her. "It's nearly time…" he said, softly.

The empty silence was filled by the low rasp of the ocean and the low moan of a distant train whistle.

When Rita spoke, her voice was small and reflective. "When I was a little girl, a day or two before my father was killed, he came into my room one night, proudly carrying a large, elaborately wrapped present. I remember the wrapping paper. It was white, shiny paper with red and blue circus animals on it: elephants, lions, camels and horses with headdresses of red feather plumes. The red velvet bow was so wide and bright that it dazzled my eyes. I thought it was one of the most beautiful things I'd ever seen. It seemed to shout with surprise and happiness. I laughed and applauded, and he gathered me up into his arms and I kissed him on both cheeks. Daddy said, 'It's for you, my princess.'

Rita turned to Clint. "When I tore off the wrapping and peeled back the mound of tissue paper, do you know what I found at the very bottom? A pair of dice."

Clint shoved his hands into his khaki pants pockets, tilting his head, not understanding.

Rita continued. "Daddy said, 'If you don't throw the dice, little princess, you can never expect to score a six.'"

Rita folded her arms, smiling. "I still have those dice... They're in a jewelry box back in 1948. Maybe they'll bring me luck."

Clint waited for more.

"I threw the dice when Everett Claxton said he'd put me in his show, if I'd sleep with him. I said he reminded me of my father, who was murdered. It was a lie, of course. Everett didn't remind me of my father at all. Anyway, he blushed, I didn't sleep with him, and he put me in the show anyway. We became good friends. I threw the dice when Tony Lapano signed me. As it turned out, that wasn't a fortunate toss of the dice, but you win some and you lose some. I threw the dice when I moved to Hollywood. A lot of girls didn't make it and had to go back home with their tails between their legs. I also threw the dice with Ted, marrying him after only five days. He was killed."

"All I'm saying, Clint, is I didn't have to toss the dice with you. You are that big lavish box with the big red bow and all those circus animals on it. I just wish the game was over and I didn't have to throw the dice again when that damned portal comes dancing by."

Clint crossed to her, took her by the shoulders and drew her into him. He held her close, feeling her beating heart.

"Whatever happens, Rita, know that I love you. We've got to believe that if the fates went to all the trouble to get us together in such a bizarre way, then it must be that we're meant to be together and meant to stay together."

They held their embrace for long minutes.

They were on the beach at ten minutes to eleven, dressed in raincoats, throwing darting glances about, looking for any sign of a blue, shimmering light. A low wooly fog was rolling across the dunes, pushed by a wet wind, and Rita and Clint strained their eyes, struggling to pierce it. They saw nothing.

Rita was on high alert, every sense tuned and alive to sight and sound. Clint climbed the damp sand toward the dunes, searching in every direction.

"Do you see anything?" Rita shouted.

"Nothing."

Rita's shoulders sagged. Maybe Oscar was just some senile old man who was making the whole thing up. What if what had happened to her was a one-time event and it would never repeat itself?

Rita pressed on, hearing the sea roll in loud, throwing gray slabs of waves onto the beach. She pushed her hands into her coat pockets, searching up and down the beach. In a slow turn, she glanced up toward the crest of the dunes and froze when she saw it. There it was, dancing erratically like a wild thing, shimmering blue light tumbling across the dunes, heading directly for Clint.

She screamed out for him, but he was a white ghost lost in the fog. Frantic to reach him, she hurled herself forward, racing toward the dunes. Did he see the light?

Did he know it was coming straight toward him? Could she reach it in time?

"Clint! Look out!"

Rita's lungs were burning as she ran, gulping in air, her feet digging into the sand in what seemed like slow motion strides, as if she were trudging through molasses.

The glowing, boiling wave of light was almost on him, and she was still too far away to reach it. Did Clint know? Did he see?

She shouted, waving her arms. "Clint! The light! Look out! The light is coming at you!"

Rita didn't see the stray beach debris, a bleached limb of a tree. It snagged her right foot and she went sailing, propelled forward, her hands extended to break her fall. She hit the sand hard, bursting the air from her lungs.

In horror, she lifted her head and watched as the silent charging mass of gleaming light engulfed Clint's ghostly figure, swallowing him up into the mouth of the tunnel.

And then it was gone, and Clint had vanished. There was only the wheezing wind, the thundering surf, the far-off squeal of a seagull.

Rita lay still on the beach as the dark, angry sky opened and rain pelted down, drumming on her body, her hair soon a wet, tangled mass, the side of her face caked in sand. One horrible thought chased another until her mind locked up. She had come to the end of thought.

The sea hurled waves across the beach, the wind howled as if wounded, and stringy fog blew over her like fleeing ghosts, skimming the beach and the dunes, shrouding the houses in veils, as if they were in mourning for the dead, the helpless and the lost.

Rita lay exhausted, not aware that a second blue rolling portal was swarming across the beach toward her.

PART 2

CHAPTER 22

1948

Rita lay still, cold and shivering. She made a small murmur of complaint. Her head was throbbing—too heavy to lift, arms like marble. Body one big pulsing bruise. She had no sense of time or place. She breathed with effort, feeling death closing in on her like a gathering force of pain and dread.

A voice from above seemed to float down to her. Something was said, but the words buzzed like bees, and then seemed to growl. Then more words rambled about her ears like little marching soldiers barking orders. She heard herself ask for help just before she felt a sharp prick in her arm. She drifted off into a black pool of silence.

Sometime later, she was lifted. She yelled out in pain as she was carried through darkest night—a night that blew cold and strong—a never-ending corridor of night—and swimming lights, and high-pitched voices, and the frightening wobble of a siren.

Faces swam in and out of her consciousness. Movie cameras dollied in for a close-up. She saw the clapper-board slide in, click shut, and heard someone shout "Action! Roll 'em!"

A man with a bandito mustache and cowboy hat suddenly appeared in her face, a gleaming knife thrust in her face.

"This won't hurt, Miss Randall," he said, with a bright, evil grin. "Just a little cut here and a little cut there, and then everything will be fine. You'll see. Trust me."

Rita awoke thrashing and whining. A white angel with bright red hair and black bulging eyes held her shoulders.

"They should have strung you up, you know. Strung you up from the highest tree, but no... you got off lucky. The director yelled 'CUT' just when they wrapped that rope around your pretty little neck."

A tall, thin scarecrow of a man with a long, poker face, wide wondering eyes and a wrinkled smile, spoke to her in a metallic voice.

"Can you get me in the movies? I can play all sorts of parts, you know. I can be a man, or a woman, or a dog, or a cat. See? So versatile. Now, Miss Randall, one more little shot in the arm, and you and I will go dancing, arm and arm, down that lovely yellow brick road."

Timeless minutes later, Rita was wandering lost under a dark moving sky under sycamores, on a path that narrowed and led to an angry, heaving ocean. Petrified, she turned to run back the way she came, but a tall, handsome man stood in her path, with the flat of his hand up, as if to stop her.

"I'll find you, Rita. Don't worry, I'll find you again."

Rita's eyes fluttered open, and little by little she explored her surroundings. She was in bed. A warm, soft bed. Her headache was gone. Her limbs were stiff, but she could move them. She was hungry. She was alive. Sunlight slanted in from the blinds and made rectangles of light on the floor.

"How are you feeling, Rita?" a male voice asked, from somewhere within the room.

Rita slowly rolled her head to the sound. A man approached from her right.

He was a broad, sharp-nosed man, with salt and pepper hair and searching dark eyes. Rita studied him, and she thought he gave the impression of authority. She knew the face, but she couldn't match it with a name.

"It's good to see you awake. It's been a while."

Her eyes were still glazed with sleep. She tried to speak, but the words wouldn't form to translate her thoughts.

"Don't talk, Rita. You still need lots of rest. There'll be plenty of time to talk later."

Rita? Was that her name?

"Rita?" she asked, in a breathy voice.

"Yes, Rita. Can I get you anything?"

Rita thought about that. Allowing her eyes to rest on the man for a time, she strained to recall him. She felt caught in a dream, remembering bits and pieces from the past, but she was unable to string them together to make any logical sense.

"Where? Where am I?"

"At the Lenox Hill Hospital in New York City."

135

"I don't remember..." Rita said, her voice trailing off.

"It's just the medication. You've been hallucinating. It will wear off soon. You were a sick little girl, Rita."

Rita worked to put a name to the face. "Who are you?"

He laughed, a nervous laugh. "Who am I? You know who I am, Rita. Of all people, you know me."

Rita's eyes were a blank. "I'm sorry."

"It's Everett. Everett Claxton. Of course you remember me. I found you in my living room in Amagansett. I don't know how in the hell you got there, but there you were. I thought you were dead."

Rita's eyes were restless with confusion. "Amagansett? Dead?"

"Yes. I called an ambulance. Thank God I found you when I did, or you would have died."

Frustrated at her lack of memory, Rita closed her eyes and turned away. "I don't know... I don't know who I am."

Presenting an optimistic smile and tone of voice, Everett clasped his hands together.

"Are you hungry, Rita? I can have them send in whatever you want."

She opened her eyes and tilted her head to look at him again. Her eyes remained dull and tired.

"Just some coffee and toast."

Everett rubbed his hands together. "All right then, Rita, you shall have it. Now, I also have a little surprise for you."

Rita tried to smile but failed.

"Out in the hallway is someone you will definitely want to see. I'll be right back. Don't go away," he said with a chuckle, proud of his little joke.

A moment later, Rita heard a little girl's gleeful cry.

She managed to lift her head to see Laura. She breezed into the room, pudgy arms outstretched.

"Mommy!"

Rita struggled up on elbows as Laura threw her arms around her mother's neck, pressing her warm cheek to Rita's.

"Why did they put you in here, Mommy? I'm so happy, happy, happy to see you."

Rita lifted her heavy arms and embraced her daughter. Inside, Rita felt a furnace of terror. She couldn't recall who this little girl was.

"And that's not all, Rita," Everett said, a big smile on his face. "See who brought Laura, all the way from California."

When Laura released her mother and drew back, Rita stared up into a tanned, handsome face. He wore a blue striped double-breasted suit, white shirt and gold and blue striped tie. His raven hair was smoothed back with pomade and parted on one side. His smile was wide and meant to dazzle.

The man spread his arms, dramatically, like an actor who'd just leapt from offstage into the full flood of spotlights. "Hey, baby, I've been beggin' those saw bone doctors to let me in to see you. I told them that one look at me, and you'll spring out of bed and dance around the room with me. I said, you let old Tony Lapano in to see his girl of girls, his star of stars, and she'll make a miraculous recovery."

Tony did a little tap-dance over to the bed, stooped and kissed Rita on the lips. "Hello, doll. You don't worry about nothin' from here on. Ole Tony is going to take care of everything. No more of those big pills that make you crazy and no more of those white coat quacks fakin' like they know what the hell they're doing. Tony's here, now, and everything's going to be top drawer, baby."

Rita's eyes were wide and turbulent. She shivered, and tears swelled in her eyes. She had no idea who this man was, but something far in the recesses of her mixed-up head told her something was very wrong. She felt a wild, menacing storm forming in her chest.

"Hey, don't cry, Rita baby. Everything's going to be fine now that I'm here," Tony said, taking Laura by the hand. "Laura and me will have you outta here in no time, and back in Hollywood makin' pictures where you belong."

CHAPTER 23

1948

Clint's hands were outstretched, bracing for impact. He burst through a blue, shimmering force field, the thin membrane exploding into spinning shards of glass, whirling, sizzling around him in bright flecks like thousands of sparklers. He landed on his feet, off balance, steadying himself with effort. His body quivered and twitched, and a rush of cold wind swept over him like a wave, scattering his hair, making his teeth chatter.

As he struggled to focus, the glittering shards fizzled, faded and melted away, leaving him in a kind of large blue/black vibrating capsule. He reached out to touch it and his hand passed through.

His breath came fast; heartbeat fast; mind raced. Where was he? Still his teeth chattered. He made a small effort to escape, just one foot out to take a step.

The capsule disintegrated, and he found himself standing in a screened porch in the dead of night. His ears picked up the sound of the sea, and he wrapped himself with his arms around his chest hoping to build warmth.

Standing on wobbly legs, he swayed and almost fell. Spotting the outline of a canvas chair, he stuttered over and dropped into it, sighing with relief and exhaustion.

Thinking was impossible. Reasoning was impossible. His mind, his memory, was a jigsaw puzzle. All the pieces had been tossed up into the air and they'd landed in chaotic fragments. Nothing fit. No clear picture of what had happened or where he was.

He needed rest. He needed to relax his bruised mind and wild, galloping emotions. He needed sleep. Clint leaned back, shut his eyes and dropped into instant slumber.

He was only vaguely aware of a light. Sunlight? There was a far-off voice, like an echo, and a mumble of words.

His eyes slitted open, and he saw a gun pointed at him, and the barrel of the thing seemed enormous, like a cannon. Clint sucked in a startled breath and dared to lift his eyes. He saw an over-sized man, with hostile eyes and salt and pepper hair, dressed in a blue silk bath robe.

"Who are you?" the man growled. "And what the hell are you doing on my deck at 6:30 on a Sunday morning?"

Oddly, Clint did a side glance and saw a gray tabby cat, curled up on a rug, looking back at him indifferently.

"Talk before I blow your brains out and then call the cops."

Clint swallowed, stuttering out his name. "I'm... I'm Clint West."

"Is that supposed to mean something to me? What the hell are you doing here? How did you get in?"

Clint cautiously glanced about, trying to fit the scattered pieces of his mind together. Part of his atoms or whatever, still seemed to be circling, and his thoughts were spinning about with them. He was present enough to know something remarkable had happened. He recalled the beach and the rushing, blue, glittering wave overtaking him. He was certain he had time traveled. But where? When? And what had happened to Rita?

"I'm not a burglar. It was a mistake. I was looking for someone and I guess I just stumbled in. I'm sorry. Please lower that gun. I'm not going to hurt you."

"You're damn right you're not. Get up. I'm going inside to call the police."

"Don't do that. Please. I'll leave. It was a mistake. Like I said, I was looking for someone."

"Who? Who are you looking for?"

"A woman named Rita."

"Rita who?"

"Rita Randall."

He was first astonished, then alarmed, then angry. "Did you beat her up?"

"What?"

"You know what I mean. Did you beat her up, because if you did, I am going to shoot you, and no court in this land will convict me."

"I don't know what you're talking about. Is she here? How is she?"

The man took a threatening step forward, speaking through clenched teeth, looking at Clint with a splendid hatred. "Tell me now who you are and what you want or so help me God, I will shoot you."

It was in that desperate moment that Clint's mind cleared just enough for recognition to dawn. He knew this man. But where? He strained to think, to remember.

"I'm only going to give you five more seconds before I start shooting."

"What happened to Rita?" Clint insisted. "Just tell me

what happened to her and if she's all right."

"I'm not telling you anything."

"Is she here? Is Rita here? We were together. We got separated. Is she all right?"

The man hooded his eyes. "I found her in this room, unconscious, close to death. I have no idea how she got here. I called an ambulance and they took her to a local hospital. From there she was taken to Manhattan to a hospital. She had no memory of what had happened to her. She didn't know me, and she didn't even know her own daughter. A week later, she did remember Laura, but no one else."

Clint recalled Oscar Bates' words, "*I was lost once myself, in the future, and I was lucky to get back. When I did get back, I was all banged up and had lost my memory. I didn't know who I was or where I'd been.*"

Clint sank a little. Why hadn't it happened to him? Overall, he seemed all right. So why had Rita arrived before him, injured so badly, and why had she lost her memory?

On a desperate reflex, Clint wanted to dart off after her. But there was the little problem of the gun pointed at him.

And then Clint's brain cleared, like clouds parting, revealing a dazzling blue sky. He now recognized this man. "You're Everett Claxton."

"So…?"

Clint let that sink in. If this was Everett Claxton, then Clint had definitely time traveled because, according to Wikipedia, Everett Claxton died of a heart attack in 1959 in Malibu.

Clint tried not to stare in dazed astonishment.

"Where do you know me from?" Everett asked.

Clint pushed aside his pressured mind. First things

first. He had to get to Rita as fast as he could, which meant convincing Everett to lower the gun. Clint decided to go for flattery.

"You're the great director, Everett Claxton. You directed *Payback on Front Street*, and one of my favorite movies, *Danger Town*."

Some of the malice left Everett's expression, but it was replaced by suspicion.

"How do you know about *Danger Town*?"

"I've seen it. It's a great movie."

Everett's eyes narrowed. "Are you completely out of your mind?"

"It's one of Rita Randall's best films," Clint blundered on.

Everett grew nasty again. "Rita Randall has just arrived back in Hollywood. We're not scheduled to start shooting *Danger Town* for another two weeks. Unless her memory improves, that date will have to be pushed back to who knows when. Now for the last time, tell me who the hell you are."

Clint shut his eyes and massaged his forehead, suddenly weary. "What's the date?"

Everett's brows lifted. "What?"

"What day is this? What year is this?"

"So you *are* out of your mind."

Without thinking, Clint blurted out his frustration. "For God's sake just tell me, when did Rita arrive?"

"Arrive where?"

Clint opened his eyes, feeling so exhausted and confused he dismissed the gun that was still pointed at him. "Here. She must have landed here… I mean arrived here. When? What day?"

Everett's expression fell into confused suspicion. He wasn't sure who or what he was dealing with, but he sensed this strange-looking man held mysteries and he wanted to find out what they were, for Rita's sake.

Clint tried another approach. "Did Rita say anything? Did she say what had happened to her?"

"She spoke in riddles."

"What kind of riddles?" Clint asked.

Everett's face registered a memory. He cocked his head, staring with new interest.

"A man with a beard… She looked at me a couple of times and said, 'Where is the man with the beard?'"

Clint sat up, alert. "What else?"

"She said she'd lost him."

"Did she say his name?"

"No… Now tell me. Who are you and how do you know Rita?"

"I can't tell you," Clint said.

"Can't? In case you can't see straight, I have a gun pointed at you. I will shoot you."

Clint put his head in his hands. "Okay, fine, if I tell you, you'll either shoot me or you'll call for the guys in white coats."

Everett laughed darkly. "I'm going to call them anyway. With that long hair and beard, you look like some man from the last century."

Clint looked up boldly. "Not the last century. The twenty-first century."

Everett did a slow blink, his expression a combination of doubt and confusion.

"What did you say?"

Clint squared his shoulders, sharpening his eyes on Everett. "Mr. Claxton, you will marry fashion designer Lucy Gibbs in 1950 and you'll have one son, Daniel. I believe you are currently meeting Mrs. Gibbs in secret, because she is married to a Wall Street banker who is the jealous type."

Everett was visibly shaken. "How do you know this? Nobody knows this. Nobody. A son? Impossible."

Clint continued. "You are currently trying to end a secret relationship with Ann Dumont, an up-and-coming starlet who is only 19 years old. You do seem to like secret affairs, Mr. Claxton."

Everett opened his mouth to speak, but nothing came out.

"Don't worry, Mr. Claxton, Ann will not divulge the affair because you have guaranteed her a minor, but good role, in *Danger Town*, as Rita's younger sister. Of course, only you and she know this."

Everett swallowed. Sweat had popped out on his forehead and the gun trembled in his hand. Clint did not like that.

"I'm not going to hurt you. Please lower that damned gun and tell me what the date is."

Everett stood dead still. Clint could see the muscles in his jaw working—could almost hear his startled mind working.

When Everett spoke, his voice had a little quiver in it. "It's Sunday, March 28."

"What year?"

"Don't you know the year?" Everett said forcefully, his voice tinged with anxiety.

"No, I don't."

"It's 1948."

Clint let that settle. "What day did you find Rita?"

"Sunday, March 7."

Clint did quick calculations in his head, his eyes sliding away. "Well, what do you know about that. He's still alive…"

"Who is still alive?"

Clint thought the name. Tony Lapano. Clint shot Everett a look. "Did Tony Lapano visit Rita in the hospital?"

"Of course he did. He's her agent. He took Rita and Laura back to LA by plane after she was released from the hospital."

"Did she know him? Did she recognize him?"

"No..."

Clint rose to his feet, feeling the burn of a new urgency. "I need to get out of here. I need to get to LA as soon as possible to see Rita."

"Sit down. You're not going anywhere until I get some answers."

Reluctantly, Clint eased back down. Keeping the gun aimed at Clint's head, Everett tugged a chair over and sat down opposite him. "You're not going anywhere, pal. Now tell me what the hell is going on. And don't leave out anything."

Clint settled back in his chair with a heavy sigh, his eyes focused on the barrel of the ugly looking gun.

"I presume we're in Amagansett, Long Island."

Everett nodded. "Yes..."

"Okay. If you have a phone book, I'd suggest you find the number for an Oscar Bates. He'll be able to explain it to you much better than I ever could. Knowing you're a man who likes secrets, he will tell you one of the secret of secrets, and it's happening right in your own backyard, right out there on the beach."

CHAPTER 24
1948

Rita Randall felt a stab of fright as she and Tony Lapano entered The Players, a two-level restaurant and supper club located on Sunset Boulevard. She leaned on Tony's arm while he displayed his usual vast, substantial smile.

The restaurant was designed by the eccentric but wildly talented writer/director, Preston Sturges, who'd also hired the chefs and worked on both the menu and the menu's design.

Rita wore an elegant, full length, side-slit emerald evening gown, with suede strap heels and a pearl choker with matching earrings. Her hair shined with luster. Her face was lovely but tense, her gaze searching and uncertain. She felt as though she were moving in a confused, cloudy atmosphere, her full memory still not completely returned. It was selective at best; at other times, a blank. Tony had drilled her on movie stars' and directors' photographs, helping her memorize their names and latest movies. She hoped she wouldn't have to carry on a long conversation with any of them.

Tony was dressed in his usual pin-striped suit, crisp white shirt, burgundy tie and matching scarf blooming from his breast pocket.

The restaurant's décor was restrained, vaguely gentlemen's club in tone. The tables, with white tablecloths and table lamps, occupied two long interior rooms that were filled with a dinner crowd of the rich and famous.

The maître d', whose face reminded Rita of a Russian Wolfhound's, led them across the room with flair, his back erect, his chin up, the menus tucked neatly under his arm. As Rita passed the tables, she received nods from Orson Welles, Marlene Dietrich, Hedy Lamarr, Humphrey Bogart, Lauren Bacall and Barbara Stanwyck. Stanwyck motioned for Rita to come over. Rita hesitated. Tony placed a hand on her lower back and gave her a little shove. Barbara looked at Rita curiously, perhaps calculating Rita's fixed, straining smile.

"How are you feeling, kid?" Stanwyck asked. "I heard you went through a rough one back in New York."

Rita nodded. When she opened her mouth to speak, Tony abruptly spoke for her.

"She's ace, Barbara. Never been better. Just look at her. Top drawer all the way."

Stanwyck gave him a cool glance. "Knock off the Charlie McCarthy act, Tony," Stanwyck said, referring to Edgar Bergen's popular ventriloquism act with his dummy, Mortimer Snerd.

"So tell me, how are you, Rita?" Stanwyck repeated. "You looked absolutely stunning on the new cover of *Movieland.*"

Oddly, Rita recalled Barbara's distinctive husky voice

more than her face. "I'm much better, Barbara, thank you."

Rita swiftly sought to change the subject. She glanced around. "The Players is still going strong," she said. "Everybody's here tonight."

Stanwyck made a sour face. "This goddamned greasy spoon is ruining Preston. He should be out making more pictures, not wasting his time here."

"He can do both," Tony said, with a spread of his hands. "He's crazy that way."

Stanwyck ignored him, leaving her warm eyes on Rita. "You let me know if you need anything, hear? We Brooklyn girls have to stick together."

"Yes," Rita said brightly. "Thank you."

Rita and Tony were sat at a table near the rear of the room, only two tables away from the solitary Howard Hughes, who had followed Rita carefully as soon as she'd entered the restaurant. Tony whispered to Rita that he'd talked to Preston the night before and reserved the table.

Rita did not recall Howard Hughes, except from the photo of him she'd studied. Tony had told her to smile often at the man, since he was taking over leadership of RKO Radio Pictures.

As Rita studied the menu, she also studied Tony. She still didn't remember him; nothing from the past. But he had appeared in her hospital room with Laura, declaring that he was her agent, and everyone else had corroborated that.

The longer she sat there perusing the menu, the more her beating nerves burned, bringing a cold sweat of fear. It was if her memory existed but was submerged, and as she peered down into the deep dark water of her mind, all she could see were vague swimming shapes.

She took it on faith that Tony was her agent and loyal

friend. Since March 7, when she'd been taken to the hospital, she'd had to take many things on faith. No matter how many photographs she studied, no matter how many movie magazines and popular magazines she'd read, portions of her mind were drowning under that subconscious sea.

Tony leaned in. "How are you feeling, baby? How's the memory? Do you remember this place?"

Her expression was strained. "Yes... well, some of it. Most of the faces and names are foggy."

"Well, don't worry about it. That's why I brought you here. Being here will help jog your memory. That's why I got you out of that house. You can't keep yourself locked away, baby. This town forgets who you are in a couple of months."

"Do they all know, Tony? Do they know I can't remember things?"

"No, doll. No, they don't know. I've told you already, a hundred times. I managed to keep it out of the papers. They think you almost drowned. Now, how many times do I have to tell you?"

Rita twisted her hands. "I'm just nervous. My head still feels like it's stuffed with cotton or something."

"You've got to get back to work. That's the best thing for you. This is April 10 and *Danger Town* starts shooting on April 26. You've got to be ready."

A tall waiter drifted over to take their orders.

A while later, they sat quietly, Tony munching marinated herring, and Rita pushing around a salad. She had not touched the martini Tony had ordered for her.

"Drink up, Rita. It will do you good."

"I don't want it."

"Drink it!" Tony demanded. "I know what's best for you. You've got to loosen up. You're all tensed up, coiled like a spring. Drink it. It will give you some pep."

Later, after Rita had chewed a few bites of roast beef and nibbled on the soufflé potatoes, Robert Mitchum walked over, stooped, and gave Rita a peck on the cheek.

"How are you, sweetheart? I heard the ocean almost dragged you away."

Mitchum pulled up a chair and sat next to her, ignoring Tony.

Since the last time Rita had seen Bob, she thought he'd grown into the weariness of his cautiously hooded eyes. She remembered Mitchum. He was easy to remember. *One of a kind*, Rita thought.

"Yeah, I was almost a goner," Rita said, weakly.

"Well thank God, you're back with us. I hear you're going to be starting *Danger Town*."

"Yes… I wish you were making it with me," Rita said, wanting Mitchum because she remembered him.

"Yeah, darlin', it would have been fun. They want me to do another picture like *Out of the Past*. I said, sure, but don't give me a bad script."

He changed the subject, grabbing his tie and holding it up. "Hey, what do you think of my tie?"

Rita looked at it. It had bold horizontal stripes of green and glittering gold.

"Nice," Rita said. "Different."

He lowered his chin to look at it. "It is like no tie anyone has ever seen before. I thought I'd wear it because I went to the track today."

"How did you do?" Tony asked.

"Hey, with a tie like this, I was able to hustle up a little action. I made a few thousand. Now, it's my lucky tie."

"You never had no trouble getting action," Tony inserted.

Mitchum looked him up and down with mild disdain,

then he turned his full attention back to Rita.

"Hey, Rita, when are you going to dump this guy and get a real agent?"

Tony laughed, uneasily, pointing a finger at Mitchum. "Funny guy. Real funny guy."

Mitchum replaced his tie, ignoring Tony, then jerked his head toward a table nearby, where Joan Crawford sat with a square-faced man, whose eyes were glazed from booze.

"Look at Joan. She's exercising her mouth like she's trying to swallow his ear. I told her last week that in her last picture she looked old. Her jaw dropped like she had a weight tied to it. I love to provoke her. She gets mad as hell."

He pushed up. "Hey, sweetheart, I've got to go. For dessert, get the Napoleon from the pastry tray. It's the best thing in the place. Oh, by the way, I was over at Tom Breneman's Restaurant a couple nights back. I met this guy at the bar. He had long hair and a beard. I thought he was in the middle of making a picture. Turns out, he said he's a writer working with Everett Claxton. He's okay. He didn't bullshit me and he bought me a drink. When has anybody in this magic town ever bought me a drink? Old long hair told the bartender to give me scotch in a water glass with no ice, just a little plain tap water as a chaser. Imagine that? The guy knew what and how I liked my booze. Anyway, we got to talking, and he asked me if I'd seen you."

Rita's eyes filled with interest. Tony stiffened.

"Me?" Rita said, her mind working. "He asked about me?"

"Yeah, he said if I ran into you to say, 'The guy with the long hair is in town.' He said you'd know what it meant. All right, sweetheart, you take care of yourself.

And let's try to do another picture together. It was a good time."

After he was gone, Tony looked at her, and his gaze hardened. "So what the hell did that mean?"

"I don't know."

"Well, you must know if some guy is asking about you. Who is he?"

"I told you, I don't know."

Tony squared his shoulders. "I don't like it. Maybe he knows something. Maybe he's trying to blow your entire cover. He's probably some rag reporter looking for a story and a name."

Rita became subdued, as her mind drifted. There was something about Bob Mitchum's mention of a beard and a writer that intrigued her. It awakened an antique memory. She picked at the memory like a thief trying to pick a lock.

"I hope you're not lying to me about your memory, Rita. I hope you're not playing me for a sap, because I don't like being played for a sucker."

Rita looked at him with a new curiosity. "Why don't people like you, Tony?"

He leaned in toward her. "Why? Because they're all jealous, that's why. Because I've got connections and the prettiest girls in Hollywood. Let me tell you something about this town, Rita. The more successful you become, the more they try to knock you down. Well, nobody's gonna knock old Tony down. I mean nobody."

Rita stared at him, wishing she could recall their old relationship. She'd asked her sister, Martha, about him and she'd said Tony had been good for her career, and that Laura liked him because he was funny.

Tony snatched up his glass of wine, now in a dark mood. "I know all the joints and all the bartenders in this town. I also know Mickey Cohen's gang. Some guy with a beard won't be hard to find, baby.

You can bet I'll track this wise guy down and when I do, I'll send him to the hospital."

Rita looked away, hating the sound of his voice, hating her trance-like vagueness of mind.

CHAPTER 25

1948

Clint lay on his couch, hands laced behind his head, staring at the white stucco ceiling. He'd rented a one bedroom in the back rear of a Los Angeles bungalow court built in the 1920s, with flat roofs, tile roof arches over the doorways, stucco exteriors and a fountain on the walk.

The court had been built in two neat rows facing one another. A central walkway ran between the houses, and each dwelling was fronted with a small patch of lawn, helping to set apart each home as its own distinct unit. His neighbors were writers, directors, camera operators, and aspiring movie stars who had poured into the greater Hollywood area. Thanks to Everett Claxton's connections, Clint had found the place and rented it from money Everett had lent him.

Clint's eyes were wide open, every sense on alert. He heard a dog barking, the low murmur of traffic and, next door, a manual push mower spinning a cylinder of sharpened, grass-cutting blades that whispered over the lawn. His grandfather had had one of those mowers and, even then, it had been an antique.

Before Clint had flown to LA, Everett had fronted him the money to stop in New York City to buy clothes and necessaries for his airplane trip West. Clint had been excited to see and experience 1948 New York in the flesh.

It was a dizzying spectacle of elegant fashion, retro shiny cars, clunky looking yellow cabs, romantic nightclubs and people piling into air-conditioned movie theaters on hot days, since their apartment windows contained only fans.

As usual, New York City's streets were full of motion and energy. But the air was a little sootier because of an absence of gas emissions laws or standards; the dress was noticeably more stylish and formal; and cigarette smoking was the norm, with cigarette commercials crackling through the radio and plastered on many of the massive billboards on Times Square.

Now in LA, as Clint lay staring, thinking and strategizing, he couldn't entirely shake off the moods and images of the last few incredible, whirlwind days. He could almost hear Everett Claxton's agitated voice back in Amagansett, as if he were standing next to him.

"I tell you, I don't believe it! The whole thing's a damned fantasy. A fiction. A bad movie plot. Who can believe such a thing?" Everett had ranted. "Time travel? Time portals? It's just too implausible. Too fantastic. I don't believe it!"

A young Oscar Bates sat unperturbed at his patio table, pen in hand, spiral notebook before him. He'd just documented an account of everything Clint had communicated about his and Rita's time travel experiences.

Everett and Clint were standing by in Oscar's modest, gray-shingled beach house that looked out on a splendid view of beach, sea, and sky.

Oscar was a tall, thin, sandy-haired man of only twenty-five years old, looking nothing like the withered old man of 2019. This Oscar was thoughtful, vital and quick, and his eyes seemed to take in everything. He spoke directly, with clipped words and low speech. It was obvious that this young man was highly intelligent and mature beyond his years.

Oscar slowly lifted his eyes from the page, meeting Everett's owlish stare. "Believe it or not, it's true. I believe Clint, because I have time traveled. We are currently conducting two time travel experiments in Montauk."

"Who is we?" Everett asked, in a challenge.

"Scientists like myself from Princeton, MIT and other universities. Some government staff." Oscar narrowed his stern, almond eyes on Everett. "It's a top-secret organization. Do not tell anyone what is going on here. I stress, do not tell another living soul."

"Is that a threat?" Everett asked, defiantly.

"Yes, Mr. Claxton. That is a threat."

Everett's face dropped into distress. "I don't want to know about this or be a party to it. None of it."

"Then don't," Oscar said, pointedly. "Sell your home and stay in Los Angeles."

Clint spoke up abruptly. "Mr. Claxton, I need your help. I have to get to LA and to Rita."

"I tell you she doesn't remember anything about her past. She didn't even know me. She didn't know her own agent, and I'm certain she isn't going to know you."

Oscar pushed back from the table and stood up. "The last time I time traveled to the future, it took me a little over a month before my full memory returned. A woman who time traveled to 2160 returned with no memory whatsoever of her present or past, but she recalled every detail of her experience in 2160."

In a startled silence, both Clint and Everett shot Oscar inquiring glances, hoping he'd elaborate on some of the details of the future, but Oscar didn't, and he continued, ignoring them.

"Our experiments suggest that Rita will regain her memory at some point soon. I can tell you from experience that it is distressing and frightening to forget, and very jarring to suddenly remember. It's best if she has a good and trusted friend with her when her memory does return."

Everett pointed at Clint. "Why didn't he lose his memory when he time traveled? Why just Rita?"

Oscar made a vague gesture with his hand. "If I knew all the answers, I wouldn't be here talking to you. I'd be the ruler of the world."

Everett's face twisted and went vacant. He left the house and went strolling along the beach, attempting to take it all in and make some sense of it.

While he was away, Oscar and Clint compared notes and strategized about the best way for Clint to proceed.

Everett returned a little over an hour later. He built himself a gin and tonic and thoughtfully wandered over to the two waiting men.

"All right… Clint, you say that unless you stop her, Rita will shoot Tony Lapano on June 25, because he will try to rape her?"

"Yes…"

"Can you stop it? Can you stop him?"

Clint pocketed his hands. "I know that if I can get out to LA and see Rita, she'll eventually remember me. From there, we'll have to work it out together. Tomorrow is

April 1. That gives Rita almost three months to regain her memory before the night of June 25. Between the two of us, I'm sure we can change events and prevent the shooting."

"Is it possible to change the past like that? Isn't the past set in stone, so to speak?" Everett asked.

Oscar smiled, his expression eager. "Well, gentlemen, let's find out."

"That's not a very comforting answer," Everett said.

Oscar shrugged and turned his gaze to Clint. "If you are successful in stirring Rita's memory and preventing the shooting, what will you do then?"

Clint removed his hands from his pockets and raked a hand through his hair. "Simple. I'll ask her to marry me."

Everett rolled his eyes. Oscar knew what Everett's next question would be.

Everett's lips formed into a wry grin. "Will you live happily ever after in 1948, or will you return here, try to find the time portal, and escape to 2019?"

Clint stared coolly, not answering.

Still on the couch in LA, Clint sat up, his mind jumpy and tangled. Flying in a DC-6 from New York to Chicago, from Chicago to Las Vegas, and from Vegas to LA had been strange and unnerving. He kept reaching for a cell phone he didn't have. Smoking was allowed on the plane. Everyone was dressed to the nines, men in suits and ties, women in fashionable dresses, hats and stylish shoes, as if off to a wedding.

The airplane food was excellent, the stewardesses all female and willowy, with impeccable uniforms and perfect manners. It wasn't that flight attendants in 2019 weren't also friendly or skilled, but the overall style in 1948 was more formal, every action seemingly choreographed, rehearsed and mastered, the smiles, magazine-model perfect. Clint was more comfortable with the informal style of 2019.

Once in LA, Clint was enthralled by the 1948 LA. In the taxi he saw street after street with antique, decorative streetlights, quaint hotels, row houses and stately Victorian homes. He could see clear, distant green hills. The sunlight seemed to sparkle, and the air was fresh. Seeing the streetcars excited him; he was like a kid at Christmas. He'd seen them only in photos or on *YouTube* videos. There were fewer people, less traffic and no freeways, except for the Arroyo Seco Parkway, built between Los Angeles and Pasadena in 1940.

Clint stared at it all in wonder, feeling light-headed and out of place. There were seconds when he felt stuck in a vintage movie or lost in some virtual reality.

Sadness arose when he realized that this lovely and colorful city of 1948 had vanished, replaced by 2019's architecture of high, blank walls, skyscrapers, sharp angles and glass. The LA he had lived in was a futuristic city, one that these people could have never imagined or envisioned. He had walked through a door and entered a world where dead people now lived and breathed, people who, in his time, had been dead for many years. This LA was not his LA, and it certainly wasn't Jenny's, who wouldn't be born for many years in the future.

Clint recalled a line by Thomas Hardy he'd memorized in college.

Childlike, I danced in a dream...

Clint lifted off the couch, stood and stared into the middle distance, as if lost. When his heavy, black rotary telephone rang, he glanced at it, nervously, then lifted the heavy receiver.

"It's Claxton. I'm in LA. How are you?"

"Like a cat on a hot tin roof."

"Good title for a movie," Everett said.

"Yeah, well it will be a movie in the 1950s, starring Elizabeth Taylor."

"Don't bring up the future with me. I'm still struggling with the present. Now listen. So you've got the driver's license Oscar managed to get you, right?"

"Yes... From Long Island."

"It'll do. I've got you a job with RKO as a script writer. You're on the bottom of the scale and you should know that almost nobody out here respects writers much except actors. Some of them think they can do better, but let's not get into that. Anyway, here's the deal: get over to Hudson Sales and Service car lot on Wilshire. I don't remember the address, look it up in the phonebook. A car's waiting for you, bought and paid for. It's nothing grand, a 1940 Ford three-passenger coupe, but it will get you around town. Show up tomorrow morning at The New Writers Building on the RKO lot. There'll be an ID and pass waiting for you. You'll have a pleasant enough office—large paneled woodwork, with a room for a secretary."

"A secretary? What will I do with a secretary?"

"Her name is Margaret Stern and she's got a personality like a serrated knife, but she's good. She'll help you. You'll have plenty of legal pads and pencils. You'll have an Underwood typewriter. Can you type?"

"I use a laptop."

"Don't start with future words I've never heard of, and don't know what the hell they mean. Write in longhand, and Margaret will transcribe. Or use the typewriter, and Margaret will retype the script in the right format and correct your typing mistakes. Got it?"

Clint inhaled a nervous breath. "You haven't wasted

any time, have you?"

"I'm not doing this for you. I'm doing it for Rita. She makes my movies better and she makes this town better. I'd marry her if she'd have me, but she won't. Anyway, you'll meet other writers who work in the same building. Some work at home. I've arranged it so you'll start a new script. You'll get a brief outline and some notes on what the studio wants. It'll be a B movie gangster picture, so don't overwrite the thing, and don't use your 2019 slang. Eventually, I'll bring Rita in to meet you. From there, my hairy young friend, you'll be on your own. Oh, and by the way, you'll hit it off much better with everybody if you get a shave and a haircut. I know an excellent barber."

"Can't do that," Clint said. "I want Rita to recognize me. Without the hair…"

Everett cut him off. "…All right, good point. Do you need more money to hold you over?"

"No, thanks. I should be fine until I get my first paycheck."

Everett's voice softened. "I hope Rita recognizes you right away so we can get this whole thing over with before I start shooting *Danger Town*. I'll be going to see her in a couple of days. I'll be in touch."

After Clint hung up the phone, he paced the bungalow like a caged lion. What would he do if Rita didn't recognize him? If she *never* recognized him? After all, they had known each other for only a few short days.

Clint reached for his cell phone again. Of course it wasn't there. In this time, people used those heavy, black, rotary phones. There was no Wi-Fi or streaming, no computers or communication satellites, no satellites orbiting Mars. No astronaut had landed on the Moon. There were only three TV stations. There were no credit cards.

A hamburger cost 15 cents and coffee 10 cents. Everything was new, strange and vaguely out of sync. The people in this time were foreign, with different modes of speech, dress and manners. He'd have to be careful who he spoke with or hung out with. Any perceptible person would swiftly perceive that he was oddly different.

That night he ate dinner at a greasy spoon down the street: meatloaf, creamy mashed potatoes with a crater of real gravy, peas and coffee. It wasn't bad. His teen-age waitress, an attractive brunette with pouty red lips and fluttering eyelashes, often looked his way.

"Are you in the movies?" she finally asked when she dropped the check.

Clint stared at the check. It was $2.35. He didn't look at her. "No... Just passing through."

"I'm going to be in the movies. I have a screen test coming up in a week," she said with bubbling confidence.

"Good luck with it."

When he didn't offer more, she sashayed away.

It was after midnight when Clint yawned himself down the hall and opened his bedroom door. The room was filled with cool air and moonlight, and as he drifted off into welcomed sleep, the shining blue mirage of Rita appeared at the foot of his bed.

She stared at him, her blue eyes glowing. "If you don't throw the dice, Clint, you can never expect to score a six."

CHAPTER 26

1948

Four days later, Clint was at his desk working on a movie script entitled *Hot City*, a lame story about a baby-faced mobster who, during a heatwave, was hellbent on violently taking the city away from a ruthless mobster who'd ruled it for years. As it happened, both men were in love with the same girl, Dotty, a damaged blonde who, in turn, was in love with a mild, handsome piano player, who got her a job singing in a nightclub.

This style of writing was all new to Clint, and he literally rolled up his sleeves and went to work.

One of the many jaw-dropping adjustments to living in this time and working at the studio, was seeing the classic movie stars wander through town or the RKO studio lot. Of course, he'd seen them only in black and white photos or old movies, and they were long dead in his time: Humphrey Bogart, Ava Gardner, Barbara Stanwyck, Clark Gable and Errol Flynn. When one passed, he'd stop dead in his tracks, gawking like a stage-struck teenager, overcome by surprise and wonder. It was strange and stressful, making him feel like an alien in a world of shadows and light, and death, and rebirth.

The title of a poem by Emily Dickinson often came into his mind, *The Loneliness One Dare Not Sound.* There was no one he could share his experiences with. He was an island surrounded by a sea of the past, a very dead past that was miraculously alive again.

Clint's thin secretary, Margaret, was bony and hard-featured. She was also middle-aged, efficient and aloof. Her crinkly gray hair was always up in an old lady's stubborn bun, and her expression was one of distrust, dislike and disdain.

"Did anyone ever tell you to get a haircut?" she asked, when her disapproving eyes first took him in.

Clint grinned boyishly. "And a grand how-do-you-do to you."

Her entire face frowned, and Clint had never seen anyone's entire face wrinkle into a frown.

Margaret smoked like a chimney, a cigarette always dangling from her thin, tight lips, the long ash clinging precariously, but somehow never managing to flake off. Her voice was scratchy and rusty, like an old creaky hinge, and she bit off words precisely, if coldly. The wire-rimmed granny glasses that sat perched on her long, pointed nose had one arm broken off, but her beady, bird eyes never missed a period, comma or typo.

Clint figured she must have felt insulted, banished to work with him, a nobody of a writer of whom she obviously didn't approve. She glanced at his hair and beard often with utter repugnance, and as she scooped up fresh typed pages, she'd leave the room, mumbling curses, with a little shake of her head.

On Friday morning, April 23, Margaret stepped into his office and dramatically held up two pages.

"You're not writing Shakespeare, you know," she said sharply. "Your dialogue is too long and flowery. Use quick verbs, no adverbs, less description, more slang. You're not writing a novel. This is a hard-boiled, two-bit script about two losers, a tramp with a heart of tarnished gold, and a scared piano player mouse. But he kisses her with thick, burning lips. He kisses her like Clark Gable kissed Scarlett O'Hara in *Gone with the Wind*, so she isn't going to leave eighty-eight keys, even when that dumb, violent mug threatens to shoot her."

Margaret pivoted, exited, and slammed the door, leaving Clint scratching his beard.

A while later, as he was struggling to write dialogue for Dotty, when her piano player lover said he'd give her the sun and the moon if she asked for it, Clint's office door opened again, and a man stepped in. He was a good-sized man, about Clint's height, six feet two, but he was heavier and older, maybe in his middle forties. His black hair was short but carelessly combed, his ruddy face was somewhat pock-marked, and his expression was a peculiar combination of world-weary curiosity and lazy humor.

"So you're the tall, hairy one," he said, closing the door behind him. "MGM's about to film *Little Women*, I hear, with Liz Taylor and June Allyson. With that beard and long hair, you should screen test for Laurie, although I also hear Peter Lawford's got it. Okay, then why not Heathcliff in *Wuthering Heights*? Some studio is always kicking around the idea of filming another *Wuthering Heights*. Yes, you've got a bit of the Heathcliff in you, I think."

Clint leaned back in his chair with a sigh, not happy to be interrupted as he struggled with his tawdry masterpiece. "And you are?"

"Robert Bolin Bolt, better known as 'The Drunkard.'"

He came forward, sat comfortably on the edge of Clint's desk, and offered his hand to shake. "You can also call me Bobby, but I prefer Drunkard."

Clint extended his hand and they shook, Bobby's hand nearly crushing Clint's.

Clint swiftly withdrew his hand, flexing it to increase the circulation. "I'm Clint."

Bobby had the gleam of mischief in his dark eyes, and his thick, bushy eyebrows, nickname and loose-fitting shirt all suggested an unpredictable nature.

"Of course you are. Who else could you be?"

Clint had no idea what that meant. And then, with a jerk of his head toward the door, Bobby said, "How did you wind up with the wicked witch of LA?"

Clint shrugged. "Just lucky, I guess."

"You do know that she hates you."

"Yes, she makes that obvious, every minute of every day."

"It's okay, she hates everybody, except Claxton. Don't ask me why. Her eyes get all gooey whenever he comes around. Imagine that. Margaret and Everett Claxton. Well, okay, don't imagine it. It might hurt."

Bobby leaned in, conspiratorially, and whispered. "Rumor has it that Claxton and Margaret had a thing going on a few years back."

Clint looked at him doubtfully.

Bobby raised those bushy eyebrows. "I know, I know. I don't believe it either. Actually, I think it's because old Margaret wants Claxton to screen test her daughter."

"I didn't know she had a daughter."

"Oh, yes, and guess what? She's a class-A looker. Not smart like her mother, mind you, but a looker nonetheless. Another rumor has it that the papa is none other than Errol Flynn. I'm not sure I believe that either, but then, on the other hand, knowing old Errol as I know him, maybe I do believe him. We are good drinking buddies you know. But I'm getting sidetracked. Well, anyway, I once attempted to ask Margaret's daughter out, and when Margaret heard about it, she came at me with her claws out, her shark teeth gleaming, saying she'd shoot me in the back if I ever even thought about such a thing."

Bobby swung off the desk and let his eyes settle on Clint's typed pages. He reached and snatched up a couple before Clint could stop him. Bobby took them to the one window, held them up to the light and read, mumbling and humming.

Bobby glanced up. "Did you kill off the mother in the first ten pages? I always love a movie when the mamma gets it right off."

Clint gave him a bending smile. "Obviously, you have mother issues."

Bobby gave Clint a dismissive wave of his hand. "Don't get me started with old mother dear. Okay, let me get back to this hot-from-your-fingers script."

Clint waited, impatiently, tapping a finger on his desk.

"Not bad. Not bad," Bobby said, looking up, his brows knitted, eyes squinted. "You write like a novelist, like F. Scott Fitzgerald wrote, poor slob. He couldn't write good movie dialogue if you held a gun to his head. And was he ever wordy. If one word would do, then surely ten would do better."

Clint disagreed with Bobby's assessment about Scott Fitzgerald's writing, but he stayed silent.

Bobby returned the pages to the stack, finger combing his hair, which remained unruly.

"Not bad, Clint. Needs more grit, verbs and slang, but

not bad. That dialogue about the piano player's burning lips is a winner. I mean, what doll-face doesn't like kissing a guy with burning lips? The director will love it. Hell, I'm going back to my little hovel of an office and practice by burning lips kiss in the mirror. I've got a hot date tonight, and if I can manage to warm up my cold, clammy lips and crush them against hers, I think she'll come around. She may not even throw a wicked punch, like most of my girlfriends do."

Bobby turned and started for the door. As he reached for the doorknob, he paused, turning about with a smart-assed grin.

"Do you know how many times I've written this scene? That is, the scene where the guy or the girl walks to the door, grabs the doorknob, pauses dramatically and then turns back to the camera with a look of contrition or anger or, God help us, helpless flirtation. Probably a few hundred times. But... directors love it. You should add it to your script. They'll think you're a genius."

Bobby turned suddenly serious, his voice low and even, his eyes clear. "You've made some enemies in town, Clint. I don't know how you did it, having just arrived, but you've got some bad guys out watching you. I came to warn you, and to tell you to get out on the town now and then and make some friends. Friends come in handy out here. So meet some people. Have a few drinks. Date some of the local girls. There are positively oodles of them. I'm your first friend, Clint. Remember that. It might come in handy in the future. Now, for my final scene exit."

Bobby turned his back on Clint, grabbed the doorknob, paused, and glanced back over his shoulder. With a dramatic lift of his chin, and in mock anger, he exclaimed, "All you men are the same. You're all wolves and rats, who wouldn't know a good and true girl if you tripped over her in church while she was praying for her black-hearted lover's soul. I never want to see you again!"

And then he was gone, slamming the door behind him.

Clint was grinning and pondering that weird interchange, when his phone rang. He snatched it up.

"It's Claxton. Rita won't leave the house. I wanted to get her down to see you this morning, but she won't leave. And worse, her memory hasn't returned. Hell, it's been over a month since I found her lying there back in New York. March seventh. Didn't Oscar Bates say she should start to remember after a month?"

"Yes..."

"I tell you, I can't get her to leave the house. She's moody and scared."

"Can I come over?"

"No. No, I'm afraid it would spook her, and I'm going to need her stable enough to start shooting *Danger Town* on Monday."

"Can I come to the set? Maybe if she sees me there, it will help jog her memory."

Everett paused. "That's not a bad idea. Not bad. Let me think about it and get back with you. By the way, how's the script coming?"

"Don't ask."

"Is Margaret helping?"

"In her own lovely and friendly way. Why didn't you hire her to write the thing? She knows what she's doing, and what I should be doing."

"Because she's a woman."

"Yeah. So?"

"I don't know what it's like where you come from, pal, but around here studio bosses don't want women writing scripts. They want the pretty ones on the screen, showing their assets, and the others as secretaries or in wardrobe."

Clint stayed silent.

"Anyway, Clint, Margaret's doing me a favor because I'm doing her one. She's one of the best, Clint. Learn as much as you can from her."

At four o'clock the same day, Clint had had enough script writing. He stood and stretched, collected three of his typed pages and exited his office. Margaret had already left for the day, and he dropped his pages next her typewriter and an ashtray clogged with ugly cigarette butts. He didn't know why, but he grabbed the dirty ashtray and dumped the butts into the trash. On the way out of the office, he seized the doorknob and paused, remembering Bobby's exit. Clint stopped and swung around toward Margaret's desk.

In his best Humphrey Bogart impression he said, "You know something, sweetheart, one of these days you and me are gonna be an item, whether you like it or not. So, you might as well get used to the idea, see?"

With a shake of his disbelieving head, Clint left the office, slamming the door.

The afternoon sun still had some sting to it. He started for his car, dreading the drive home. The black, old, gangster-looking vehicle came with a column shift and a stubborn clutch. Having never driven a column shift, whenever he shoved the car into gear, he heard a terrible grinding sound. The car also had no power steering, and it maneuvered like a tank. How he missed his 2018 Mustang.

As Clint reached his car, he saw a man approach from his right. Clint turned to see him close the distance. The parking lot was quiet, with only a few cars and no other people.

The man was handsome in a mobster kind of way, with a sinister grin and a cheap elegance, almost a laughable caricature. He wore a blue, pinstripe suit, white shirt and silk tie, with an impressive gold pinky ring flashing in the sun.

He stopped within three feet of Clint, sizing him up as he chewed gum.

"Would you be Clint West?" he asked, his gaze sure and threatening.

From the look of the man, Clint was sure it was Tony Lapano. Rita had described him and spoken of him often, back in 2019, always with frustration and fear.

"I would be, and I am," Clint answered.

"Oh, a wise guy. I figured you'd be a wise guy."

"And what's your name?" Clint asked.

Clint faced Tony's cold stare, and his surly and aggressive manner wasn't laughable. Clint saw evil intent in Tony's eyes.

"It don't matter what my name is. All you have to do, pal, is remember my face and what I'm about to tell you."

Clint was taller than Tony and he had more pounds than Tony, but Clint observed that Tony had a toned body and good muscles on that frame. Clint did not want to fight him. He would if he had to, but he didn't want to. Clint had boxed in college and when he was in the Marines, and he knew some Karate, but he was by no means an expert in either. No doubt, this guy was a street fighter, no rules, no mercy.

"What can I do for you?" Clint asked.

Tony kept his sardonic grin. "I'll tell you what you can do, wise guy with all that hair like some shaggy dog. You can leave Rita the fuck alone."

"And what makes you think I know Rita Randall?"

"Because I'm not stupid, okay? Because I hear things

and know things in this town, and a little birdie told me you were looking for her. So don't look for her. Don't find her, and don't talk to her, okay, pal? Do you understand what I'm saying, wise guy?"

Clint nodded. He wondered if Tony carried a gun. Clint concluded he did. There was nothing clownish about the inner thug Tony, even if the outer Tony was a smoothly polished act with expensive clothes and a dazzling smile. Most people probably saw through his act. Then why hadn't Rita? What had she told him back in 2019?

"Tony never struck me or was unkind. He got me my start in pictures and he was good to Laura. I didn't care what he did in his personal life."

Tony spread his hands. "Did you hear me, pal? I want to make sure I don't have to repeat myself at some future time. I want to make sure you understand completely everything I said."

Clint nodded. "Yes, Tony, I heard you."

Tony's eyes flared at the mention of his name. "Now, how do you know my name?"

Clint tried to stop the words, but they tumbled out as if someone else had written the dialogue and he was hired to speak them.

"Because I hear things, and I know things in this town, and a little birdie told me you were looking for me."

Tony took a menacing step forward. His slitted eyes burned with rage. His hands formed tight fists. When he spoke, his voice was filled with venom.

"Listen to me, wise guy. You fuck with me and you'll wind up swimming to the bottom in some oil lake on Signal Hill. You got that?"

Clint held his stare, but his heart was slamming against his ribs, both from fear and anger.

"Sure, Tony. Whatever you say."

Tony squared his shoulders and stepped away. "Okay, then, pal. I'm glad you understand me. That's good, isn't it? Now, you go write your useless scripts and maybe you wanna think about leaving town in the near future. You think about that, pal, okay?"

As Clint drove under the palms of Wilshire Boulevard, the beat of anger and doubt whipped up the red in his face. He had to get Rita and Laura out of this town and back to Amagansett. Oscar would be waiting, and he'd already offered to help them return to 2019.

CHAPTER 27

1948

Early Wednesday morning, April 29, Rita sat in her dressing room before a lighted mirror, staring at herself. Her makeup was completed, her black and white satin gown was fitted to perfection, and the little fur hat, like a fez, was tilted left, giving her a sassy stylishness. Everett had already called her to the set, but she couldn't seem to drag her body off the chair.

She dreaded leaving her room for the lighted set, where the crew would linger, stare, and judge every move she made and every line she delivered. Her memory loss had left her feeling insecure, self-conscious and shy. She covered that insecurity by keeping an aloof distance.

Everett had told Rita that she knew the entire movie crew, having worked with many of them several times before, but she'd struggled to recall them, remembering only a few.

When they had begun shooting *Danger Town*, she noticed the odd stare, the nervous smile, the half wave. They were observant, or perhaps they had heard the gossip about how she'd nearly drowned when she was in New York. Whatever it was, they knew something was very wrong with her, or that she'd become a snob, when, in truth, she was just plain scared and confused, and trying not to show it.

Every day added frustration, fear and confusion, and she felt haunted and vulnerable. Her dreams were a series of fleeting faces and blurred images; of distant places and towering ocean waves thundering toward her. She hadn't had a good night's sleep in days, and she refused to take narcotics, aware that Hollywood was awash in them, aware that it was easy to get addicted, just as Judy Garland and others had. She was dealing with enough problems without adding to them.

She flinched when she heard a light knock on her door.

"Miss Randall..." Pete Atkins, the assistant director called. "Everett said it's time. We're all waiting..."

With a straining effort, Rita stood, turned to face the door and inhaled a bracing breath. She slowly wrapped her fingers around the doorknob, pulled the door open and left the safety of her room.

She moved gingerly past cables and canvas chairs, past actors, cameramen and gaffers, all lounging in chairs. They'd been animated only seconds before but were now silent, watching her with rapt interest as she approached the set. She was soon standing under the full flood of overhead lights.

Everett left his Director's chair and went to her, wrapping a comforting arm around her shoulder, speaking in a calm, reassuring voice.

"How do you feel, darling?"

Rita nodded. "Fine."

"Ready to go for a take?"

"Sure…"

Everett turned, with a clap of hands. "Let's go," he called, and the crew sprang into action, manning the cameras and the lights. The lighting technicians went to work, climbing six-foot ladders to make final adjustments as they prepared for the scene.

Everett glanced about, stern authority in his voice. "Make sure you light Rita mostly from the left in this scene. Watch the shadow."

Rita's thirty-two-year-old costar, Dan Clark, appeared, a cigarette stuck between his lips, his dark hair careless, dark suit rumpled, as if he'd stumbled home drunk.

"Hey, Rita. Let's do this in one go. I ain't had my breakfast yet, and I really do have a whopper of a hangover."

Dan was good looking, in a street-rough kind of way. He'd done many gangster films, the last being with Lana Turner.

Rita smiled nervously. "Okay, Dan. I'll do my best."

The set contained a sofa, a chair opposite, a fireplace that came to life when a crew member switched it on, and a coffee table that held a whiskey bottle, half-filled with Lipton Tea. A window covered by half-opened blinds was back lit with a low lamp that cast rectangles of light across the carpet, adding atmosphere in the black and white movie.

Everett clapped his hands again. "All right, we're going for a take. Quiet. Quiet on the set."

Rita's eyes shifted restlessly as she glanced beyond the lights and the set, seeing the silhouettes of wardrobe, technicians and sound men standing around, waiting. The heat and glare from the lights were intense. Yes, she did want to do this scene in one take and get back to the privacy of her dressing room.

"Okay..." Everett shouted. "Quiet! And..."

The cameras rolled, and the clapperboard was snapped shut.

"Action!" Everett called.

Dan stood on rocky legs, cigarette still dangling between his lips, a glass half-filled with the tea in his hand, hair disheveled, eyes glassy. He stood by the chair, Rita before the couch, her face taut with fear.

"Everybody knows what you are," Dan growled at Rita. "The whole town knows. I'm the only sucker who didn't know about you, baby. Well, I'm not a sucker anymore," he snarled, his fist punching his chest. "No, not anymore. Tell me, baby, tell me you haven't been two-timing me with the great and rich Carson Caine. The Carson Caine that owns this town and everyone in it, including you. Yeah, deny it! Deny it, so I can take one more drink before I squeeze that pretty little neck, until you scream out with the truth. ... Scream out the truth while I kill you!"

Rita took two steps back, still on her mark, as the camera moved in for a closeup to show her terror.

Rita's voice was tight with fear. "No matter what I say, no matter how many times I tell you, you won't believe me. I've never had a thing with Carson Caine. He's not my kind of man."

Dan pulled the cigarette from his lips and crushed it out in the ashtray. "And who is your kind of man, baby? Tell me. Who?"

Rita ventured a step forward. "It's you, Johnny. It's always been you. You and nobody else."

Dan cocked an arm and hurled his glass into the fireplace. Rita cringed as it shattered.

"Stop the lies, baby! For once, just stop the lies!"

He lunged at her, but Rita stumbled back and scampered away. Dan was off balance, but he recovered, whirling, jabbing a pointed finger at her. "Not this time, baby. You won't escape me this time."

Rita had a line, but she didn't speak it. With her lovely face in a closeup, it was clear she was distracted by something other than Dan and his threats. She was taken by someone off camera, just to the right and behind Dan's right shoulder. The lighting had changed, and for only seconds, offstage, a face was illuminated. It was a face from a dream. A face that startled her, beguiled her. She stared, frozen.

From behind the camera, Everett leapt from his chair, anxiously willing Rita to continue, with his gesturing hands. They were so close to completing the scene. The entire cast and crew looked on, captivated, following Rita's eyes.

"CUT!" Everett bellowed, the scene ruined. Exasperated, he turned, craning his neck to see who or what had distracted Rita. Then he saw him. "Son of a bitch!" Everett snapped, slapping his leg.

Clint West stood off set, on the periphery, his face gently lit by an overhead spot.

Everett threw his hands to his hips, waiting, fuming, but Rita didn't move. Clint didn't move.

Finally, with all eyes still stuck to her, Rita started toward Clint and then stopped. He took steps toward her and stopped. They stared at each other, still and silent.

CHAPTER 28
1948

Under a windy evening sky, a light rain fell, raising the humidity and snarling traffic. The streetcar, called "Yellow Cars" by the locals, was traveling from Lincoln Park to West Washington Boulevard. It bumped and rumbled over uneven tracks, its windows beaded with drops, its passengers lost in low conversation, newspapers, magazines or sleep.

Clint sat towards the back, his eyes closed, a movie magazine open on his lap. He'd just read an article about Rita and her new movie in the making, *Danger Town*.

Earlier, back at the RKO lot, he'd climbed into his car and cranked the starter. The engine wouldn't kick over. It wobbled, coughed and belched an ugly cloud of black smoke from the rattling exhaust pipe.

He'd left the car there, not wanting to return to his office to call for a tow truck. Margaret was still in her office, and he didn't want to have to explain what had happened, not that she would have cared. She was in her usual grouchy mood, and, anyway, he was glad to be out of there.

It hadn't looked like rain when he'd set off on foot, and he'd been lucky. A downpour began just as he mounted the streetcar steps. He sat, swaying with the streetcar, inhaling the cigarette smoke, hearing the hum of voices all about him.

As it had most of the day, his mind kept circling back to Rita and the encounter he'd had with her on the set early that morning. Their eyes had met, and everything had come to a grinding halt. Under the studio lights, she was pure fascination, a secret, alluring radiance glowing from her.

For a minute, as she held his eyes, he was sure she recognized him. But then she had a sudden change of expression, as if she didn't know who he was or where she was.

It was Claxton who appeared at her side. He ignored Clint, his full, concerned attention on Rita.

"Are you okay, Rita?"

Rita passed Clint one final puzzled glance, then turned away. "Yes... Yes. I'm sorry about the scene. Let's do it again. I'm fine now."

And they did the scene again, and she was perfect, abruptly leaving the set for the safety of her dressing room as soon as Claxton yelled "CUT! Print it."

The streetcar bell clanged loudly as they approached a stop. Not Clint's. His eyes opened, and he glanced down at the magazine article, rereading it, fighting mild depression. Rita had not recognized him. How long would it take? Maybe her memory would never return. His eyes rested on the article.

He thought it was good, compared to some of the

others he'd read. *Movie Fan Magazine* summed up what other fan magazines were writing about Rita, much of the copy released by the studio as forward marketing for *Danger Town*.

> *Rita Randall has always been a lovely paradox, on screen and off. She's tender yet elusive, welcoming yet aloof, splendidly attractive yet modest. Whenever she turns those deep blue, questioning eyes on you, you simply melt and walk away breathless.*
>
> *What theater-goer isn't taken in by her enigmatic smile and honey-glazed vocal tones? This is what has made Rita Randall the Queen of the Bad Girl/Good Girl movies. Is she really so bad? We know she isn't all good. She is often shown suffering at the hands of a man, a victim of a fractured romance, unrequited love or physical aggression, and yet there is steel in her eyes and strength in her performance that suggests, 'You may kill me, but I'll die fighting.'*
>
> *In most of her films, Miss Randall has been the emotional catalyst for much of the film's tension, and whenever she enters a scene, she does so with full sensual presence, sending out waves of an energy that is capable of lifting most men off their seats.*
>
> *This is one reason why her movies pack theaters, and why this writer predicts that Rita Randall is headed for that stardom which is granted to only a fortunate few.*

When the streetcar bell clanged again, Clint arose and stood by the exit door. Outside, in the now misty rain, it occurred to him that perhaps even if she regained her memory, Rita might not want to return to 2019. Why should she? As the magazine reporter had stated so pointedly, it was possible that Rita could become one of the greatest Hollywood stars of what was known as Hollywood's "Golden Era." Clint stepped down from the streetcar and started home.

Tony Lapano was very much alive. Rita had time traveled to March 7, 1948, more than three months before that fateful day of Friday June 25. Surely, Clint could find a way to prevent Rita from shooting Tony and, in the meantime, he had to stop Tony from killing him.

Clint glanced about, warily, as he turned onto the court center walkway, heading for his front door. He searched his pocket for his key, inserted it and shoved the stubborn door open, the wood frame having swelled from the high humidity.

As soon as he entered, he knew he wasn't alone. Goose bumps rippled up his scalp. In the gray, dim light, he stiffened, bracing for an attack. If someone had told Tony Lapano about Clint's visit to the set that morning, then he was probably a dead man."

CHAPTER 29
1948

"Hello, Clint," she said giving him a slow, melting smile, as recognition awakened in her lovely eyes. She stood in Clint's living room, in shadow, away from the gray light leaking in from the windows. She was elegant and mysterious in her tailored blue trench coat and cobalt blue headscarf.

Clint gave her a gentle, worried smile.

They didn't start for each other, each questioning the reality of the moment. Was it a dream? Had they time traveled again? Was she on a set, searching for her lines?

Her eyes were clear and warm. His, blinking in curious fascination.

Speaking at a near whisper, he said, "Rita… How did you…?" His voice fell away.

"Everett gave me your address and a key. I parked around the corner. Fortunately, rain drives people indoors in this town. I don't think anyone saw me come in."

"… Do you remember?" Clint asked, nearly holding his breath. "I mean, is your memory…"

She interrupted. "…Don't you want to hold me, darling?"

His face was sensuous and tender. He went to her, wrapped her in his arms and drew her in close, inhaling her fresh scent. He slid the scarf from her head and kissed her damp hair. They kissed, hungrily, their faces warm with desire, their breath coming fast. Clint felt her excited lips open, sweeten and blossom.

With a dramatic, abrupt eagerness, he swept her up into his arms, as she wrapped hers around his neck. They started for the bedroom.

Later, they lay close, naked, covered by the sheet, listening to rain strike the windows like little pebbles.

Rita's mind wandered, a hand resting on Clint's hairy chest. She hooked a leg over his, feeling a soft purring comfort, a sensation she'd always felt after making love with Clint.

"It's so good to feel you next to me again," she said.

Clint turned, lifted on an elbow and kissed her nose. "Do you remember everything?" he asked. "Has your full memory returned?"

"I think so… Well, there are still some hazy images and faces. But you'll help me fill in the gaps, won't you?" she asked, turning her face toward his.

He took her hand and kissed it, holding it to his lips. "Always, and in any time or place."

"You are such a romantic, Clint, and I love it."

"Why not? I'm with you. You make me romantic."

"And you, Clint West, are a very gifted lover."

"God, how I've missed you, Rita."

He moved on top of her, and they made love again.

An hour later, they were eating in Clint's small dining room, a dinner of scrambled eggs, bacon and coffee. A yellow candle glowed between their faces.

Rita smiled at him. "... Like I said, such a romantic you are. Candlelight and everything."

"A confession," Clint said. "I bought the candle the other day because a neighbor told me the electricity shuts off now and then for no apparent reason. I thought I might need it."

The sound of drumming rain on the roof was accompanied by a low rumble of thunder. Rita held a cup to her lips and Clint in her eyes. "How did we get separated?"

"I don't know..."

Clint leveled his eyes on her glowing, candlelit face. "I'm so sorry you were so badly hurt. Everett told me everything. Do you remember what happened?"

She shook her head. "The last thing I remember is seeing you swallowed up by that blue misty wave. I was terrified and crushed. I thought you'd left without me. I didn't remember another thing until I woke up in the hospital, feeling like every bone in my body had been broken. I couldn't move or think. It was hell. I thought I was going to die. What happened to you?"

Clint gave her a condensed account, but went into detail when he described his meeting with Oscar and Claxton, and how he'd traveled to LA. He didn't tell her about his encounter with Tony, not wanting to alarm her and spoil their reunion and romantic mood.

"What was it like trying to remember?" Clint asked.

"Like trying to remember before I was born."

"This morning, when you saw me... did that shake your memory loose?"

Rita nodded. "I saw you, and I felt this kind of explosion in my head. I nearly fainted. Do you know how people who have almost died say that their whole life flashes before them? That's what it was like. But with you, it took a few seconds before I recalled time traveling to 2019. That still seemed like a dream to me. The longer I stared at you the more I realized it wasn't a dream, and that you were real."

"Why didn't you come to me?" Clint asked. "Why did you pretend you didn't know who I was?"

"Because I needed time to recover. To think. To get my balance back. My knees almost buckled. That's why I turned away. I also didn't want the entire cast and crew to know about you. I was in no shape to explain anything to anybody."

Her face dropped into worry. She slid her empty plate aside and crossed her arms.

"I also remembered Tony. The images crashed in on me right after I recognized you. I recalled that awful, terrible night in every detail, and it made me sick. The terror was so severe I almost vomited. Not very romantic, I know, but there it is."

She forced a little smile. "In those few minutes and afterwards, I did some of the best acting of my life. I wanted to grab your hand and run off that soundstage, pick up Laura and take the first plane to New York. I wanted to return to 2019, to our perfect and private life there."

Clint let all that sink in. "And now? What now?"

Rita sighed. "Everett asked me the same thing in my dressing room this afternoon. He knew. He is a very observant man. He knew I recognized you."

"What did you tell him?"

"That I would finish *Danger Town*. After that, I said I didn't know."

Clint said, "He knows what happened on June 25. I told him everything back in Amagansett."

Rita lowered her head. "Yes, he told me that too, and he kept pacing my dressing room with his hands locked behind his back, cursing Tony. I told him not to say anything or do anything. I made him promise. I told him that you and I would work it out."

"Did he stop pacing and relax?"

"Of course not."

Clint drained his coffee, his eyes not moving from Rita's conflicted face. When she spoke, her voice was strained and whispery.

"Can we change the past? Is it possible? What did Oscar say?"

"Oscar shrugged. He had a sort of 'why not, let's see' attitude."

Rita pushed her chair back and got up, reaching for her empty plate. "I'll clean up."

Clint stood. "We'll both clean up."

There was no dishwasher, so Clint washed, and Rita dried. Neither spoke for a time.

"Clint...," Rita said, avoiding his eyes, "Tony asked me to marry him a few days ago."

Clint froze, shooting her a look of alarm. "I was afraid of that."

"At that time, I had no memory of him or of you. Laura liked him, and my housekeeper, Maude, said he would be a good father to Laura, and he'd been a great help to my career. I just... I don't know..."

"What did you tell him?" Clint asked.

Rita sat on a wooden kitchen stool. "I told him I'd think about it."

Clint turned away, wiping his hands on a towel. "So that's why he threatened me."

Rita's face almost came apart. She shot off the stool. "He did what?"

Clint faced her. "He met me in the parking lot last Friday."

"Friday… That was the day he took me out to dinner and asked me to marry him. He had a ring and everything. He said he was ready to call studio publicity."

"And did he?"

"I told him to wait. I told him I needed a little more time. I knew something was wrong. I could feel it in my gut, but I was just so lost and confused. And then he told me I'd already said I'd marry him before I left on vacation to New York."

Clint cursed.

"Of course I didn't. I remember now. He was trying to manipulate me. He's a snake in the grass."

Clint watched Rita's face turn from anger to fear. "Clint, will Tony try to rape me again? Will I have to shoot him again? Do I have to repeat what already happened?"

Clint put his hands on her shoulders. "No, Rita, no. I think you've been given the chance to change what happened. You're in a different world this time. I'm here, things are different. I don't understand why or how it works, but I believe we have the opportunity to prevent it from happening again."

Rita's eyes wandered the room, searching for answers. "Maybe Tony won't try to rape me this time."

"We can't give him that opportunity. We have almost two months to change the circumstances."

Clint dropped his hands and turned away from her. "Of course, the biggest problem we have right now is trying to keep Tony from killing me."

Rita went to him in a rush, her arms wrapping him

tightly. "You don't know Tony like I know him. He's friends with every mobster and rat in this town."

A squeal of wind rattled the windows.

Rita's soft voice was in his ear. "Clint, let's get Laura and go back to Long Island. Let's try to find the portal and return to 2019."

"There are risks there too. Remember what happened to you last time? And what about Laura? What if something should happen to her?"

Rita pulled back, her eyes searching his face. "Then what are we going to do? By now, I'm sure Tony has heard you were on the set this morning."

Clint shrugged.

"Clint, I think we should take our chances and take that plane ride back to New York. The sooner the better. I'll hold onto Laura. I'll protect her."

Each considered the possibility.

A few minutes later, Rita called home and asked Maude to let her speak to Laura. Rita told her complaining daughter that she'd be home late and to let Maude put her to bed.

"I want you to put me to bed, Mommy. Come home now."

Rita spoke soothingly. "I'll be home before you know it, honey. I just have a few things to do."

"Tony called," Laura said.

Rita stiffened, passing Clint a worried look. "And how is Tony?"

Clint drifted to her side, anxiously waiting for more.

"He asked where you were."

"What did you tell him?"

"I said you weren't here."

"Did he say anything else?" Rita asked.

"No. He said he was going to bring me a present

soon."

"That's nice of him. Go to bed now, honey. I'll be home soon and kiss you goodnight."

Minutes later, as they sipped white wine, Rita sat on the couch, staring into the carpet. "I keep thinking that Tony's going to come to the house sooner than later. I'm going to have to be ready for him, but not with a gun."

"Do you want me to stay there with you?"

"No, it could just make things worse."

Clint's telephone rang, loud, sounding like an alarm. They both glanced toward it, tense.

"Don't answer it," Rita said, her urgent eyes lingering on Clint's face, her heart thumping in her ears.

CHAPTER 30

1948

Clint set his wineglass down and went to answer the telephone. "I'm not going to hide away like a scared dog, Rita. Whatever comes, we might as well face it now rather than later."

His pulse quickened as he lifted the receiver to his ear. "Hello?"

"Clint? It's Everett. Where in the hell have you been? I've been trying to reach you for hours."

Clint released a little sigh. "What's up, Everett?"

"What's up? Who are you, Bugs Bunny? Look, have you seen Rita? I've been trying to reach her too."

Clint cupped a palm over the speaker. "It's Everett. Wants to know if you're here."

Rita relaxed her shoulders, shaking her head no.

"No, I haven't seen her."

Silence.

"Clint. Level with me here. I'm a friend. Anyway, I

know she's with you because I gave her a key and the address. She's in love with you and she has her memory back."

Clint glanced at Rita and shrugged a shoulder. Resigned, she nodded.

"Okay, Everett, she's here."

"Good. Put her on the phone. I have great news. I'm bursting with good news."

Clint held up the receiver. "He wants to talk to you. He has some good news."

Still reluctant, Rita left the couch and took the phone.

"Hello, Everett."

"Why don't you trust me, Rita? After all we've been through."

"I'm sorry… These have not been easy times, and part of me is still lost in a fog."

"Well, you won't be when I tell you who I just got off the phone with."

"Okay… Who?"

"Howard Hughes."

"And?"

"I'm sure you are aware that all of Hollywood has been buzzing about who will play the part of Annabel Fleming in *Shadows over Meadow Green*."

Rita swallowed. It was the part every Hollywood actress wanted, and many had already screen tested for it. The gossip was that Howard Hughes had purchased the movie rights of the best-selling novel for an exorbitant price.

"Yes, of course I know of it."

"Take a deep breath, Rita."

Excitement suddenly boiled up in her. "What, Everett? Tell me."

"Hughes wants you for the part."

Rita shot Clint an excited gaze. "Me? But... I haven't screen tested for it."

"He told me, matter-of-factly, like he always does, that he doesn't give a damn about the screen test. He wants you. He said you were born for the part."

Rita dropped to the couch in a little bounce. "I don't believe it. Are you sure he hasn't gone crazy? Gene Tierney told me that, after his plane crash in 1946, he's different."

"Okay, fine, so he's different. We all change. Who cares?"

Clint questioned her with his eyes, leaning in, trying to hear.

Everett went on. "This is your ticket to stardom, Rita. This is your Gone with the Wind part."

"When? I mean, how? I mean... I'm so stunned. I thought Merle Oberon and Loretta Young were up for it. I even heard he was thinking about Ava Gardner."

"Get it in your head, Rita. Howard wants you and only you... But, like most things in life, there's a catch."

Rita frowned, thinking the worst. Her voice dropped into dark suspicion. "What does he want? As if I don't know."

"Not that, Rita. He won't make the deal with Tony. He recommended you drop him immediately and meet with Victor Bracket. He likes Victor and, as you know, Bracket only handles the biggest stars. Victor is also known for getting two-to-three year studio terms—that allowed actors to work at other studios simultaneously. Victor knows Howard, and Howard respects his business savvy. Howard says you need to dump Tony and climb the ladder to Bracket. His words, not mine."

Rita shot up. "Tony's not going to go for that," Rita said, feeling her emotions yo-yo up and down.

"Howard said he could arrange it. He said he'd call Tony personally. You know Howard."

"No, I don't know Howard, but I do know Tony. You know what Tony's going to do. He's going to hit the roof and threaten me, you, Clint and Howard."

"Annabel Fleming is yours, Rita. Everybody knows Tony is basically a two-bit con man who is in the business for the parties and the girls… His girls. I heard he asked you to marry him."

Rita's voice was flat. "Yes."

"He's a loser and a punk, Rita. I'll ask around and get some muscle to protect you and Clint. He'll come after me too. Hell, maybe it's time somebody had a good talking to him. Somebody he'll respect. I know some people. Tony's kind of people. Meanwhile, Howard wants to see you bright and early tomorrow morning. I've delayed the shooting schedule until eleven."

After Rita hung up the phone, she turned to Clint in a kind of trance.

Clint waited. "So?"

"Howard Hughes wants to see me tomorrow. He wants me to play Annabel Fleming in *Shadows over Meadow Green*. That means my contract will have to be renegotiated."

"Yes… And?"

"Howard Hughes wants me to change agents. He won't make the deal with Tony."

Clint raised an eyebrow. "Tony won't like that."

Rita gave a little shake of her head as if to clear it. "Have you read the book?"

Clint nodded. "I skimmed it the other day. Good story. Perfect for a movie."

"I don't trust Howard Hughes. I've talked to Ava Gardner about him. He once punched her and dislocated her jaw. Ava smashed an ashtray over his head and knocked him out. She told me there was blood on the walls and on the furniture. She thought she'd killed him. She even called Louis B. Mayer in a panic. But Hughes recovered. Then he proposed marriage. Ava declined. So you see, as my old stage manager back in Brooklyn used to say, 'The man is not altogether, together.' He's a little or a whole lot crazy."

Clint pocketed his hands while Rita reached for her wine glass and drained it.

"But it's the part I've been waiting for. It's the part that could make me a star."

Clint slid down beside her. "Tony could be a problem."

Rita sighed, heavily. "Yes, a big problem. It's not good."

She looked at him with uncertain eyes. "In the future, did I make the movie? Was I chosen to play Annabel Fleming in *Shadows over Meadow Green*?"

Clint looked away.

"Tell me, Clint."

"It's a different past, Rita, remember? You didn't get offered the part in the past, before you time traveled to 2019."

As the reality sank in, Rita ran a hand through her hair. "I feel like I'm on a merry-go-round, spinning out of control."

Clint stroked her hair. "I know the feeling. At least we're on this merry-go-round together."

"Who did play Annabel in the future? Do you know?" Rita asked.

Clint gave her a small, frank smile. "It was Gene Tierney. But, as I said, in the previous past, you weren't offered the part. At least so far, we've returned to a different world."

Rita lowered her head in despair. "I don't know what to do. I don't know what to do about Tony."

CHAPTER 31

1948

At 9:10 a.m. on Thursday morning, Rita and Everett were in Howard Hughes' spacious office, sitting in wing-back emerald leather chairs, Rita nervous, Everett anxious. Howard Hughes sat in a swivel chair facing them, his focused eyes examining Rita's every feature, her hair, eyes, eyebrows, lips, neck and outfit. She was dressed in a modest white blouse with padded shoulders, a dark skirt, silver earrings and simple heels.

Rita thought Hughes a handsome man: tall, with good features, dark hair combed back smoothly from his forehead. But his eyes held mystery, intensity and a kind of faraway look, as if his mind were lost in visions.

"As I told Everett, Miss Randall, I want you to play the part of Annabel Fleming. You're right for it. You look like her, in my mind, I mean. You're exactly what I think about when I imagine her."

Rita noted he was very pleasant and civilized, speaking

in a low, clipped Texas accent.

"I'm very happy and pleased," Rita said, trying to speak evenly, although she heard a little tremor in her voice.

"I didn't read the entire book," Howard said, offhandedly. "I read Annabel Fleming's parts, and that's what sold me on it. I don't really care all that much about the story. What I care about is that you'll be beautiful in it. You'll wear beautiful clothes. And we'll make your hairstyles into works of art. The camera will love you, Miss Randall."

Rita was surprised he didn't call her by her first name.

And then, out of the blue, he changed the subject. "Do you like to fly, Miss Randall?"

Rita was a bit taken back. "Well, yes… well, it makes me nervous, mostly during takeoffs."

He nodded, his eyes boring into her. "Takeoffs?"

"Yes."

"I see."

Hughes slid his gaze over to Everett. "You'll direct the picture, Everett. Did we discuss that? Did I mention that yesterday?"

"Yes. Thank you, Howard."

"You can hire the writers, but I want a copy of the script sent to me every three days. That's three days, Everett. I need to look at the script every three days."

"Of course. Three days."

"You pick the writers. I'll choose Miss Randall's wardrobe. And what's the makeup lady's name you used on Deadly Restitution?"

"Ida Cohen."

Howard pointed enthusiastically. "Yes, I saw that picture again two days ago and I was pleased by Miss Randall's makeup. Expertly done. Yes, use this Ida Cohen for makeup on *Shadows over Meadow Green*."

"Fine, Howard. I'll call her."

"Good. Good."

Howard leaned forward, folded his hands, and placed them on his meticulously neat desktop. He turned his full attention back to Rita.

"Takeoffs…" he said thoughtfully. "Yes, you have to get that right, Miss Randall. Yes. As an aviator, I make sure my takeoffs are pitch perfect. You have to feel the takeoff, Miss Randall. You have to listen to it—allow the engines to speak to you with sound and vibration. The airplane has a voice, you know. It speaks, and the aviator has to listen. That's very important on takeoff."

Rita watched his expression suddenly change, his eyes shifting from left to right before they settled on her once more.

"Miss Randall, do you know I spent nearly $4 million to produce *Hell's Angels*? When it opened in 1930, it was one of the most expensive movies of its time. Do you know what else? It was a hit. But I knew it would be. I just knew it. So will *Shadows over Meadow Green* be a hit, Miss Randall. I like the romance in it. I like the air action. We'll use a DC-3 for the air crash scene. Maybe I'll fly it and crash-land it into that field where Annabel first meets her on-the-run lover."

Everett cleared his throat. "Do you have a shooting date in mind, Howard?"

He glanced up at the ceiling, staring at it. "Let's get the script written. Yes, let's do that right away."

Howard's eyes dropped swiftly back to Everett, his gaze direct. "Every three days I want to see the script, Everett. Please make sure you arrange that. You can do that, can't you?"

"Yes, of course, Howard. That can be easily arranged.

I'll have it delivered to you in the morning of every third day."

Howard's attention returned to Rita. "The trouble with this movie business is that I do not think I am cut out to sit behind a desk. I like flying, and if I could fly this desk, I would. But movie making is a business, Miss Randall, and the purpose of a business is to make money. If it happens to make art, too, that would be secondary and accidental."

Everett gently cleared his throat again. "Howard, have you had the opportunity to speak with Tony Lapano?"

"Lapano?" he asked, calmly. "Oh yes, Tony. I called him last night, around midnight, I believe. Yes, it was 11:58 p.m. when I called him. I told him that, per my wishes, Miss Randall will be severing all ties with him and, accordingly, in all future picture negotiations, she will be represented by Victor Bracket."

Rita swallowed a big lump, waiting. Howard didn't raise his voice or seem the least bit concerned about Tony's response.

Everett lowered his voice. "Was Tony... shall I say, open to the change, Howard?"

"Tony? Oh, he told me he would sue me and Rita for breach of contract. I told him that he was at liberty to do so, but I stressed, quite fervently, that I would win in court. I offered him five thousand dollars to sever the contract."

Rita and Everett were, literally, sitting on the edges of their seats, waiting for Howard to continue. When he didn't Rita spoke up.

"Did Tony agree to that? To the five thousand dollars?"

"Not entirely."

Howard glanced at his watch. "He should be here at

any moment. He's late by twelve minutes. I asked him twice to be on time. Yes, I did mention that twice. I don't know why he would be late."

At that moment, a knock on the door lifted Howard from his chair. His secretary, a middle-aged dour woman, was in the act of announcing Tony when he rudely brushed by her and entered, his face tight and flushed with fury.

Howard remained standing as Tony marched into the room and planted himself behind Rita and Everett, forcing them to turn and face him. He tossed them both angry glances. Rita had not seen Tony since her memory had returned on Wednesday morning. Since then, she'd avoided his calls and ducked away when he came onto the set. Seeing him revolted her, and she was grateful she wasn't left alone with him, as he raged.

"You can close the door, Mrs. Dowling," Howard said softly.

With a shake of her outraged head, she did so.

Tony threw his fists to his hips, scowling down at Rita.

"So this is why you haven't returned my calls? This is why you've been avoiding me. This is how you pay me back for all I've done for you, baby? I bring you up from nothin', a nothin' girl from Brooklyn who was nothin' until I found you and now that you have a shot at stardom, you kick me into the gutter? You stab me in the back, and you don't even talk to me. And you have the nerve to have this guy," he shouted, pointing at Howard, "call me and tell me you're leaving me for Victor Bracket. Just like that? What is that? Huh? Why did you do this to Tony?"

Rita stared back at him fiercely, bitterly, as if he were an enemy. She had been unable to erase the dark emotional scars that remained. A part of her even reveled in the fact that she'd stopped his violent attack by shooting him. She recalled again the bizarre image of him lying on her living room floor dead, shot through the chest.

She was unable and unwilling to feel any compassion for him, now that she knew what kind of man he was. Only the day before, a young actress on the set confided that Tony had raped her two months before. She'd allowed it so she wouldn't be blacklisted, like other girls who'd refused him.

A searing heat flushed her face. Rita was about to blast him, but Howard cut her off. She would have lashed out, spilling everything, past and present, and everyone in that room would have thought her irrational and crazy.

Howard said, "Tony, we're all doing business. Picture making is a business. In business, things change. People come and go. Miss Randall is making a change. I have offered to pay you for it, and I don't have to offer you anything."

"Well, I don't like the price, okay, Mr. Hughes?" Tony snapped.

"What's your price, Tony?"

"I don't have a price, okay?"

"Tony, every man has his price, or a guy like me couldn't exist. My last offer is seven thousand. It's a good price and a generous one. Take it now or leave this office. I know editors of movie magazines and newspapers, Tony, and they can destroy you. This is a small town, so take the money and leave like a gentleman."

Tony glared at Everett. "I know you're the one who talked Rita into this, Claxton. I know who you are, and what you are, and you'll pay for this. You'll pay for this one way or the other. Nobody fucks over Tony Lapano and gets away with it. Nobody."

He turned his wrath to Rita. "Just when I was getting you great scripts, you leave me. The best scripts I was getting you, okay? Yes, I was getting scripts that every actress in this town was chasing. You'll be sorry you left Tony."

Rita's expression didn't soften. She knew he was lying, all bluster and smoke and no fire. The big directors and producers didn't want to work with him, and the ones who did work with him, did so because they were given a little bonus: one of Tony's "girls."

Rita stared, baffled and disappointed in herself. Why had she stayed with him for so long?

"Miss Randall is blameless, Tony. We are all blameless. I am simply conducting a business transaction and I need to get on with it. Will you accept my offer, or should we call our attorneys and begin litigation? Will you take the money?"

Tony huffed out a loud sigh through his nose, his eyes burning. "You bet I'll take the money, but none of you have heard the last of me. Not in a long shot."

After he'd stormed out of the room, slamming the door, Howard calmly returned to his chair and the meeting.

"Miss Randall, Victor Bracket is waiting for your call. He has your contract. If all is agreeable, please sign it and we will begin working on RKO's next big success, *Shadows over Meadow Green*."

Rita gave Howard a transient smile, feeling a chaos of emotion. Clint would be waiting for her in his office, waiting to hear the news. In her soul, she felt a storm brewing, and yet she seemed helpless to stop it. She wanted to play the part of Annabel and she wanted Clint. Whenever she thought of Clint and Laura as her family, she was filled with happiness.

Was she risking that happiness? Was she being selfish, remaining in this time to film *Shadows over Meadow Green*, and putting them all at risk?

Tony would seek revenge. She knew that without any doubt.

CHAPTER 32
1948

"We should get a place together," Clint said.

They lay on Clint's bed after making love. Rita had moved on top of him and was tracing his lips with a finger.

"Do you think so?"

"Yes… And we should think about getting married."

"Why?"

Clint lifted his head in surprise. "Why?"

Rita gave him little pecking kisses, speaking at a sexy, breathy whisper. "Yes, lover, why?"

"Because we love each other. Don't we… love each other? Didn't you tell me you loved me while we were making love?"

"Yes… I did, and I do."

"Okay… Then?"

"You haven't met Laura yet."

"I know. You keep putting it off."

"I know, darling."

"Why do you keep putting it off?"

"I don't know. Worried, I guess."

"About what?"

"That she'll get, I don't know, upset."

"I won't upset her. I'm sure once we get to know each other we'll get along fine. In time, I'm sure we'll grow to love each other."

"I'm sure, too."

"Then?"

"Okay. Come to dinner tonight. I'll cook. This will be the perfect night."

"Why perfect?"

Rita kissed him softly. "Because you'll be there."

"Well now, aren't you being quite the romantic this morning?"

"It's Saturday."

"Yeah, so?"

"So on Saturdays, I'm a romantic."

"That makes no sense."

She kissed him again. "I know, but it was a line I had in *Wrong Turn to Waco*, and I always wanted to use it."

"I've never seen that movie."

"You didn't miss much. At the end, my car went plunging off a cliff. It was a lousy picture."

"I don't believe it. It couldn't have been a lousy picture with you in it."

"Now who's being the romantic?"

"But I am a romantic. I mean, naturally, and not just on Saturdays."

Rita twisted up her face in mock insult. "Oh, and I'm not?"

Clint pulled her down and kissed her. "You, Rita Randall, are a lovely mystery and I want to marry you and have babies with you."

Rita stared deeply into his eyes, suddenly serious. "Clint…" She stopped, her voice falling into the silence.

"Yes…?"

"How do you think it would be if we lived in your time? I mean in 2019? Do you think we'd be happier there?"

"As long as we're together, we'd be happy. I know it."

"I want your babies, Clint. Whenever we make love, I want your baby."

"So, what are you saying?"

"Don't you see? If we're going to start a family…"

He cut in… "We have to get married, especially in this time. In my time, it's no problem if we're not married, but in this time, we have to be married if we're going to have children."

"Okay, yes, we'll get married, but don't you see, we're going to have to choose a time and stay with it. We can't just keep time traveling back and forth as if we're flying from LA to New York. My point is, look what happened to me the last time I entered that time portal."

"That won't happen again. If we have to use the portal, we'll go in together. We won't be separated like the last time."

"Okay, but what if I'm pregnant? What if we have two or three children? Don't you see? We have to decide what time we're going to live in, and then stay there."

Clint turned his head away. "Yeah, I see what you mean."

Rita laid her head sideways on his chest, sighing. "I wonder if I'm the only woman on this planet who has ever had this problem?"

The silence lengthened, each lost in private thought.

Finally, Clint spoke up. "I can stay here. We can build a life here. We don't ever have to time travel again."

"Can you, Clint? Are you sure?"

"Yes. Your career is taking off. You'll be the star you've always wanted to be."

"But will you be happy? Most men find it hard to be the wife of a star. I've seen many marriages bust up because of it, both ways."

"I'm a writer, Rita. I can write anywhere. Now that Everett has signed me to be one of the three writers to work on *Shadows over Meadow Green*, that will help. I also have an idea for a novel that I'm writing with you in mind. Everett can sell it to RKO and you'll be the star in it. Yes, we can make it here. I can be happy here, as long as we're together."

Rita lifted her head. She kissed his eyebrows, his nose, his mouth. "You, my darling, are the sexiest and most wonderful man I have ever known. I know Laura will love you, like I love you."

"I propose that instead of having dinner at your house, we have a picnic dinner on the beach. It might be easier for Laura and me to get to know each other. We can play, swim, build castles and watch the sunset."

Rita brightened. "I love it. Yes, let's do it. I'll fry some chicken, make potato salad and a fruit salad. Oh, and Maude baked a chocolate cake yesterday. There's some left. You bring the pop and the wine."

"Pop?"

"Yes, soda pop. Anything wrong with that?"

"Nothing. I've just never heard anyone call soda, pop."

Rita grinned. "Well, you have now, baby doll. Get with it. This is 1948."

Rita drove home, anxious to get started on their picnic dinner. Despite the shining day, her sparkling happiness and her love for Clint, she couldn't shake off a certain feeling of fragility. Since Thursday, two days ago, she'd not heard from or seen Tony. But he was out there, adding a constant menace and paranoia to her every thought and act. Everett continued to insist there was nothing to fear from him, but that was little comfort.

She glanced frequently into her rearview mirror, her mind turning again to the possibility that she, Laura and Clint could return to Amagansett, 2019. They would be safe there forever.

CHAPTER 33

1948

They took Rita's car and drove to Malibu. Clint let Laura sit in the front seat with her mother, while he relaxed comfortably in the back, taking in the sights, amazed at the sparse traffic compared to the endless mass of cars in 2019.

Earlier, back at the house, he'd met Laura for the first time. When Laura saw him, she backed away, nervous and shy. Then she pointed at his hair. "Where did you get so much hair?"

Clint grinned, pulling a 12-inch doll from behind his back, holding it up.

"This is for you."

Laura's eyes expanded on it in wonder and curiosity.

"Look at that, Laura!" Rita said, largely. "Isn't she beautiful?"

Clint lowered to his knees, meeting Laura face to face, smiling warmly. He presented her with the doll. "Go ahead. Take it. It's yours."

Laura hesitated, looking up at her mother for permission.

"Go ahead, honey. It's a present from Clint."

Laura gently took the doll, looking it over with brightly shining eyes. It wore a cheerful white and blue flower dress, and had auburn braids with bangs, beautiful slate-blue eyes that moved back and forth and opened and closed, and long, extravagant lashes. Laura touched its button of a mouth, its hair and its eyes.

"Say thank you to Clint," Rita said.

Laura held the doll to her chest, her glowing eyes finding Clint. "Thank you. I love it. She's my new, my very own Dollie."

Laura continued staring at Clint's hair.

Clint ran a hand through it. "Want to feel it?"

Still shy, Laura waited, thinking about it. "I don't know."

He bowed his head. "Go ahead. Touch it. It's okay."

Laura glanced up at her mother for courage. Rita nodded, and Laura ventured forward, holding her Dollie in one arm, reaching tentatively to touch Clint's hair with the other. At the touch, she squealed and jumped back.

"I like it!" She said giggling.

Clint extended his hand. "Shake?"

Laura considered it, and then tilted her head a little to the left. "Can I pull your beard?"

"Just like you always want to pull Santa's beard?" Rita said.

Laura nodded. "Yes…"

Clint jutted his jaw out, squeezing his eyes together dramatically, anticipating pain.

Laura snickered. "Santa's beard is white."

"Go ahead, Laura, pull," Clint said.

Laura inched forward and, with wiggling fingers, she touched the beard, then jerked her hand back as if she'd touched a hot stove. "I'm scared, Mommy."

"Go ahead," Clint encouraged. "Give it a little yank."

With his eyes still squeezed together, waiting, Rita looked at her daughter and put a finger to her lips in a shh gesture.

Laura put a hand to her mouth, giggling.

Rita stooped, reached, grabbed Clint's beard, and yanked hard.

"OUCH!" he yelled, eyes popping open, hand on his beard. "That hurt."

Rita and Laura burst out laughing.

Clint saw the mischief in Rita's eyes as she backed away, ready to run for it.

He shot to his feet, pointing at her, playfully threatening. "I'll get you for that."

Laura hopped about, gleeful and laughing.

The ice had been broken.

Clint turned back to Laura with a friendly grin. "Hi there, Laura. I'm Clint."

Laura squinted up her eyes. "That's a funny name."

"I'm a funny guy," Clint said, making a rubbery, crazy face, tongue out and lopsided, eyes wide.

Laura applauded, laughing. They shook hands and were instant friends.

Rita drove the twisting, cliff-hugging road that threaded through Big Sur, where mountains plunged into the Pacific and the phenomenally beautiful coastline came into view. Waves thundered in, beaten to froth on ragged rocks. In places, the road's narrow shoulders and sharp drop-offs were unnerving, no place for RVs or other oversized vehicles of 2019, Clint thought, as he poked his head out the window, taking it all in.

Clint was surprised when Rita turned left onto a dirt road and drove about 20 yards to park next to a picturesque, three-bedroom bungalow that offered breathtaking views of the vast Pacific Ocean.

"I bought the land about two years ago for $8,000 and built the bungalow right after. I haven't had the time to enjoy it as much as I want to."

"Do you know how much this place would be worth in 2019?" Clint said, carrying the picnic basket up the flight of steep wooden stairs to the bungalow patio.

Rita held Laura's hand as they ascended the stairs, gazing out at the sparkling sea. "I have no idea."

"I have no idea either, but certainly in the millions."

The rest of the day was spent at the beach, with Clint and Laura digging holes in the sand, inspecting bugs and collecting seashells. After eating, Rita napped while Clint and Laura walked along the back trails, finishing up at the beach. Rita joined them as they ran along the edge of the water and built a sandcastle.

By late afternoon, sunlight cast a hazy sheen across the water and all three lay on beach towels napping. The sunset spread across the sky in bursts of pink and reds, the multi-hued cotton-candy clouds lush and gilded.

Inside the bungalow, Clint started a fire in the fireplace and Rita left to put an exhausted, fussy and sleepy Laura to bed.

She returned fifteen minutes later, smiling, glowing from a new tan, her hair tousled, her mood sexy. She found Clint staring out the window at the moon-sprinkled ocean and the distant silhouette of rolling hills.

"Is she asleep?" Clint asked.

"Yes. She's had quite a day. A good day. I hope she never forgets it."

Rita took his hand, lacing her fingers into his, resting

her head on his shoulder. "It's a beautiful place, isn't it?"

"Yes. Why don't you come here more often?"

"I had no one to share it with. Now I do."

Later, they lay close on the extravagant tan throw rug before the fire. A log shifted and hissed. Rita's face was aglow, her lips open and waiting for Clint's kiss. They kissed and played for a time, whispering secrets and little jokes, and laughing. Rita lolled her head back, relaxed, gazing up into Clint's radiant eyes.

"Do you know what this reminds me of?"

"Tell me."

"Everett's beach house back on Long Island. Remember when I came bursting in from nowhere to 2019, and our eyes met? I think I may have fallen in love with you right then—at first sight—just like in the movies. I remember looking into your eyes and I felt something electric, something familiar, something safe. It was as if I'd known you before, in some other place and some other time. I had the strange feeling then that something had forced us apart; forced us to separate for a time. And when I looked at you that next morning, I couldn't stop an irrational feeling that I was in love with you. It felt so right to be together again. Did you feel that too?"

Clint nodded. "Yes, I did."

He gently touched her cheek. "I think we have time traveled before, Rita… perhaps many times before. We separate, forget for a while and then, when we see each other again, we remember. And each time, we fall more in love. And each time, we have it in our power to begin the world all over again."

Rita sighed out a longing. "I wish we could have stayed in that beach house forever, and never had to come back to the real world, whatever the real world is. Right now, I don't care about making pictures or being a star or anything else. This has been a perfect day, one of the best days of my life."

Clint was intoxicated by her, lost in a hazy world of desire and longing.

Rita's smile slowly faded.

Clint noticed. "What happened to that beautiful smile?"

Rita sat up, suddenly serious. "Clint, if anything should happen to us…"

"Nothing is going to happen."

"But if it does. If we somehow get separated again, because maybe it did happen, and so maybe it could happen again, let's always…"

He interrupted. "…We're not going to be separated, Rita."

"But if we do, then let's always remember this beach house. No matter what happens to us, let's always remember this place and, if we're ever separated, we'll know we can return here and find each other. Let's make this beach house our place, no matter where we are, or what time we're in."

Clint leaned and kissed her. When he spoke, he kept his burning lips close to hers, only a breath apart. "All right, Rita. As you wish. This will always be our place. It will be our safe house, no matter what happens."

CHAPTER 34

1948

Clint finished the script for *Hot City* in early June, adding the final scene at the bungalow where Rita, Laura and he now spent most of their weekends. Rita read it on the patio facing the sea one bright Saturday morning, while Clint and Laura romped on the beach. When they returned, wet and sandy, Rita sprang up from her chair and ran into Clint's arms.

"I love it!" she exclaimed. "If I wasn't going into production for *Shadows*, I would demand to play Dottie. She's edgy and smart, and she gets her man in the end. I love the dialogue. It's much better than *Danger Town*."

"Give a lot of the credit to Margaret. She coached and bullied and insulted me every hour of every workday, especially on the dialogue. Anyway, I modeled Dottie after you," Clint said, giving her a peck on the lips.

Laura tilted her face up to her mother, tugging on the hem of her white sundress. "Mommy, Clint said he would get me a dog. He said I have to ask you. I want a dog. Can I have a dog?"

Rita smiled, stroking Laura's wet hair. "Yes, Laura, but only if Clint teaches you how to take care of it. And don't get one of those big dogs. And no puppy. Oh, and we have to ask Maude."

Laura frowned. "She don't like dogs, Mommy."

"She doesn't like dogs, Laura," Rita corrected.

Rita narrowed her eyes on Clint. "Make sure the dog is at least two years old. I don't want the thing tearing everything up."

"He can live with me," Clint said. "That way Maude won't have to get involved. Now that *Hot City* is finished, I can do most of the writing for *Shadows* at home. I'll bring the dog out on the weekends, so Laura can play with it."

Laura leaped up, clapping her hands, her curls bouncing. "Can we, Mommy? Can Clint get me a doggie?"

"If Clint wants to, he can." Rita winked at him. "He's a very big boy. And he's a wonderful writer."

Clint stepped back and performed a courtly bow. "Thank you, my lady."

As June progressed, Rita and Clint grew progressively edgy. It was difficult to ignore the fact that the last time *Danger Town* had wrapped, Rita had shot Tony in self-defense.

But this was a different time—the time portal had changed that. Tony was no longer in the picture. Since the incident in Howard Hughes' office, Tony had mostly vanished from Hollywood. The gossip was that he was living in Las Vegas, keeping a low profile. Everyone knew he'd left town to save face after Rita had been cast as the lead in *Shadows over Meadow Green* and Victor Bracket had become her new agent.

Most thought it was about time Rita dumped Tony. It

was obvious that Tony had been more interested in using Rita as a show piece to further his own career than in helping Rita advance hers. Rita's fellow actors were relieved that she wasn't going to marry him, and they welcomed this long-haired newcomer. Word had circulated that Clint was a talented writer.

But Tony had his friends: a few club owners, mobsters and production staff, who regarded Rita as a traitor and back-stabber. They considered Clint an upstart writer, and the true reason why Rita had dumped Tony. Clint was an easier target than Howard Hughes, who didn't give a damn what anybody thought, and who had the money to buy or prosecute anyone.

As it had happened on the previous Friday afternoon, June 25, 1948, *Danger Town* wrapped. This time, Clint was waiting for Rita by the soundstage. They walked to Rita's car, holding hands. Clint held the passenger door and Rita stooped in, heaving out a sigh of relief. For the second time, she'd completed the picture, confident that this performance was better than her first, and happy that Tony was nowhere to be seen.

Clint slid behind the wheel, closed the door and started the engine. He exited the security gate, turning onto Gower Street, moving through the gears with ease, loving the straight six engine, four-speed manual transmission. He'd fallen in love with the 1940s models: the Packard, the Delahaye Roadster, the Nash, the Hudson. Driving was a new joy, and he loved exploring the old, two-lane roads that preceded superhighways.

Rita turned to him. "So where are you taking me on this late sunny afternoon?"

"A surprise."

"Oh, I love surprises."

"Just so you know, I dropped Jeter at the house.

Maude was okay with it and Laura went crazy with happiness. She has friends coming over to play with her and Jeter."

"Tell me again why you named the dog Jeter? I have the hardest time remembering that name."

"Derek Jeter is one of the greatest baseball players of all time. He retired from the Yankees in 2014, just in case you're keeping up with future events. Anyway, when I saw the dog at the animal shelter, he somehow reminded me of Derek Jeter. If you put a Yankee cap and uniform on him, I'm telling you that any Yankee baseball fan would say 'Hey, he looks like Derek Jeter.' Well, okay the black circle over his left eye isn't Jeter, but everything else is. The dog even runs like Jeter."

Rita shook her head, smiling. "You are a little bit crazy, I think."

Clint gave her a side grin. "A whole lot crazy and getting crazier all the time."

Rita leaned her head back, closing her eyes, feeling a spreading contentment. "This June 25, 1948 is certainly turning out better than the last one."

Clint glanced at her uneasily. "Let's hope it stays that way."

They drove along Palisades Park in Santa Monica, north towards the Lighthouse Restaurant. It was set on the Long Wharf outcropping off Roosevelt Highway, later called the Pacific Coast Highway. The restaurant lay at the point where the Santa Monica Mountains sloped down to the shore, where the sea glistened and gentle waves rolled in.

Clint turned into the crowded lot and parked. Rita noticed six outside tables with striped umbrellas and couples close and touching, sipping summer drinks. Guests in summer attire roamed lazily toward the sea, high on the sun and cocktails.

"I'm told it's a bit trendy, but what the heck. The manager I talked to on the phone said he'd arrange a private table for us in the back, facing the sea. He said he was a fan of yours."

Inside, Rita and Clint were efficiently escorted through the crowded bar and a side dining room with a wall of windows and splendid views, and into a private room with exotic floor plants, seascape paintings on the walls and a white linen tabletop with a vase of fresh flowers. A large picture window offered romantic views of beach, sky and sea. After Rita and Clint were seated and given menus, they exchanged looks of private satisfaction.

"Well done, sir," Rita said. "I love it."

"I say we order a bottle of champagne."

They told the stocky waiter that they were in no hurry and then ordered clams and salad and filet of sole. Before the main course was delivered, they poured the last of the Champagne, lost in lively conversation about movies, writing and Laura.

By the time the orange sun began its descent into the sea, Clint pushed his chair back and got up. Rita watched him curiously as he reached into the lower right pocket of his powder blue sport coat and drew out a rectangular jewelry box, wrapped in shiny silver, tied with a rich, royal blue bow.

"What do we have here?" Rita asked, eyes glowing.

Clint handed the box to her. "I saw it, it reminded me of you, and I bought it."

Rita took it, staring at it in bright anticipation. "I wonder what it is."

She gently unwrapped it, tugged off the bow, opened the lid and parted the silver tissue. Her eyes lit up, mouth opened. "Oh my... Clint."

Clint rounded the table and stood behind her, as Rita gingerly removed the glistening 14-karat white gold and rose cut diamond bow necklace. It had a sky-blue topaz and rose cut diamond halo dropping from the bow.

"Oh, Clint, it's absolutely beautiful. It must have cost you a fortune," Rita said, holding it up into the light and watching the fire dance in the diamonds.

"Yep, even with the 1948 prices. Here, let me help you put it on."

Clint draped it around her neck and fastened the clasp. As Rita stood up and turned to him, the evening golden sun gilding her, Clint stepped back. He fell in love with her all over again. His eyes warmed, his face softened. "Rita Randall... I love you."

She went to him, fell into his arms and kissed him, their bodies pressed close, breath intimate.

"Now, will you marry me?" Clint asked.

She whispered in his ear. "Yes... Yes... A thousand times, yes."

They danced for a time to silent music, neither speaking, each lost in the magic of that perfect moment of love and romance that is usually found only in the movies.

After their entrees arrived, they ate slowly, smiling and winking and talking about the future, about Laura, about redecorating the beach house in Malibu.

When Tony Lapano entered the room, Clint saw him first. Rita saw Clint's startled face and followed his eyes, turning. It was as if a cold winter wind had blown in, freezing them into ice. Rita shivered.

Clint sat up, alert, expecting an attack.

CHAPTER 35
1948

Tony Lapano wore a white, single breasted tux with wide trousers, a black bow tie, a rose boutonniere in his lapel, and a white silk scarf in his breast pocket. He was alone, standing by the door, only a few feet away. He smiled, but there was no joy in it. Despite his handsome face, the smile made him ugly, and his very presence seemed to suck the light and the life from the room.

"Hello, lovers," he said, darkly. "What a lovely couple. Can I say it? Beauty and the Beast. Yeah, it fits, doesn't it, Clint? With all that fucking hair. I thought you'd have gotten a haircut by now. No? Well, of course not. I mean, Rita likes it, doesn't she? She likes that beast look. I bet she gets all hot and panting when she grabs hold of it while you're doing her, right?"

Rita's fear turned to sharp anger. In defiance, she straightened her spine and threw back her shoulders. "What do you want, Tony?"

"Want?" he asked, spreading his hands as he always did when he was about to put on a show. "Now, what would I want? I heard you were here. I said to myself, hey, I should drop by, you know, for the good times. Yeah, so I came by to say hello to my old friends. Hey, Rita, baby, I heard you were real good in *Danger Town*."

He tapped his right ear. "That's right. Tony still keeps his ear to the ground. Yeah, I hear things, even though I'm living out of town. Hey, maybe because you're in love with the beast here? With the hairy dog. I mean, that's what I hear. That's what my friends tell me."

Clint pushed his chair back and stood up. "Thanks for stopping by, Tony."

"Hey, that's what friends are for, right, beast?"

Clint let out a breath of annoyance. "I'm sure you have other friends to see, Tony. Don't let us keep you from them."

Tony's face flamed red. His gaze hardened. "You know what, beast, I've been trying to find out who the hell you are. I've got friends, see? I have friends who have been looking into your past, professional gumshoes. And do you know what? They've got nothing. They can't find nothing on you. It's like you don't exist. Now tell me, beast, how is that possible? What are you hiding? Did you kill somebody?"

Tony aimed a finger at Clint. "Trust me, beast. I'm going to keep digging around until I find out what hole you crawled out of."

"Get the hell out of here, Tony," Clint said, his voice sharp and angry. "I'm sick of looking at your face and I'm sick of your macho bullshit. You're like some evil antagonist in a bad B movie, who repeats the same stupid lines over and over again. Maybe you should hire some writer to write you some new dialogue. Now get the hell out of here."

Tony's eyes flared with heat. "I'm gonna take you out, beast. You can count on that. I'm taking you out, do you hear me?!"

Rita shot to her feet. "Get out, Tony! Get the hell away from me and don't ever try to see me or Clint again, or so help me I'll shoot you in the head. Now get out."

Tony turned a wild, sardonic eye on her. "Okay, Brooklyn girl. Okay. But you still ain't heard the last from old Tony."

After he'd boiled out of the room, Rita and Clint sat in silence, listening to the soft sigh of the sea. Clint's eyes moved, one thought chasing another.

"I wonder how he knew we were here?" Clint asked.

"He has friends all over the place. Rats and sons of bitches. I wouldn't be surprised if the manager or one of his friends called him after you made the reservation."

Clint looked at her apologetically. "I'm sorry, my love. I wanted this night to be special for you."

Rita reached for his hand and squeezed it. "Well, maybe you can put that scene in one of your scripts. Your acting wasn't half bad," she said, hoping to mock them out of their mood.

Clint forced a smile, as the light left the sky and candlelight flickered. Clint drew in a breath. "I think we're going to have to chance it. I think all three of us are going to have to try to return to the future. Tony will try to kill me, and probably you. I saw it in his eyes. He wasn't bluffing and, as you said, he has friends all over the place."

Rita's expression turned grave. "I know... He's crazy. He's crazy enough to take Laura. He's crazy enough to do anything. I've never seen him so crazy. Let's start for home and pack. Let me drive. I know a shortcut."

With Rita at the steering wheel of the car, they drove the twisting Palisades Road, headlights stabbing into the night, the mighty car bending and swerving around mountain curves, with drop-offs that plummeted into deep canyons. Rita's worried eyes were locked ahead, Clint's watching the pavement race by, the white dotted lines hypnotic. For a time, he ignored the car's mounting speed and the narrow shoulder, the back wheels skidding, flinging dirt and pebbles back into the endless black night.

"You're driving fast," Clint said, softly, glancing about nervously.

"I know these roads. I've got to get to Laura."

Clint caught the note of hysteria in her voice, and he thought, if only they could text or email. Before they'd left the restaurant, they'd called home to check on Laura, but there was no answer. There should have been an answer. Maude was there. Laura's two friends were there, so why didn't anyone pick up the phone? They were probably in the pool, splashing about, squealing, and Maude no doubt was sitting poolside watching them. That's probably why she didn't hear the phone. Rita told him it had happened before, but after Tony's threatening visit, Rita was taking no chances. She was certain he'd do anything to get revenge, even kidnap Laura.

Rita took the turns closer, tires squealing, the headlights swinging left and right.

"Rita, you'd better slow down."

Rita straightened up, her eyes round with fear. "I can't."

"What do you mean, you can't?"

Rita frantically pumped the brakes.

In the soft amber glow of the dashboard, Clint saw Rita's left foot engaging the brake pedal, but it was low, sluggish and unresponsive.

"The brakes are going, Clint," her voice tight with fear. "They're going! What do I do?"

"Keep your eyes on the road. Keep pumping them."

"I am. I am, Clint. Nothing's happening."

The car hurtled on, picking up speed, careening down the steep, winding road, swerving over the double lines.

Clint feared the worst. Someone must have tampered with the brakes.

"Try the emergency brake."

She yanked on it, but the car didn't respond.

From the opposite lane, glaring headlights shot toward them. On instinct, Clint grabbed the wheel, nudging the car right, desperate to avoid a collision. But it was too late. The oncoming car grazed the Alfa Romeo. On impact, Clint's door burst open. Off-balance, he was flung out, bouncing on the road, tumbling toward the edge of a cliff, pain shooting through his body.

Grimacing, he struggled to stand, but his left foot buckled, and he collapsed, looking on helplessly as Rita's car veered right, out of control. He watched in frozen horror as the car burst through the wooden guard rail, bumped across a narrow rocky space and went plunging over the cliff, out of sight.

When he heard the explosion and saw the bright flash of orange light rocketing up, Clint screamed like something wild and wounded. He raged, crawling with a painful effort toward the edge of the cliff, toward the broken guard rail, his face twisted in agony. His heart shattered.

PART 3

CHAPTER 36

1948

Clint lay on his back in his hospital bed, still and silent, his glazed, grieving eyes open and staring at the ceiling. He'd lost track of time, but Everett Claxton, who'd visited three times, told him he'd been there for five days. That was yesterday, Clint believed. A kind nurse told him that he'd be released soon. Clint wanted out of there. The sooner the better. He'd filled the silent nights with screaming nightmares that brought swift footsteps of night nurses and more drugs.

The endless days brought needles and doctors and more nurses, and none seemed to have faces, just smooth skin pulled tightly to their necks. It was the drugs that made him crazy and violent, so they said. But he knew better. He'd heard his own screaming cries in the night—his frantic shouts for Rita, as the image of her car plummeting over that cliff haunted his dreams and his tortured waking hours.

Rita's image was everywhere in that room; sliding up and down the walls; dancing at the foot of his bed with the beat of a big band; laughing, pointing at his bandaged head, the cuts on his face and thigh; the swollen knee that knifed with pain.

"You look so funny, Clint," she said, her entire body alive with laughter.

He reached for her, but she avoided him, always just beyond arm's reach. She'd lift a finger and waggle it back and forth, like a clicking metronome, while speaking in a low, castigating voice, with the expression of a scolding grade school teacher.

"You shouldn't have grabbed the steering wheel, Clint. I would have missed that car. I know that road. I would have steered us away from the car and into the high bank that was only a quarter of a mile away. I wouldn't have died, Clint. Why did you grab the steering wheel? You killed me. You killed us. Why did you do it?"

Clint wept, and stared, and hurt. The physical pain was nothing compared to the emotional pain that cut him, or the rage that burned through him like hot molten lava. Clint knew who'd cut the brake fluid line. He knew it was Tony or one of his mob friends.

Two stone-faced detectives had visited, both wearing dark suits and black fedoras. They asked him questions he couldn't or wouldn't answer.

"Who was driving at the time of the accident?" one detective asked, his face long, somber and bored.

"How fast was the car going? Had you been drinking?"

Clint rolled his head toward them, his eyes fierce. "Did you check the brake lines? You know, in 2019 cars have a dual master cylinder and so cutting a single brake line for a given wheel doesn't end in a complete failure. Do you know that?"

They looked at him vacantly. They knew he was drugged.

One detective's chin lifted in a proud angle. "What do you know about the brake lines?"

Clint just shook his head. "Nothing. I don't know anything about it."

When the second detective spoke, he revealed crooked teeth. "Mr. West, when you leave the hospital, we'll need you to come down to the precinct and fill out a complete report. We'd also like to learn a few personal things about you, like where you were born, where you grew up. Why you left New York."

Clint narrowed his cold eyes on them. "You must be good buddies with Tony Lapano."

Their eyes filled with hostility.

"Get out of my room," Clint said, harshly, turning away from them.

After they'd gone, Clint's hands formed fists, his body slowly gathering new strength. He'd already formed a plan. As soon as he was well enough and strong enough, he'd execute that plan.

Clint had sustained a concussion, a sprained ankle, several deep cuts and bruises, and a banged-up knee that held a brace.

A young doctor told him he'd been lucky. Clint told him to get the hell out of his room. Rage burned through every vein, muscle and organ. He held onto the anger, allowing it full reign, nurturing it, allowing it to fester and spread like a virus. Clint needed the anger. Craved it. Without it, the knifing pain of regret and loss would overwhelm him and drive him insane. In time, he'd get his revenge. He'd be patient and he would surely get his revenge.

On Friday, July second, Clint was still in the hospital seated in a chair, staring ahead at nothing. When Margaret Stern entered, Clint sat up erect. She was the last person he'd expected to see. Her expression was unchanged. She still wore the same sour, miserable face. There was no cigarette dangling from her lips and her hair was bunless, falling without shape on her skinny shoulders.

She closed the door behind her and went to him, her cotton print dress too big for her skinny, shapeless frame, her eyes filled with the spark of a feisty young woman.

"What the hell are you still doing in here?"

Clint squinted up at her, his eyes sensitive to light. He was fighting a blurry headache and he was certain he hadn't heard her correctly. "What did you say?"

"You should be out of here by now. You should be back at work. I've got two script ideas and plots on your desk. I sure as hell am not going to write them."

Clint shook his head. "What are you doing here?"

"I just told you. Get your sorry ass out of here and get back to work. Work is the best thing for you now. Hell, it's always the best thing. People and things will always fall apart and disappoint you. Work won't. Work is always there, until the day you drop dead."

"Are you trying to piss me off, Margaret? Because I can tell you that you're really pissing me off."

"I don't give a damn if you're pissed off or not. I wouldn't be here if I didn't think you could become a damn good script writer. So get your ass out of this hospital and back to work."

With that, she turned and started for the door. Clint wondered if she would pause at the door and glance back, just as Bobby the Drunkard had done, in imitation of his scripts.

She didn't. She yanked the door open and left, like a sturdy, defiant soldier.

But then, to his utter surprise, Margaret reappeared. She entered thoughtfully, with the hint of a grin that looked more like a smirk.

She stood measuring him, as if he were a code she was trying to crack.

"I have a daughter. She's not ugly like me. She's a looker, as all the men will tell you. You haven't met her, but you should. I think she'd take to you. I think you'd take to her. Her name is Peggy. You could do a lot worse than Peggy."

And then Margaret whirled about and away she went, leaving Clint, dumb with disbelief.

Clint was still recovering from Margaret's visit when, twenty minutes later, Bobby the Drunkard appeared, holding a bouquet of fake, plastic flowers.

He crept forward, appraising Clint with his wide, dramatic eyes. "Hey, there, buddy boy. Look what the drunkard brought you."

He advanced and presented the bouquet to Clint. "Flowers. How about that?"

Clint looked at the sorry-looking plastic flowers and then up at Bobby. "What is that? They're plastic."

"Yep. I got them from the prop department. But aren't they *purdy*?" he said, instead of *pretty*. "Take them. Stick them in some water and just watch them grow, grow, grow."

Clint didn't take them. "Are you drunk?"

"Of course I'm drunk."

"And nuts," Clint said, with a shake of his head, folding his arms and looking away.

Bobby bristled, mockingly, pointing a finger at Clint like Uncle Sam, and with his stern, challenging stare. "Not nuts, Clint. Nope, I guarantee you one hundred percent that I am not nuts."

Bobby glanced about as if searching for something. On a side table near the bed, he spied a glass, half-filled with water. He stepped over, snatched the glass and jammed the flowers inside, returning the glass to the side table. The flowers looked hideous, as if struggling for dignity.

Bobby took a step back, gazing at the bouquet in exaggerated admiration, hands extended, face filled with dramatic emotion.

"My God, Clint, just look at them! Aren't they lovely? I tell you, there is nothing in this world more beautiful and captivating than a lovely glass filled with plastic flowers. Now if that doesn't cheer you up, my boy, then nothing will."

Clint sat staring, incredulous.

In a swift change of mood, Bobby lowered his arms, fixing his sincere eyes on Clint. "Do you know, friend Clint, that I like you. I do. And I've always loved Rita. We were good pals. We even got drunk together once. Well, I got drunk and she drank coffee until she was buzzing about like a bumble bee, albeit a darling and a beautiful bumble bee."

Bobby sat on the edge of Clint's bed and dropped his head in his hands. "I'm so damned sorry about it all, Clint. I'm so damned sorry that it turned out this way."

When he lifted his head, his eyes had filled with tears—and they were genuine tears. "If you need anything, Clint, anything at all, I want you to call me. Call me or just come over to my big old house filled with tasteless furniture, bad art and a good swimming pool. You come over night or day."

Bobby stood up. "Meanwhile, old Howard Hughes still wants you to work on *Shadows over Meadow Green*. Hell, everybody is pulling for you, buddy. Even hatchet face, Margaret Stern, is on your side, and I have never seen that before. Do you know that she was fond of Rita? She said Rita was one of the most underrated actresses in this town."

Clint felt the weight of Bobby's sympathy and it touched him, but he didn't speak.

Bobby stood over him, hands in his pockets. "You'll come back to us, won't you, Clint?"

Clint lifted his eyes. "I don't think so, Bobby. I've got things to do."

Bobby nodded, resting a gentle hand on Clint's shoulder. "You do what you've got to do, my good writer friend. But don't forget us, okay? Don't forget your true friends."

CHAPTER 37
1948

Clint hid in the shadows near the garage, beside gnarled branches of hedges and plants. He waited, feeling a scented night breeze move across his face, listening like a predator to the distant sea roar; the occasional call of a night bird; the low moan of a freight train whistle on its way east.

They were romantic sounds—sounds for a movie love scene—not the sounds of revenge. Those effects would have included wind squealing around the garage, a crack of lightning, and a heavy, constant rain falling thickly, exploding off the concrete.

It was after one in the morning and Clint had been waiting at Tony's cliffside house for over an hour. He'd parked his car down the road about a half mile, in a shadowy area with a glorious overlook view, where lovers were known to go for privacy.

He knew Tony would come. Clint had heard that Tony had left Las Vegas and returned to Hollywood about three weeks after Rita's funeral.

Tony had attended Rita's funeral. Clint had not. He'd left the hospital only the day before and even though Bobby, Everett and others had come by Clint's apartment to pick him up, Clint sat on his couch, emotionless and aloof, his cane beside him. They waited for him, appealing to him to go, but Clint refused. Finally, he turned and said coldly, "Go on, get out of here. I'm not going."

Clint had remained cloistered in his apartment for nearly four weeks, recovering, thinking and stalking about, bracing his right leg with a cane until he could limp around without it.

He'd left the house once, and that was to visit Laura, before Rita's in-laws came to take her back East to Boston. It had been a tearful goodbye, with Clint on his knees, holding the little girl tightly in his arms, kissing her hair and her cheeks, wet from tears.

Jeter sat on his haunches, a loyal friend, his sad liquid eyes moving, his tail limp. He was going with her.

Clint held Laura at arm's length, managing a warm, encouraging smile. "You, my dear heart, are going to be just fine."

Laura searched his eyes. "Why won't you come too?"

"I can't, Laura. I've got to go somewhere else, and it's very far away. If... well, if things don't work out, I'll come to see you. I promise. We'll go out to the park and play with Jeter."

She rubbed her red eyes. Maude said she spent much of the day sad and crying. She smiled only when she and Jeter played together.

"Is Mommy in heaven?" Laura abruptly asked.

Clint nodded. "Yes... she's with the angels."

"Angels are pretty, aren't they? I'm going to bring my angel from the Christmas tree. Aunt Maude said I could."

"Of course you can."

They played in the backyard for a time, played tag around the pool and played toss with Jeter.

Before Clint left the house, he slipped into Rita's bedroom where she'd kept her .38 caliber Smith & Wesson Snub nose handgun. Thank God it was still there. He slipped the gun into his blue blazer pocket, cast his eyes about her room one last time and left, fighting tears.

When he heard a car engine, Clint peered out from the side of the garage, every sense on high alert. A faint light at the end of the drive swelled, until headlights appeared. He reached into his sport coat pocket, feeling the cool grip of the handgun. He'd been visualizing this moment for many weeks, planning it, living it and breathing it.

Tony's candy-apple red two-seater Roadster drew up to the garage and stopped. Clint heard a woman's high shriek of laughter. He heard a man's muffled voice.

The outdoor landscape lights illumined the area and gave Clint a good, clear view of two silhouettes seated inside the car.

Tony emerged, standing loosely, obviously boozed up. In an over-exaggerated gesture, he gently closed his door, insuring that the car wouldn't shatter.

The passenger door burst open and a young woman popped out, giggling. With effort, she drew herself up to an unsteady height, patted her blonde curls and slammed the door.

"Hey, baby, take it easy on the door. You don't slam the door like that. This is a fucking one-of-a-kind car, you know."

She was a debauched girl, with a smear of lipstick and

wild, wandering eyes. She stood on wobbly legs, a hand braced on the car to keep her aloft.

"Yeah, yeah, yeah, Tony, baby. So sue me," she said, in a slurred, girlish voice. "Sue me, sue me and call my lawyer, Tony baby."

Tony wasn't amused. "Hey, that's not funny, Clara. You're tight as hell. If you can't take the martinis, then you shouldn't drink them."

Clara stuck her tongue out at him. "Bitch, bitch, bitch, Tony baby."

"And don't call me Tony baby."

"Okay, Tony baby," she shouted with a defiant lift of her chin. "I bet you didn't bitch at Rita Randall like you bitch at me, Tony baby," she said, taunting him.

"I said shut up. Don't you talk to me about Rita, okay?"

"I'm just as good an actress as Rita Randall was, Tony, and you know it."

Tony aimed a finger at her like a gun. "You talk any more about Rita and so help me, Clara, I'll squeeze that pretty neck of yours until you're dead. Now shut up about Rita."

Clint had had enough. He left the shadows and crept forward, eyes cold, face set in deadly determination.

Tony was turned away from Clint, so it was Clara who spotted him first, her batting eyes struggling to focus.

"Who's that?" she pointed.

Tony turned about, following her finger.

Clint stepped into a pool of light.

Tony saw Clint's fiery face, and he knew he was caught. Instead of showing the sudden stab of fear, Tony put on his best face, his practiced face, his ingratiating smile, hoping his eyes didn't show alarm.

"Clint... Well, look who's here. Clint West."

Tony's voice was thick and slow, and despite the million-dollar dazzle of a smile, Clint saw Tony was scared.

"Who's he, Tony?" Clara asked, rocking her head left and right, analyzing him.

"Clara… Let me introduce you to my friend, Clint West. Clint meet Clara."

Clara bubbled up. "Hey there, Clint. I like that wild hair. Who has hair like that, Tony?"

Clint slid his gaze toward her. "Beat it, Clara."

She didn't understand. "What?"

Clint's voice was sharp. "Get out of here. Go."

Clara shrank back in slight offense, with a hand on her hip. "Well, that is rude."

"Get out of here. Run. Go!" Clint shouted.

And to make his point, he pulled the .38 from his pocket. "Clara… Go. Now!"

Clara's face fell apart, shock instantly sobering her. "Shit, Tony. He's got a gun. Shit!"

Clint took a threatening step forward. Clara stumbled backwards as if pushed, her legs almost buckling beneath her. She threw panicked, darting glances to her right and left, unable to move. She was the proverbial deer in headlights.

To propel her into motion, Clint raised the gun and fired a blast into the air. The explosion shattered the night. Raw terror drove Clara stumbling off down the driveway, on shaky heels. She hobbled on one foot, yanking off one heel, and then balanced on a hopping foot as she tugged off the other. She flung them away as she broke into a run, her cries and shrieks fading as she drifted off toward the main road.

CHAPTER 38
1948

Clint shined his full, grim and deadly eyes on Tony. "Now it's just you and me, Tony baby."

Tony stared at Clint like a terrified kid. His face was waxen. He tried to speak but failed. His scared eyes moved, seeking escape, and finally, when he saw there was no escape, he lowered them.

"No, Tony, there's no escape."

Tony lifted a hand as if to push Clint away. His smile had vanished into tight lips and fast blinking eyes.

"Look, Clint, I don't know what you're thinking, but I had nothing to do with it. You've got to believe me about that. The police cleared me, you know. I talked to them a couple of times and they cleared me. I'm innocent, Clint. You know how much I loved Rita. Hell, she and I came from New York, you know. She was everything to me. When I heard the news, well, you know, it broke me. Yeah, I'm tellin' you, Clint, something inside me just got broken, you know."

Clint let him blubber on.

"I never would have done anything to harm even one hair on that beautiful head. You know that, Clint. You can ask around. Everyone will tell you that."

Tony paused to catch a breath. His breathing was fast and staggered, like an animal trapped with no way out.

Clint grinned, darkly. "I did just that, Tony. I asked around and you know what everyone I talked to said? They said, Tony wouldn't do that. No, not Tony baby."

Tony's face registered small relief. He licked his lips. "I just told you that, Clint. Didn't I just tell you that?"

Clint's voice took on an edge. "They said, Tony baby would never cut the brake lines on Rita's car."

"Hell no, Clint. Hell no, I wouldn't do that. Not to Rita. Rita was special, you know. You know I loved her. Okay, so okay, you loved her too, and she loved you. Was I sore about that? You bet I was. I was as sore as hell, but I got over it. I said, okay, if that's what Rita wants, then okay. And you know what, Clint, I was plenty sore when she dumped me for Victor Bracket. Yeah, well who wouldn't be sore over that? I mean, I made her who she was, didn't I?"

Tony's voice rose in volume, as seething anger crept in. "Yes. Me, Tony Lapano. I made that woman the success she was, so that Howard Hughes himself hired her for his A-picture. For the picture of the year. I made her, Clint. I made her who she was."

"Just shut up, Tony. Rita made herself. She elevated every lousy picture she was in and you know it. Don't take credit for that, and don't take credit for being her agent. Any second-rate agent would have done just as well, most would have done better when they saw her talent. Face it, Tony, you were more interested in what she could do for you than what you could do for her."

Tony bristled, then caught himself. "Okay, so that's what you say. I say different, okay? I say, she was nothin' without me and she would have wound up nothin', okay, Clint? Can you take the truth? Because that is the truth."

Clint lowered his eyes on Tony. "The truth, Tony, is that you didn't kill Rita. The truth is you're too chicken shit to have killed Rita. That's why you hired somebody else to cut those brake lines. And, Tony, let's both face the truth here. You're a low-life, loud-mouth son of a bitch, and you always will be."

Tony's face changed from tight control to animated mounting rage. "And what are you, you fucking hairy nobody? Some two-bit writer with no talent. You come into town from nowheres-ville and suddenly Rita's hanging all over you."

Clint nodded, grinning, taunting him. "That's right, Tony. Rita was in love with me. That didn't feel so good, did it, Tony baby?"

Tony thrust a threatening finger at Clint, the anger taking over. "Are you man enough to shoot me, hairy beast, or are you just tryin' to scare me to death?"

"Oh, I'm going to shoot you, Tony. Yes, right between the eyes. But first I'm going to shoot you in both legs and watch you squirm. Then I'm going to shoot you in the arms and then in each foot. Oh, it will be a while before I put a bullet in your head."

Tony's lips curved into a frightened, meager smile. "That ain't so funny, Clint."

"No, Tony baby, it ain't funny at all."

"Hey, Clint, I mean can you shoot so good?" he asked, trying for a joke.

Clint nodded. "Oh, yeah. I spent four years in the Marines. Did you know that?"

Tony swallowed, and his Adam's Apple moved. "No... That's a good thing, Clint. Very patriotic. Good for you. Yeah, good for you."

"I was quite good with firearms. I qualified as an 'expert.' And speaking of firearms, pull your gun from your shoulder holster, very gently, and toss it into the hedges."

Tony hesitated. "You don't miss much do you, pal?"

"Do it. Now!"

Tony slipped his hand inside his black tux jacket and, in one easy motion, drew out his Smith & Wesson .38 Special with a four-inch barrel. He held it up for dramatic effect, then backhanded it into a row of box hedges.

Tony worked to screw up his courage again, placing fists on his hips, presenting a little sneer.

"Okay, hairy man, are you going to shoot me now?"

Clint's arm slowly came up and aimed at Tony's head. "Goodbye, Tony baby."

Finally, all of Tony's courage vanished. He threw up his hands as if to stop the bullet, dissolving into a quivering mass of terror. "Don't shoot... Don't shoot me."

For a long, hanging moment, Clint held the gun firm, his finger itching to pull the trigger. Tony squinted, waiting for the bullet's impact.

In swift angry motion, Clint swung his arm left. He aimed and fired at the Roadster's right front tire, and the impact of the bullet jolted the car. The burst of air escaping the tire made a squealing sound, as if the car were crying out, wounded.

Tony leaped away, hands still covering his face. "Dammit, Clint. What the hell!"

Clint fired again, shattering the front windshield. Tony backstepped, almost falling, venturing a look of horror. "Not my car, Clint. Not my car!"

The sound of the sea was loud at high tide, as waves

threw themselves against the jagged rocks. Lost in his inner vision, Clint saw Rita's car again bursting through the wooden railing, sailing into oblivion, plunging out of sight.

Clint's arm spun toward Tony, gun poised.

"Don't shoot me, Clint. Please! Don't shoot."

Clint fired just over Tony's head. Tony felt the whistling breath of the bullet whizz by, and he dove to the ground near a row of hedges, curling into a tight ball, hands covering his head.

"I loved her. Don't shoot. I loved Rita."

Clint's shoulders sagged, and the longer he stood there looking at Tony's pathetic body, his face lost its stern, detached conviction. He took a few steps toward Tony, stopped and aimed the gun at his head.

When he spoke, his voice was low and resigned. "Like they say in the movies, Tony, you're just not worth killing. And, anyway, killing you won't bring Rita back, will it?"

Clint lowered the gun at his side, feeling sad and defeated. He couldn't kill any man in cold blood, not even Tony. Clint turned and walked up the driveway, past the car and on toward the main road, the landscape lights tracking him, his shadow growing long.

In honor of his friend Bobby the Drunkard, Clint turned back toward the car. He lifted the gun, aimed, and fired at the rear tires and back windshield.

The exploding glass was loud in the violent night. Clint left Tony's driveway and started up the road to his car. The sea roared, and the moon was nearly full in the vault of sky. Clint approached the cliffs and heaved the gun away, picturing it smash on the rocks below—smashing the gun, just like Tony had smashed Clint's and Rita's life together.

No, killing Tony wouldn't bring Rita back. But there was a full moon. And the same full moon would be shining over the sea in Amagansett, Long Island, New York.

.

CHAPTER 39
1948

Clint was traveling on the *Super Chief,* known as The Train of the Stars, en route from LA to New York. The train included a diner, the Pleasure Dome Lounge car, an observation lounge, a third lounge, and sleeping cars.

Everett Claxton had suggested Clint take the train instead of flying, believing that the four-day journey would help clear Clint's mind.

The *Super Chief* held 500 passengers and, in 1948, it was one of the fastest trains in the world. Onboard crews included train engineers, conductors and brakemen, Pullman conductors, Pullman porters, dining car stewards, waiters, cooks, bartenders, lounge attendants, cleaning crews at both ends of the line, and maintenance crews en route.

There were also barbers, maids and valets. The train had been designed for elegance, comfort and style, and Clint spent much of his journey exploring the train, a welcomed distraction from his heavy thoughts. But always, his thoughts returned to Rita, and he ached for her, her lovely smile, her soft embrace, her gentle sighs and yielding body as he made love to her.

Clint gazed out the window in a moody silence, watching the midwestern landscape blur by, lost in a fog of thought. He'd traveled so far, carried so many secrets, held so much love, and now he seemed to be returning to the same place from which it had all started.

Fragments of memories and bits of conversation cut in and out of his head, particularly his last conversation with Everett the day before he left LA.

"Do you really think you can return to 2019, Clint?" Everett asked, as they sat in Clint's bungalow apartment, his bags packed, both sipping a bourbon on ice.

"I have no idea," Clint said, with a faraway look in his eyes.

"And so I suppose it goes without saying that if you do get back to your own time, you'll then try to return to us and 1948? You'll try to return to Rita?"

Clint took a sip of his drink. "Yes, it goes without saying."

Everett gave Clint an awkward glance. "It's all too… well, too bizarre for me, Clint. How can you cope with all this…" Everett's voice dropped away, as he searched for the right words. "… Well, all this up and down, back-and-forth business? According to what happened to Rita the last time she went through one of those dreadful time portals, she was nearly killed. You could be killed."

Clint stared in a thoughtful silence. "When I get back to Long Island, I'm going to see Oscar Bates."

"For what purpose?"

Clint made a vague gesture. "I don't know. I guess because I need somebody to talk to who understands all this…"

Clint's voice fell away into silence.

"I would go with you if I could, Clint… But we'll be doing pre-production on… well, you know… *Shadows over Meadow Green.*"

The sun streaming in from the window revealed Clint's sad eyes.

"I will miss you, Clint," Everett said. "Bobby and Margaret, yes, even Margaret said she'd miss you. Okay, well she didn't exactly say she'd miss you. She said something like, 'Why the hell doesn't he stop moping around like a lost dog and get on with his life?' But for her, that's a 'I'll miss him.' Anyway, her daughter, Peggy, was anxious to go out with you, you know. I finally gave the girl a screen test."

"I've never seen her. Does she look anything like her mother?"

Everett pondered that. "I'll describe Peggy like a writer would describe her. She has limpid, bright eyes; a fine, chiseled nose; a small, crimson mouth set in an oval face, framed by a mass of blue-black hair."

Clint grinned. "I'm impressed, Everett. You have the makings of a writer in you."

Everett waved off the compliment. "I had time to think about it when I was screen-testing her."

"How did she do?"

"Not bad. She's not a natural, but if she was lighted just right, she'd be okay in comedies. Maybe a melodrama with the right actor opposite her. She's sassy, like her mother, but she doesn't have the intelligence to back it up. I'm afraid she's going to wind up with the wrong guy, in the wrong way, with the wrong future."

"Maybe you can help her, Everett. You can be the father she's never had."

"Then I'd have to deal with Margaret."

"She's not so bad. I've grown to like her."

"Before the screen test, Peggy asked me about you. Margaret had really talked you up. Even showed Peggy a photo of you."

"Where did Margaret get a photo of me?"

"The studio photo they took when you arrived. Margaret has connections. Anyway, Peggy was quite taken by your hair. Who knows, Clint, you may even start a whole new fashion in this town."

"Not until the 1960s," Clint said, knowing that anything he said about the future made Everett anxious.

And it did. Everett held up a hand like a barrier. "I don't want to know anything about the future. I'm sure you could tell me things that would fascinate me and scare the hell out of me, but I don't want to know."

At the front door, Everett rested a soft hand on Clint's shoulder. His eyes held tender affection. "Well, Clint, perhaps the next time we meet, I won't even know who you are. But I hope that doesn't happen. I hope you'll return... before Rita's accident, if that's even possible."

Clint smiled. "Thanks, Everett, for everything. And thanks for lending me your house on Long Island again."

Everett looked deeply into Clint's eyes. "Do you believe you'll find her, Clint?"

Clint stared forcefully. "Oh, yes. I'll find her. The question is, in what time will I find her? How will the world have changed? How will she have changed? How will time have changed everything? Even if I do manage to find the time portal, who knows where it might take me?"

Clint arrived back on Long Island on August 26, 1948, aware that he'd missed the full moon of August 20. The next full moon would be on Saturday, September 18, and that's when he was targeting an encounter with a time portal.

Oscar Bates was anxious to see Clint, but he was in Boston and wouldn't return until the first week of September. Meanwhile, Clint spent most of his time roaming the beaches, day and night, having developed a bad case of insomnia. He often stared at Rita's photograph that hung in Everett's den, again memorizing the shape of her mouth, the curve of her hair, the richness of her eyes.

If Rita had not already become an obsession, then she was fast becoming one, and that is exactly what Clint was after. He wanted her branded in his mind so that every thought contained some remnant of her voice, her taste, her touch, her smell. He wanted his senses steeped in her image, her scent, her magnetic smile and her sultry, loving eyes.

Clint believed that if these impressions were deeply placed into his mind, like initials carved into the bark of a tree, they would help guide him back to her when he entered the time portal.

When Oscar came to visit, Clint shared these thoughts with him, and he had agreed.

"Yes, Clint, I believe you are absolutely right about that. Some of our experiments show that strong, clear thought and impressions do help connect the time traveler to a location or a person. Not always, mind you. Sometimes the portal has a mind of its own, so to speak, but still, there is evidence to support your theory."

The men were drifting along the edge of the tide on a cloudy day, already cool and autumnal for early September. Clint wore a tweed sport jacket, jeans and gloves, Oscar a brown corduroy suit, with an open collar shirt. His shoulders were hunched against the chilly breeze.

Clint noticed Oscar's inward stare, as if he were dwelling in some inner world.

"What are you thinking, Oscar?" Clint asked. "I'm getting to know your expressions. One is troubled. One is distant. One is engaged. Right now, you look distant and troubled."

Oscar nodded, staring up at the gray moving sky, where seagulls battled against a sturdy wind.

"Clint… About the time portal thing. Well, I'll just come out and say it. It's not easy on the body."

"I know that, Oscar. I've felt it. We know what happened to Rita."

"I'm going to be honest here. We've lost two people who have time traveled more than twice. It's too destructive on the body. And you must have realized that it takes time to adjust to another time. The body—your body—was built for 2019, not for 1948. Your DNA is calibrated for 2019; you were raised in that culture, with that atmosphere, water, and food. You don't belong here, at least not for any length of time. You have lived longer in 1948 than any of our explorers have lived in the times they traveled to. I'd love to run a battery of tests on you to see what effects time travel has had on your body."

Clint stopped. "No time for that. And anyway, what are you saying? I shouldn't return to 2019, or that I should stay here?"

Oscar leveled his sober eyes on Clint. "I'm saying, if you get back to 2019 all in one piece, then you'd better stay there."

The two men held each other's eyes, Clint's were conflicted, Oscar's firm.

Clint's hair blew wildly in the wind, snapping about his face. He raked it back with a gloved hand, considering.

"No, Oscar. I've got to get back to her, and if I sound

like a romantic idiot or a fool, then so be it. I love Rita. I think I loved her the first time I saw a photograph of her. We fit together, we blend together, we breathe the same breaths."

Oscar pursed his lips. "Clint... time portals are unstable. They don't accommodate our wants and desires or issue us tickets to the exact place and time we wish to travel to. They're like unpredictable children. We don't even know why the hell they exist. For what purpose? Are they anomalies in nature? Are they mutations of some kind? Are they spiritual, demonic, or just naturally weird phenomena, like the waterfall that flows upward in County Leitrim, Ireland? My point is, you will be taking a risk—a risk that has been deadly for two other time travelers."

Clint turned his eyes away, staring out to sea. Waves came in loud, rushing the shore. A nearby man scampered up the beach, away from a charging wave.

They walked on for a time in silence. Gray clouds lowered over the dunes and distant houses.

Finally, Oscar spoke. "If you get back to 2019, and if I'm still alive, come and see me. If I don't remember you, tell me everything."

As they started back toward the house, Oscar stopped, kicking at the sand. Clint stood by, knowing Oscar was about to say something, most likely profound. Oscar's eyes came to Clint's.

"It's curious, a scientist like me, but I find it absolutely extraordinary and fascinating that you are so in love with Rita that you would risk your life to do something so remote and tenuous. I've never felt that kind of love, and I don't believe I ever shall. I envy you for it."

CHAPTER 40
1948

As Saturday, September 18, approached, Clint spent much of his time improving his diet, exercising, and resting as much as possible. His body had to be in great shape, his mind rested, his spirits positive. His life, and his potential life with Rita, depended on it.

The exact time of the full moon was 8:46 p.m. Clint was out on the beach by 8:05, searching the sea and dunes for any sign of the blue wavy portal.

He walked briskly up and down the beach, ignoring beach strollers who were lingering near the tide, lost in the rising yellow moon.

The chilly breeze was snappy and erratic, the sea oddly calm. His face was flushed and he was adrenalized, his eyes moving, straining and watchful.

As 8:46 p.m. approached, he wandered up and down, probing the night: the mist from the sea, the occasional slow-moving cloud, the liquid yellow light from the moon—but he saw nothing.

He walked purposively across the sand and upper dunes, willing the portal to appear, cursing it, calling to it, appealing to it but, by 10:12 p.m., Clint was losing hope. Still, he persisted, surveying the area, every sense heightened and awake.

It was well after 1 a.m. when, with a heavy heart, he started back to the house, his dispirited feet kicking at the sand in irritation and frustration.

He sat on the patio in a canvas chair, staring vacantly out to sea until daylight crept in, spreading turquoise and pink across the eastern sky, until the disk of a golden sun rose, blazing, warming the crisp morning air. He fell asleep sometime after 7 a.m. and awoke four hours later with a backache and stiff neck.

Clint spent the next few days wandering and lost, fighting the fear of being trapped in 1948 forever, without any hope of seeing Rita again.

The next full moon was Sunday, October 17. More determined than ever, Clint kept up his healthy diet and workout regimen. He ran along the tide three to five miles, four times a week, and vigorously swam laps in the 64-degree ocean three times a week. His stomach was taut and flat, his muscles sinewy and defined; his face was haunted, eyes burning with purpose.

He searched for thunderstorms, but none came, only cool, late autumn days with bright sun, or the occasional clay-heavy clouds bringing a light rain.

Everett called several times, his voice controlled and concerned. Clint assured him he would never give up until he found the portal.

Oscar visited twice in October, his deep, earnest eyes always filled with a combination of hope and dread.

"I would be here on October 17 if I didn't have a

meeting in Washington."

"Is it one of those high-level meetings?" Clint asked.

"Just some other scientists. Two senators and a general will be there. They're supportive and can keep secrets."

"Will you mention me and what has happened?"

"No... As far as I know, Everett Claxton is the only one who knows. I'm certain he won't talk. He'd be laughed out of Hollywood, and we know he'd never let that happen."

He stood up, preparing to leave. "You're in good physical shape, Clint. Let's hope that when the portal comes, you'll survive the journey."

On the night of October 17, Clint was strolling the dunes, bracing himself against a looping, briny wind, his face and gloved hands tingling from the cold, the collar of his tweed jacket pulled up to his ears. A white moon played hide and seek in dark, fragmented clouds and, in the gathering half gloom of night, Clint roamed like a pilgrim, seeking a second chance, seeking redemption, seeking the impossible.

Through a break in the fragmented clouds, Clint was suddenly illuminated by the dim light of the moon. He straightened up, his face alive, his eyes round with new hope.

Off in the middle distance, about a half mile away, he spotted a faint blue misty light crawling across the land. His pulse quickened. Was that a portal? Leaving thought behind, he hurled himself forward, down the slope of the dunes, racing across the undulating sand, head high, his feet digging, heart pumping.

The light rolled and tumbled, playing on the wild currents of the wind, leaping up and crackling, as if electrically charged. Was it moving away from him? In desperation, Clint sprinted off toward it, his body strong, his courage strong, his determination firm.

And then, in seconds, as if Clint had called to it, the shimmering thing flipped, rolled, gathered force and charged toward him. Clint stopped, gathering courage, holding his breath, watching the wave grow in magnitude, speed and strength, like a swelling, terrifying monster.

He was dwarfed by the towering size and energy of it, and as it closed the distance between them, it seemed to be everywhere. There was no chance to escape, to run away, although every cell in his body was screaming at him to do just that.

The blue tremulous portal rolled aggressively toward him. Resigned, he opened his arms wide, lifting his head, his eyes wide with anticipation. He stood firm, waiting to be taken. All at once, he was engulfed, his body whipped by the wind as he sank deeper into the awesome wave and was swept away.

CHAPTER 41

2019

Jack West's blue eyes stared down at his sleeping brother.

"Are you still asleep, old man?" Jack said, putting on a proper British accent, and continuing with it. He put an open hand to the side of his temple and saluted.

"Sir, the troops are assembled and ready for inspection, sir. The battle is raging just beyond those distant misty hills and we've already taken heavy losses. Will you please get your lazy ass out of bed and lead us to victory, my Captain Oh Captain?"

Jack concluded by clicking his heels together, keeping his smart salute.

Clint's eyes struggled open and his lips moved soundlessly. It took two attempts before words formed. "Where am I?"

Jack stayed in character, obviously playing a game the two brothers had engaged in as boys.

"You're at the front, my Captain, and the Zulus are fast approaching. We're almost out of ammunition, food and water, but fortunately, the women and children have been evacuated to the rear and they are safe."

Clint rubbed his eyes and, in a wheeze of sound, said "Water. Get me some water."

Jack dropped his salute and his British officer character, disappointed that his brother wasn't playing along. "Hey, and that's my best Michael Caine impression."

"Water…" Clint repeated, his face pinched in discomfort, his dry tongue making a clicking sound.

"Do you remember how we used to pronounce Michael Caine's name when we were boys?"

"Water…" Clint persisted.

"We'd say… 'My Cocaine,' remember? We'd practice our cockney accent and say, 'Do you know, my name is My Cocaine.'"

Clint's head was still holding visions, and his mouth was as dry as a desert.

"Did you get drunk last night, Clint?"

Clint managed to lift his aching head and speak through clenched teeth. "Water… Jack. Water!"

"All right. All right. Calm down."

When Jack returned, with a small bottle of spring water, Clint was sitting up, leaning his back against the headboard. He snatched the bottle from his brother's grasp and clumsily twisted off the cap. He tipped the bottle back and gulped the water down hungrily.

"You did get drunk, didn't you?" Jack said.

Clint shut his eyes, his head still reeling. "No…"

"You're as white as a ghost. What did you do last night?"

The words 'last night' were a trigger to an explosion of images and memories. Clint's eyes popped open, moving, searching the room. His room? No, not LA. Where was he? Not his room. If not his room, then whose room? New York? He was in New York. Beach House? New York, beach house?

Jack's expression changed from playful to mild concern. "Clint, are you all right? You're acting a bit weird."

Clint shot his brother a look, his eyes squinting on him. Yes, Jack was his brother. He knew that. But where were they?

"Where am I? What day is this? What year is this?" Clint said, his voice taking on a hoarse strength.

Jack pocketed his hands as he lowered his chin. "Clint... do you need to see a doctor?"

"No. No, I don't need to see a doctor. What month and year is this?"

Jack turned to the window that looked out on a bright summer day. "It's Sunday,

July 7."

"What year?"

"It's 2019. What else could it be? What the hell's the matter with you?"

Clint squeezed his eyes shut, straining his brain to think, to remember, to calculate time and place, but every memory and every image was all melted together. He lay his head back and let out a heavy sigh.

"Clint, do you want me to take you to a doctor? You don't look good."

"Rita..." Clint said, in a soft, intimate voice.

"Rita who?"

"Is she here?" Clint asked, hopeful.

"Clint, there's nobody here but you and me and Linda. She's out on the beach. You remember you said I could bring Linda and come for the day, right?"

Clint lied. "Yeah, sure I remember."

"I let you sleep until eleven."

Clint massaged his eyes. "So, it's July 7, 2019?"

"Unless my cell phone, CNN and the natural cycle of time and space have all somehow changed."

Clint opened his eyes fully. He gave his brother a cold smile, his voice soft and low. "I'm back. I came all the way back."

"From where? Back from where? What are you talking about?"

Clint's eyes slid away from any direct gaze, as new images of Rita flickered in and out, like film clips. Clint let the movie in his head continue for a time, while Jack seemed to exist on the periphery.

"Jack…" Clint said in a remote voice. "Do you remember the girl that was staying here? The girl you saw in my photographs?"

"What girl? I don't know what you're talking about."

"Her name was Cynthia, remember? You said she looked just like Rita Randall."

Jack's gaze was acute and sharp. "Bro, what have you been smoking? If I'd seen a girl who looked like Rita Randall walking around in this house, I'd have remembered. Now, are you going to tell me what's going on?"

Clint withered a little, as he began to realize that in this time, Rita had never existed.

More thoughts and memories came cascading through his head. He recalled bursting through a blue light and landing on his patio the night before. He remembered feeling nauseous and exhausted. He remembered blundering into his bedroom, struggling out of his clothes and collapsing onto his bed.

Clint's eyes expanded on this brother and then darted away, as a flood of memories washed over him. He sat up fully. "Jack… how did Rita Randall die?"

"What?"

"Rita Randall, the actress. How did she die?"

Jack stared, perplexed. "Clint... are you..."

Clint cut him off. "... Just tell me, Jack. Did she vanish in 1948 or did she die some other way?"

"Rita Randall's car went over a cliff. You know that."

Clint kept his steady eyes on his brother, as his heart thumped. "Was anyone with her? Anyone else in the car?"

"Okay, so you've been staring at Rita Randall's photo in the other room, and you're like having some kind of weird obsessive reaction or something?"

"Was anyone else with her?"

"No, Clint. She was alone."

"No!" Clint shouted, pounding a fist into the bed. "No way. She wasn't alone."

Clint flung back the sheet, his head pounding, body weak. Still, he pushed to his feet, staggered to a chest of drawers and found a t-shirt and a pair of khaki shorts. Jack watched, mystified, as Clint clumsily dressed and then weaved a path out of the bedroom, heading for the kitchen.

Jack followed, finding Clint leaning back against the kitchen island, holding his head in his hands.

"All right, Clint, tell me what this is about. Something has happened to you. Tell me."

"Do you see my cell phone?"

"Cell phone?"

"Yes, I have a blinding headache. I don't see it. I don't remember where I put it. Have you seen it? Please find it for me."

Grudgingly, Jack strolled the house, returning a few minutes later to find Clint sitting hunched on an island stool. Clint lifted his head, and Jack handed him the phone.

"It was out on the patio."

"Thanks. Is there any coffee?"

"No. I'll make some."

"Food? I'm starving."

"I'll scramble up some eggs for you. Toast?"

"Yes. Juice and anything else you can find."

While Jack went to work, Clint booted up his phone, tapped his gallery and urgently searched his recent photos, vigorously swiping through photo after photo, desperate to find any photo of Rita. His shoulders sank, along with his spirits. There were none. Not one single photo of her.

While one thought tumbled over the next, Clint ate voraciously, feeling as though he hadn't eaten in days. Jack sat opposite him across the kitchen island, watching and worried, his chin resting in his hand.

"How's your novel coming, Clint?"

Clint looked up, startled. "Novel?"

"Yes, you came here to finish your novel, remember? You are Clint West, the international bestselling novelist, aren't you? Or have you forgotten?"

"Oh, yes, right. My novel. Yes. I guess it's coming along," Clint said, still puzzled about why there were no photos of Rita in his phone. "I haven't written for a while. I've been busy."

"Don't you have a deadline?"

"Yes... I think so. Yes," he said, distractedly, staring into his phone.

As soon as he'd finished eating, Clint shot up, grabbed his phone and left for the patio, exiting out the door and onto the beach, under the full glow of sunlight, barefoot, without sunglasses or hat.

Jack followed, baffled and worried, lingering in the

doorway. He watched as Clint marched about, obviously snapping photos and shooting videos of the beach and the surrounding area. He seemed like a man possessed, tracking back and forth across the hot sand, scaling the dunes, shooting more photos, using the flat of his hand to peer into distances as if searching for something.

Later, Clint returned to the patio and wearily dropped into a chair, phone in hand. He swiped through photo after photo, eyes moving, narrowing, searching.

When Jack drifted over, Clint lifted his head and stared into distant space.

"I've lost her," Clint said, in a quiet, miserable voice. "She's not there. I've lost her."

CHAPTER 42
2019

On Tuesday, July 9, Clint drove into the Pleasant Valley Nursing Home parking lot to revisit the elderly Oscar Bates. The Nursing Home contained the same low, rambling set of buildings as the last time, surrounded by tall trees, a shimmering green lawn and a little duck pond, currently occupied by a graceful white swan who seemed to glow yellow under generous sunlight.

Clint left the car and entered the double glass doors, feeling the weird déjà vu moment. Yes, he'd already walked through these moments, or at least similar moments, and as he approached the reception desk to meet Wendy, again for the first time, he wondered if he was a shadow, or if his former self was the shadow. The difference being, this time he'd traveled through time and had a myriad of experiences that his first self hadn't had. This Clint West was older, perhaps a bit wiser, and certainly more desperate to find a way to return to Rita before she perished in that car crash.

Clint met Wendy Korman again, and their conversation was similar to that of their first meeting, with just a few alterations. Fortunately, she once again led him down the polished corridor floor to her grandfather's room.

As they approached the door, Clint felt a little catch in his throat. Would old Oscar remember the Clint West from over seventy years ago?

Oscar Bates was seated in a soft, black leather chair, with his back to the windows. Clint tried to mask his surprise at seeing this very old man again, a man who'd only been in his twenties just a few days ago, in 1948.

This Oscar was pale, hollow-cheeked and stooped. His sparse, thin, frosty hair was combed neatly from left to right and his folded hands gently trembled.

Clint's impression of this Oscar was one of vacant serenity. He was an old man who was already crossing the line between this world and the next, and seemingly content to be doing so.

But then he turned his eyes up, taking Clint in fully. His calculating stare flickered with a new light and faint recognition.

Clint bent to shake his hand, but Oscar didn't take it. He glanced over at his niece and said, in a low, rusty voice.

"Leave us, Wendy."

She did so, but reluctantly, just as she had done the first time.

Clint sat opposite him, folding his hands in his lap, feeling anxious and hopeful. He'd been a mass of nerves ever since he'd reawakened in this time. He knew he'd not fully recovered from the time travel, and his erratic heartbeat and persistent headaches told him so.

After a long silence, Clint finally spoke up. "Hello, Oscar."

Oscar finally produced a slow smile and, to Clint's surprise, a little wink.

Oscar cleared his throat. "All these years... I'm not sure I believed it would happen."

Clint nodded. "You were about twenty-five years old the last time I saw you, only a few days ago."

Oscar kept his smile. "You found the portal then?"

"Or it found me. I still don't remember very much. It must have been a rough ride. I feel as if parts of me are scattered about in two different time periods and somewhere in between."

Oscar's smile faded. "Clint... the next trip could kill you."

Clint looked down and away. "Oscar, Rita doesn't appear in the photos, like the last time. I took fifty... a hundred photos. I took dozens of videos and she's not there. I don't understand."

When Clint finally lifted his troubled eyes, Oscar met Clint's gaze and held it. "Are you ready for some cold, common facts, Clint?"

Clint didn't speak. He opened his hands and nodded as if to say, "Go ahead, give me the worse."

"My guess is the connection's been broken. If Rita is no longer in the photos, then she's gone. Or something happened in the past that we don't know about."

"What would that be?" Clint said, with emotion. "I was there, remember? I was a part of it, remember? What could have happened that I didn't know about? This is the same time frame that she first appeared in the photos. You said it was the portal connection. You said we had each other's number."

They sat in a solemn stillness.

"Oscar…" Clint said, pensively. "Do other people that roam that beach in Amagansett ever get taken by the portal like I was? Like Rita was?"

"The short answer, no. Most don't see the portals. Most of the time the portals remain out at sea or they hover close to low-hanging clouds. Why do you think we have so many stories about seaman and ships disappearing? Portals don't often come ashore. In your case, my best guess is that you attracted it. Somehow, you and Rita connected synchronistically, in two different time periods, and you drew the portals to you. But then, what do I know? Maybe you have a romantic, matchmaker portal," he said, humor in his eyes.

Clint looked at him doubtfully.

"Why did you come, Clint? Just to see how time withers a tall and straight young man into an old and gnarled bent stick?"

Clint took him in warmly. "I came because I needed a friend who understands."

"My advice, Clint. Let the past go. Be grateful you had the chance to experience it. And, if you were in love, as I know you were, give a bow and a nod and say, those were damned good days. Now advice from an old friend to a younger one: live your life now. Continue on, find another love and be happy."

Clint shook his head. "If you were in my place, would you move on? Would you live your life now and forget the possibility of returning to a woman you love more than your own life? And I can't forget what happened to Laura. She was a beautiful little girl. She never fully recovered from her mother's death. She took an overdose of drugs and was found dead in a motel room in 1970. She was only 25 years old. I have to try to stop that."

Oscar's eyes changed. They held soft pity. "I am a

scientist, Clint. Not a romantic."

Clint stood up, pocketing his hands. "Something tells me that I'm going to be seeing you again, Oscar."

"Clint… You've been lucky… Very lucky. We shut down our time travel experiments in the 1960s. We lost ten travelers. Six we know died. Three we never heard from again. One, that's me, stopped after three trips. It took me five years to recover completely. In your case, Clint, now that the connection is broken, you most certainly will never find another time portal and, even if you do, who knows where you might end up. Face it, Clint, you're not connected to Rita, or to 1948, anymore. It's over. The connection has been broken."

Outside, in the heat of the day, Clint circled the pond, engrossed in the graceful, balletic elegance of the swan, drifting on the still water, beautiful and mysterious. It reminded him of Rita, and he couldn't pull his eyes from it.

Had their connection truly been broken? No, in his heart of hearts, the connection would never be broken. As he gazed at the effortless glide of the swan, scarcely rippling the luminous water, Clint knew he'd be out roaming that Amagansett beach during the next storm or full moon. He would get back to Rita, someway, no matter how long it took.

CHAPTER 43

2023

Clint sauntered along the beach close to the waterline, under a sky the color of wet tin, near a sea the color of gunmetal gray. His long hair was restrained by a head-band, his shoulders hunched against the cold November wind, his parka collar turned up to his ears.

He'd recently endured another birthday—he was now 36-years old—and despite the birthday cards, and the calls and presents from friends, family and colleagues, he had difficulty mustering any enthusiasm for it.

He was grateful for his friends and his family, who'd put up with his moody, reclusive ways for the last four years.

Amy Parks, now Amy Parks Hargrave, flew in from LA, with her one-year-old son in tow. Clint was delighted to see her happily married and finally a mother, something she'd wanted for years.

They'd had quality time to discuss the old days and

their lives. After a couple glasses of wine, Amy admitted that she loved her husband and little boy so much that it hurt.

"I hope you find love again, Clint," she said, giving him a goodbye kiss on the cheek. "And don't forget," she continued, pointing a finger at him, "I made a vow to Jenny that I'd always look after you."

They'd parted, all smiles, declaring their enduring friendship. Clint was truly happy for her, vowing to travel to LA to meet her husband at the next opportunity.

Jack, often a pain in the neck and always working to dig into Clint's personal business, had been a good companion during long weekends, although he came less often now, having remarried about a year ago.

Clint's agent, the young, pretty and infinitely gregarious redhead, Allison Steele, had thrown a lavish party for him in September, celebrating the release of his new book, *Girl Lost in Shangri-La*. It had become an international bestseller, and Fox Searchlight Pictures had bought the film rights. As Allison exclaimed, with a glass of Champagne in one hand and a salmon hors d'oeuvre in the other, "Clint, you are now a wealthy man."

Since October, Clint had stayed mostly cloistered in the beach house, the beach house he'd purchased two years ago, having finally enticed the stubborn, puzzled owner with a lot of money.

Most days, Clint worked on his next novel. Most nights, he rambled the beach, searching for time portals. Late in the night, he watched old movies. He'd seen all of Rita Randall's movies perhaps a hundred times, perhaps more. The one he didn't watch, and never would, was *Wrong Turn to Waco*. It ended with Rita's car plunging over a cliff to her death.

There were nights he lay sprawled on the couch, a

glass of wine beside him, watching one of her movies and falling asleep to the sound of her voice.

He'd memorized all her dialogue, and he knew every move, plot point and lighting effect. There were long, lonely and sleepless nights when Clint wanted to reach into his HD TV screen and touch her. And yes, he talked to her. He even asked her opinion about a character in a book he was writing. Had he gone a little crazy? Maybe.

In October, his agent, Allison, invited herself over.

"I want to talk to you about some things. Some things that need to be said."

Allison was fit and smart and sexy. Her long, glossy red hair set off confident chipped green eyes, cute freckles and a pretty mouth. She'd come with an overnight bag, two contracts from foreign publishers, much advice on the direction of his new book, and a body radiating a sexual energy that was palpable.

It had been a long time since Clint had been with a woman, or, to be more specific, since he'd been with Rita: four years.

Allison's visit had not gone well. Clint liked and admired Allison, but he felt himself retreat from her.

Over dinner, she was elaborately conversational. After dinner, they sipped cognac and sat close on the couch. Her perfume scented the air, and it was tasteful. Her lips were moist, ripe, and ready to be kissed, and her lithe body was poised for love. Clint could clearly see that, because Allison made it obvious. When he didn't respond, she sank a little.

"You don't find me attractive, do you, Clint?"

Clint shrugged, feeling awkward. He scratched his cheek. "It's not that, Allison. You're attractive. Hell, you're a sexy beauty, as writers like to write about their female protagonists."

She folded her arms. "I'm not a character in a book, Clint. I'm real. I'm here, now, and I have been hopelessly in love with you since the first time you walked into my office, looking like a combination alpha male and puppy dog. You melted me, and you still do. I think we would make a winning couple, married or unmarried. I'll be brutally honest: I've always had a thing for writers, especially rich and successful ones."

Clint looked away, searching for words.

"You know I have a, let's say, companion," Allison said.

"Yes, a hedge fund guy, I heard," Clint said. "I read about him. Seems nice enough for a billionaire."

"We have sex, and we do things together. It's nice. He's good to me. I don't love him."

Clint fixed her with a stare. "Allison, don't tell me you love me. We don't even know each other that well."

She smiled, and her eyes held desire and invitation. "I know you well enough to know that I love you, Clint… Meaning, I would do anything for you. Just say the word and I'm in your bed. Just say the word and I'll marry you. Just say the word and I'll have your baby."

Clint tried to hide his surprise. He truly did not know what to say. Part of him—no, most of him—most of what was buried in his heart—was barren and dry. He'd often had the image of being a thirsty, high-flying bird, drifting and sailing over infinite miles of desert.

"I've heard things about you, Clint. Things you've never discussed with me. I've heard you were in love with a woman, but it didn't work out."

"I guess you could say that."

"I heard it was years ago."

"Four years ago, yes."

"And you're still in love with her?"

Outside, the wind was lively, and it rattled the windows. They could hear the sea.

"Yes, I'm still in love with her."

Allison looked at him with mild disapproval. "That's a long time. Isn't it time you moved on?"

"Yes, it is."

Clint saw a gleam of hope in her eyes.

"I could make you happy, Clint. I know I could."

She rearranged herself so that she was only inches from his face.

"I'm going to be a bold, confident bitch and say that I'm sure, eventually, and I predict it won't be very long, that you will fall in love with me. I'm a romantic at heart, just like you. Just like Jason in your last book. That character really turned me on, because I know you put a lot of yourself in him. I'm also very good in bed. I think I could surprise you there. So, why not give me a try? Why not give me a try tonight?"

And then she leaned and kissed him, her tongue exploring, hands moving, touching and teasing.

For a few sexy minutes, Clint thought about it. Allison would make a good companion. He had detached himself from the love of a woman for too long. There was no doubt about that. Even his shrink, an older, perceptive and kind woman, had told him that. He could do a whole lot worse than Allison.

She did not stay the night. At the front door, her expression was cold and strong. Her voice was tinged with expanding irritation.

"Now I know, don't I? Nothing ventured, nothing gained. I promise you this, Clint. I will be the best damned agent you'll ever have. I will make you rich and known throughout the entire world. Goodbye, Clint. Work hard and smart."

Clint watched her car disappear into the night, feeling like the loneliest man in the world. He knew Allison loved challenges. She was an A-type. He had the feeling that he was just another one of her goals—a name to checkmark after a romping night of sex. He did not believe that she loved him. But then, maybe he was no longer even capable of feeling love.

Later that night, he was out on the dunes, searching, squinting for any sign of the blue shimmering light that he had not seen for four years. As he often did, Clint heard Oscar's voice in his head. "My guess is the connection's been broken. If Rita is no longer in the photos, then she's gone."

In December, Allison Steele called him. That phone call would change his life.

CHAPTER 44

2023

"I know you're a big fan of Rita Randall," Allison said.

Clint perked up. He was eating breakfast on a stool at the kitchen island.

"Yes… I'm a fan."

"A friend told me you have a kind of obsession with her. And when I was at your place, I saw you had several photos of her."

Clint stayed quiet.

"Anyway, there's going to be an auction of some old Hollywood memorabilia at Sydney's in Manhattan on December 15. The ad is online. *Google* it. One of the items is the necklace Rita Randall was wearing when her car plunged off that cliff."

Clint shot off the stool, his mind alive, eyes staring. He was on his way to his laptop before he disconnected the call with Allison.

The auction was being held on a tree-lined side street in a classic pre-war brownstone on the Upper West Side of Manhattan.

Clint arrived early on the cold morning of December 15, in a light snowfall. He ascended five concrete stairs, opened the heavy oak door and entered a Victorian style foyer, with soft dim light, high ceilings and polished wood floors. He was greeted by a beefy man built for combat, who had a blunt nose, steely eyes and no neck. After a security scan, Clint's name was checked off by a young, stylish woman seated behind a laptop, who then directed him to a curving mahogany staircase.

"The auction will be held in the parlor upstairs," she said with a meager smile, handing him a program.

Clint was all nerves and clammy hands as he mounted the stairs. To the right was a library with floor-to-ceiling hardback books and burgundy leather wingback chairs. To the left was the parlor.

Clint passed through French glass doors into an elegant, wide parlor with cherry wood paneling, a white fireplace mantel decorated with swags of evergreen and holly, and bay windows that looked out onto the quiet street below.

Chairs were arranged into two neat rows, with a narrow aisle separating them. A tall polished lectern faced the room, *waiting like a judge*, Clint thought uneasily. Clint furtively took in his competition. There were women in the latest fashion, some in satin and suede, others in silk, with delicate lace collars. Most were adorned with diamond and pearl chokers, bracelets and broaches. All smelled of money and gleamed with polish and class.

Clint saw a well-dressed woman with a cell phone plugged to her ear, obviously ready to take instructions from some anonymous affluent person on the other end.

Interestingly, there were only three men, two dressed smartly in suits and ties, and a man in his 30s, a California sunbaked blond, wearing a Hawaiian shirt, jeans and sandals.

Clint had managed to find a frumpy, tan corduroy suit and a green turtleneck. He felt out-of-place and moody, tamping down an awful expectation. His throat was dry and his eyes bloodshot from little or no sleep the night before.

He found a seat in the front row and waited as the room slowly filled, buzzing with energy and conversation. Tea and coffee were offered in rose-colored china cups, but he declined, his gaze inspecting faces and attitudes. As ten o'clock drew near, guests perused their programs or stared into cell phones.

Clint waited in an agony of mental strain. He had to have that necklace. It wasn't just an item to be owned and displayed proudly, like a trophy before admiring and jealous friends at a cocktail party. Something in his gut told him that the necklace—the necklace he'd presented to Rita in 1948—was his mystical reconnection with her. With the necklace, he was confident he'd be able to find the time portal and return to her.

Five minutes later, the chubby, bejowled auctioneer stepped to the lectern, cleared his throat and tapped the microphone. He had tufts of white hair on the sides of his bald dome and he spoke in a very proper British accent.

Clint listened distractedly to the introduction and the thank-yous, and the brief description of future auctions. For the next half hour, Clint squirmed and swallowed away anxiety, as items were auctioned and purchased. There was applause, and the nodding of heads, and the tasteful lift of a hand, as bidding rose into the tens of thousands on jewelry, art and wardrobe.

There was much excitement surrounding three items: Donna Reed's house dress worn in *It's a Wonderful Life*; Natalie Wood's coat and hat she wore in *Miracle on 34th Street*; and the dazzling golden earrings Ava Gardner wore in *The Barefoot Contessa*.

Ten minutes later, the room gathered into a quiet hush, as the auctioneer lifted his eyebrows dramatically. "And now, ladies and gentlemen, we have a very special, unique and valuable item that has been in a private collection for many years."

Clint sat up, prepared, heart pounding. He was mesmerized, feeling the electric energy of the room. He twisted around to see people sitting on the edge of their seats, eyes wide, burning with interest.

The sophisticated gray-haired woman, sitting to his right across the aisle, appeared relaxed, hands in her lap, but her lusty eyes were already focused on the screen to the right of the auctioneer, where Rita's 14-karat white gold and diamond bow necklace with sky-blue topaz halo drop was being projected from a laptop.

Clint recalled the day he'd gently draped the necklace around Rita's neck. If he shut his eyes, her fragrance perfumed the air; he heard her chocolaty voice, her girlish laughter, the sound of the Malibu sea. He saw the golden sun falling on her like a benediction.

The auctioneer seemed to grow in height as he swept the audience with his eyes.

"As many of you know, Rita Randall is a Hollywood icon, known today as the queen of the Film Noir. Dolly Gold, a film critic in the 1940s, known to be witty, highly opinionated and sharply focused, wrote of Miss Randall…" and then the auctioneer lowered his eyes to read:

"Rita Randall, in *Danger Town*, comes swaying onto the screen with heat and sultry magnetism. Cavorting in her most iconic and vampish role, she is the despised, the loved, and the drop-dead-desirable vixen of every man, on and off the screen. Miss Randall had all the talent, skill and natural ability to have been one of our greatest movie stars, and before her tragic death, this reviewer had been looking forward to her performance in the envied role of Annabel Fleming, in *Shadows over Meadow Green*."

The auctioneer lifted his eyes, bright with anticipation. "Yes, Rita Randall died tragically when the automobile she was driving broke through a wooden barrier and she plunged to her death. As you can see projected on the screen, as well as displayed in the glass case to my left, our next item is the actual necklace Miss Randall was wearing on that terrible night. It was designed by the famous jeweler of the 1930s and 1940s, Jean-Claude Arseneault, and it is an enchanting one-of-a-kind piece: a 14-karat white gold and rose cut diamond bow necklace with a half-carat sky-blue topaz halo drop, also surrounded by rose cut diamonds. Please note that one of its 48 diamonds is missing from the lower loop of the bow, the only damage caused by the accident. This does not, in any way, degrade the necklace or decrease its value. If anything, it enhances it. Additionally, this necklace has never before been auctioned. This is the very first time, and perhaps it will be the last time."

The auctioneer paused for dramatic effect. "Now, ladies and gentlemen, we will start the bid at one hundred and ten thousand dollars."

Three hands went up before Clint's could react.

The lady across the aisle wore a designer dress. She presented an unyielding, determined face and cool, rigid eyes. Her hand had gone up like a shot.

The auctioneer nodded, alert to any movement. His face was glossy, his eyes darting about at the uplifted hands.

"The bid is now one hundred and twenty thousand."

More hands shot up.

"Very good, ladies and gentlemen. As I said, this necklace adorned the neck of the starlet Rita Randall, one of our great Hollywood stars. Do I have a bid for one hundred and fifty thousand?"

More hands periscoped up.

Clint's face was hot with panic. His jaw flexed. Perspiration popped out on his forehead. He heard his own loud voice call out.

"Three hundred thousand dollars."

Stunned silence ensued, as all eyes stuck to him. When Clint stood up, he didn't stir the astonished air.

The auctioneer recovered his surprise and continued. "I have a bid of three hundred thousand dollars, ladies and gentlemen. Three hundred thousand going once. Three hundred thousand going twice…"

The lady across the aisle spoke in a controlled, edgy voice. "Three hundred and twenty thousand."

The room buzzed with interest.

"Four hundred thousand," Clint said, still standing.

In a challenge, the woman spoke in a practiced confidence. "Four hundred and fifty thousand."

Clint didn't flinch, but his temples pulsed, heart hammered. "Five hundred thousand," he said hoarsely.

The auctioneer lifted his head proudly, as if he'd personally directed this drama and was taking full credit for its success. "Ladies and gentlemen, I have a bid of five hundred thousand. Are there any further bids for this magnificent and historical necklace worn by Rita Randall, who was taken from this world prematurely and tragically?"

To Clint's alarm, the woman across the aisle maintained her stiff composure as she spoke up, "Six hundred thousand dollars."

As he struggled to control his racing pulse, Clint wondered: *Who is this woman, and why is she so passionate about the necklace?*

But Clint was not to be defeated. "Eight hundred thousand," he said.

The woman across the aisle turned, assessing him coldly, and for the first time, tension was evident in her expression.

Clint's mind and emotions blurred into uncertainty as he waited for her response, as the room seemed to be holding its breath. The auctioneer stared, absorbed and eager for more.

Clint and his opponent stared, each measuring, estimating, agonizing.

And then, as if some of the air went out of the room, the woman's shoulders settled, and the tension left her face. She turned from him, lowering her eyes in defeat.

The gavel came down, loud and final.

Clint dropped down into his chair, fatigued, heavy, but triumphant. He sat breathing and staring, shrinking back into himself. He wanted that necklace immediately, but he knew he wouldn't have it in his hands until the transfer of funds was complete.

On the front steps of the brownstone, as snow frosted his shoulders, Clint waited for his female challenger to emerge. When she did, they exchanged cool glances.

"Why did you want the necklace so much?" Clint

asked.

The woman gave him a wintery smile. "My grandfather was Nickie Karn. Does the name ring a bell?"

It did. "Yes, Rita's daughter, Laura, was married to him, but the marriage didn't last."

"They were only married for about six months. Obviously, my grandfather remarried, but he told me, years later, that he never stopped loving Laura. He was devastated when she married Mario Cipolletti and died in 1970 from an overdose. Did you know they'd stayed good friends over the years?"

Clint shook his head, as fat flakes dusted the woman's elegant cashmere coat, and the wind whipped up the red in her cheeks.

"No... I didn't know that."

The woman's face turned to sorrow. "I've seen all of Rita Randall's movies several times and, whenever I do, I hurt for Laura. If her mother had lived, I'm sure her life would have never taken the tragic turn it did. So I wanted the necklace as a kind of token. And I'm a big fan of Rita Randall. I believe—no I am confident—that Rita would have been one of the greatest Hollywood actresses had she lived."

Clint pocketed his cold hands, staying mute.

"And you..." The woman continued. "Why did you want the necklace?"

Clint studied the woman's expression when he told her the truth. "I gave the necklace to Rita. I gave it to her the day she died."

The woman looked deeply into his eyes, trying to understand, and then she offered a Mona Lisa smile. "Of course you did. Merry Christmas."

Clint watched her stoop into a waiting limo, without giving him another look. He turned left and started toward Riverside Drive, where he'd parked his car.

As he drove back to Amagansett in a light but persistent snowfall, with his windshield wipers ticking back and forth like an old grandfather's clock, he couldn't stop the engine of his mind. Would the necklace be the connection he needed to return to Rita and Laura? If not, then he would be lost to wander through life like a shadow, like a ghost, haunting and being haunted. He'd have to learn to live without Rita. He'd have to learn to forget those magical perfumed nights and those drowsy love-making mornings; forget the softly scented sea breezes as they strolled hand in hand, dreaming of a glorious future that lingered just out of reach, on the shadowy dunes, in the misty, moon-drenched night.

On December 21, Clint was out on the dunes, marching about like a soldier ready for battle. The waves thundered in, the wind was sharp and cold, and dark clouds swam across the sky, obscuring a moon that would be full the next night.

Clint faced the sea, tall and straight, his feet rooted in the sand. Holding Rita's necklace, he thrust a hand toward the sky, shouting into the cavern of the night, as snow began to fall.

"I have it! I have the necklace. Take me back."

Clint began walking in a wide circle, as if in some ritualistic dance. "Take me back to Rita! Do you hear me? Take me back."

A big December wind circled him, pushed at him, rippled his long winter coat, whipped his hair and face. He kept circling the space, his hand held high, as a chaos of snowflakes swarmed around him, biting into his face.

"Take me back. Take me back to Rita!"

And then he saw the blue, shimmering portal dancing toward him.

Rita wandered the tide line, bronzed and lovely, her expression pensive. She wore tight shorts and a blue cotton top; her luscious blonde hair spilled out from under a slanted, white, wide-brimmed hat.

The Malibu beach was warm, heat shimmering off the white sand, and there was a good sting in the sun. Rita turned occasionally to watch the curling waves and to listen to their roaring voices, full of spray and melody, the water thudding the beach and spreading into foaming pools. She listened, acutely, as if the waves might be willing to reveal their hidden secrets or answer her many burning questions.

The sun threw yellow sparkles on the surface, like little golden nuggets. Rita wanted to splash into the water, swim out and scoop them up in her hands, just as she'd done years ago when her mother took her and Martha to Coney Island.

She moved with no direction in mind; her gaze often searching the area as if she were expecting someone, but, of course, she wasn't.

When she saw the figure in the distance walking along the lower beach toward her, she slowed down, her keen eyes focused on him. He walked with a slight limp, had long hair and a beard, and he wore a billowing, white shirt and pants rolled up to his calves.

Her hat caught the wind, was whipped off her head, and went skipping across the sand. The man kept coming toward her, and the closer he came, the more Rita grew alert and curious. She squinted, her pulse rising.

As he closed the distance between them, Rita stayed rooted in the sand, the heat of the day hot, the ocean wind circling, seagulls crying overhead.

He stopped only a few feet away, staring, his eyes tired, face handsome, expression weary.

"Rita?" he said, in a deep, resonate voice that she felt in the depths of her soul.

"Who are you?" Rita asked, uneasy.

"It's me... Clint... Clint West."

Her eyes fluttered as her mind worked.

"Do you remember?" Clint asked.

"Remember?" she said, softly, confused. "Remember what? What are you doing out here? This beach is private."

Clint's red-rimmed eyes blinked. "Do you remember us? You've got to."

"What are you talking about? I don't know you."

"You must remember."

Suddenly frightened, Rita pivoted and started toward the house.

"Rita," Clint called. "Don't you remember? They are your words. You said that if we were ever separated, we'd always remember this beach house. No matter what happened to us, you said we'd always remember this place, and we'd know... We'd know we could return and find each other. You said, let's make this beach house our place, no matter where we are, or what time we're in. Don't you remember, Rita? I've come so far."

Rita stopped.

Clint continued. "We agreed that this will always be our place—our safe house, no matter what happened."

Rita stopped, slowly turned and stared, trying to understand. Her eyes expanded on him.

Clint limped toward her. His eyes ached with gritty fatigue, and he was still in pain because of his time travel journey from 2023 to 1948.

"Rita… You said if we ever get separated, we can always return here and find each other, no matter where we are, and no matter what time we're in. Don't you remember? You've got to remember."

She hesitated then, reluctantly, she started back to him, shading the sun with the flat of her hand, searching his eyes.

He smiled warmly. "Do you remember, Rita? Do you remember me? Do you remember us? You said we fell in love at first sight, just like in the movies?"

As the waves charged the beach and withdrew; as high clouds slid forever across the blue vault of sky, and the wind rippled the tall, glistening dune grass, time slowly melted away.

In that infinite space, Rita and Clint smiled like secret lovers, their faces close, eyes yielding and tender with recognition; the sunlight glittering in them.

As the sea thundered in, Rita slowly lifted a hand and touched his cheek, and he took her hand and kissed it.

Rita ran her fingers through his long, thick hair, sighing with pleasure, tracing his nose, mouth and jaw with a finger. When she spoke, it was soft and intimate. "Yes… I remember, Clint. Yes, I remember everything."

They held each other's eyes, exploring, loving, and then, with clasped hands, they moved off down the beach, strolling along the edge of the sea, lost in the magic of romance and love, into the rising mist of the day.

EPILOGUE
1948

The car went winding up the road under a full moon night, tires screeching, rear end fishtailing. He gunned the engine, shooting past black trees, the headlights frantically sweeping across a cluster of thick trunks and jutting rocks.

His face was tight with purpose, his glassy eyes squinting. He mumbled curses and threats. By the time he whipped the 1947 Triumph onto Rita Randall's circular drive, his wild eyes held a roguish, lusty anticipation. He came to a skidding stop, shoved the car into gear and killed the engine.

"All right, baby, now it's my turn, and I've been waiting a long time for this."

Tony Lapano shoved the car door open and crawled out. He raised himself to his full height, adjusted his crooked tie and weaved an uncertain path to the front door. With the meat of his palm, he pounded on it.

When the pounding persisted, Rita swallowed, feeling the cool walnut grip of the gun she held in her hand. She crept to the bedroom door and peered out into the dimly lit hallway. She left her room, barefoot, wearing pink silk pajamas, a satin robe, and the necklace Clint had brought back with him from 2023. As she edged along the wall toward the living room to get a good view of the front door, there was another loud knock.

When she heard the voice, Tony's voice, she cursed, lifted the gun and aimed it at the door.

"Rita, let me in!"

It was June 25, 1948.

"Let me in, Rita, or so help me God, I'll kick the damn thing open!"

Rita stared soberly, waiting, the gun heavy in her hand.

She heard the thud of his foot as he drove it into the doorframe.

"One way or the other, I'm coming in. Hey, baby, it's time you and me get down to the basics. It's time you and me start having some real fun together. No more make believe, like in the movies."

The door took another blow from Tony's kicking foot.

"Dammit, let me in, Rita, now, or I'm coming through the window."

When Rita finally heard Clint's voice outside, she blew out a sigh of relief.

"Hello, Tony baby. You're up late, aren't you?" Clint said.

Rita reached for the lock and released it, the metallic click sounding loud in the sudden silence. She twisted the doorknob and opened the door.

Tony stood perplexed, a shiny-faced, loose-limbed and lazy-eyed drunk.

He stared at Rita, trying to understand. Then he

swung his gaze to Clint, who stood near the open door of Tony's sport's car.

"What the…?" he exclaimed. "What the hell are you doing here, Clint?"

"I thought you knew, Tony baby. Rita and I got married last weekend. In secret, to keep the swarm of reporters and crowds away."

"Married? What the hell do you mean, married? You two just met a few weeks ago."

Rita lowered the gun at her side, finger on the trigger. She raised her free arm, wiggling her fingers, revealing a diamond-studded wedding band that glistened in the garden light. "That's right, Tony. Married."

Tony's large, mean eyes swung first to Rita and then to Clint. He jabbed a threatening finger at Rita.

"I'm gonna ruin you, Rita, okay? I know everybody in this town and I'm gonna ruin you. You'll be a washed up nobody when I'm finished with you. You'll never work in this town again."

Rita's grin was meager and bored. "Don't waste your time, Tony. I just signed a contract with Howard Hughes to star in *Shadows over Meadow Green*. You'll be hearing from him. We begin shooting in two weeks, and Clint is the head writer."

Tony's hard expression began to fall apart. "That don't mean nothing! Nothing, okay? I'll stop it, and you know I can."

Rita shook her head in pity. "Go home, Tony. Just leave me alone and go home."

Clint stood by the Triumph's open door. "It's time for you to go, Tony. I'm sick and tired of seeing your face."

Tony pivoted and moved threateningly toward Clint, his fists clenched, eyes burning. His attack was swift, but clumsy. He swung a right wildly, and Clint easily blocked it. He swung a left and Clint slapped it away. Desperate, Tony charged, growling. Clint snatched Tony's wrist, turned it up between his shoulder blades and shoved him, three steps and head first, into the side of the Triumph. Tony bounced off with shocked eyes. He stumbled, backstepped and dropped to his knees.

Clint went for the garden hose. He turned the nozzle and directed the spray at Tony's head. The cold water instantly snapped him awake. He frantically slapped water from his face and dripping hair.

Clint shut off the water and tossed the hose away. He went to Tony, heaving him up to unsteady feet. Staggering, Clint aimed Tony toward the car's open door. He ducked Tony's head and dropped his wet body behind the wheel of the Triumph. Dazed, Tony glanced up as Clint shut the door.

Tony heard Clint's voice above him.

"Tony, this movie is about to end, and I'm going to play director here. You are going to crank the engine and drive away into the night, toward the ocean and under that beautiful big white full moon. Have you got that, Tony? Do you understand?"

Tony nodded, still punch drunk.

"Okay, and then Rita and I are going, arm in arm, back toward the front door. We'll pause, embrace, kiss passionately, and then exit into the house. And then the camera will do a slow fade and THE END will rise to the screen. The music will swell, lush violins, and the credits will roll. And guess what, Tony? Your name will be right up there on the big screen, just under Rita Randall and Clint West. Hey, buddy, you might even win an Academy Award for best supporting role. Okay, Tony?"

Mouth open, Tony nodded mechanically.

"Okay now. Ready? Lights! Action! Roll'em!"

Tony started the engine and drove away into the moon-drenched night, his red taillights slowly fading into the rising mist of the sea.

Clint turned to Rita, his smile tender. "I don't think we're going to need that gun."

As Clint strolled over, she slipped it into the pocket of her satin robe. He drew her into his arms.

"Well, my love," Clint said, "… as they say in the movie business, that's a wrap."

When they kissed, it was warm and sweet.

Timeless.

The next morning over breakfast, Rita and Clint read in the morning paper that Tony Lapano's candy-apple-red, two-seater, 1947 Triumph 1800 Roadster had broken through a guard rail and plunged over a cliff, exploding into a fireball. An eyewitness said, "The car was weaving all over the road. I had to swerve onto the shoulder to miss it."

Ava Gardner was quoted as saying, "I saw Tony about one in the morning at Barney's Beanery, in West Hollywood. He was drunk. He was lurching about like a drunken sailor. As he was leaving, I told him he shouldn't drive, but he told me to shut up. Well, at least Tony died spectacularly, like in the movies. Good for him."

Thank you for taking the time to read *Time Change*. If you enjoyed it, please consider telling your friends or posting a short review. Word of mouth is an author's best friend and it is much appreciated.

Thank you,
Elyse Douglas

Other novels by Elyse Douglas that you might enjoy:

The Christmas Diary
The Summer Diary
The Other Side of Summer
The Christmas Women
Daring Summer
The Christmas Eve Letter (A Time Travel Novel) Book 1
The Christmas Eve Daughter (A Time Travel Novel) Book 2
The Lost Mata Hari Ring (A Time Travel Novel)
The Christmas Town (A Time Travel Novel)
Time Sensitive (A Time Travel Novel)
Time Shutter (A Time Travel Novel)
The Summer Letters
The Date Before Christmas
Christmas Ever After
Christmas for Juliet
The Christmas Bridge
Wanting Rita

www.elysedouglas.com

Made in the USA
Las Vegas, NV
12 October 2021

32205800R00176